Cougars

Dear Reader:

It is my pleasure to present *Cougars* by Bestselling Author Earl Sewell. For the past few years, there has been a fascination with the new aspects of what used to be referred to as "May-December Romances." In the past, a shroud of negativity and gossip surrounded relationships involving an older woman and a younger man. It has always been practically expected that, as men age, they will trade-in their aging women for younger models; so-called upgrades. Some men are on their third or fourth marriage by the time they turn fifty, as their wives decrease in age. However, people used to look down on women who acted similarly and they were accused of "robbing the cradle."

Well, times have changed. In *Succulent: Chocolate Flava 2* (February 2008), I wrote a short story entitled "Cougar" about a woman in her 40's who was obsessed with bedding younger men. Since then, there have been at least two television series (that I know of) and it has now become trendy. Many people still do not realize that Cougars are women over 40 who like younger men and Bobcats are women in their 30's who enjoy the company of much younger men. Forty is definitely the new twenty in today's society. I am in my forties and I am certainly not over anyone's perception of a hill!

Earl Sewell has done a fabulous job of exploring this topic in the following pages. I hope that you will enjoy the book and I appreciate your support of Earl and all of the Strebor authors I publish. If you are looking for a great place to hang out online, please join the Zaniacs on www.planetzane.org. Also, visit me on the web at eroticanoir.com. If you would like to purchase other titles, please visit www.zanestore.com.

Blessings,

Zane

Zane
Publisher
Strebor Books International
www.simonandschuster.com/streborbooks

ALSO BY EARL SEWELL
Have Mercy

ZANE PRESENTS

Cougars

EARL SEWELL

SBI

STREBOR BOOKS

NEW YORK LONDON TORONTO SYDNEY

SBI

Strebor Books
P.O. Box 6505
Largo, MD 20792
http://www.streborbooks.com

ISBN 978-1-59309-269-6
ISBN 978-1-4391-4129-8 (ebook)
LCCN 2009942985

First Strebor Books trade paperback edition March 2010

Cover design: www.mariondesigns.com
Cover photograph: © Keith Saunders/Marion Designs

10 9 8 7 6 5 4 3 2 1

Manufactured in the United States of America

For information regarding special discounts for bulk purchases,
please contact Simon & Schuster Special Sales at 1-866-506-1949
or business@simonandschuster.com

The Simon & Schuster Speakers Bureau can bring authors to
your live event. For more information or to book an event, contact
the Simon & Schuster Speakers Bureau at 1-866-248-3049 or visit
our website at www.simonspeakers.com.

To all of the Cougars and the men who adore them.

"Sometimes we just fall in love with lies."
—Dr. Cornel West

Acknowledgments

Cougars is my twelfth novel and I'm amazed that I still have my sanity. Like with most of my novels, when I began writing this one, all I had was a title. I first heard the term "cougar" while having dinner with some friends. The subject of mature women dating younger men arose and the phrase was tossed around. I thought to myself, *wow, that would be a catchy book title and subject matter*. I began this novel by chatting it up with a number of forty-something women about dating men in their twenties. As soon as I mentioned the idiom "Cougar," a funny little smile would form on their faces and their eyes would twinkle. The first thing that came to their minds was the exhilaration and pleasure of having sex with a younger man. I found this interesting because many of the women were only interested in the sexual aspects of the relationship and not the commitment piece. This is the mindset of men in their twenties and I found it intriguing that a woman in her forties could be just as informal about sex as guys. They didn't mind having intimacy without intricacies. In fact, many of the women preferred it that way. Once I was armed with enough information, I sat down and plotted out this novel, which I hope you'll enjoy.

There are many people I need to thank but first and foremost, I have to give praise and glory to God for giving me such a wonderful gift.

To dear friend Kris Brown whom I've known for twenty-four years, thank you for taking the time to answer all of my questions about the pharmaceutical industry. Your insight into the profession was invaluable and made the process of writing this book easier for me.

To the Honorable Sheila Janine Harrell, thank you so much for taking time to speak openly with me about your profession as well as your thoughts about career women dating younger men.

To the Sweet Soul Sisters Book Club, Diva Divine Book Club and Circle of Sisters Book Club, thank you all for your continued support and encouragement.

To Linda Wilson, for being my right arm while writing this book. Thank you for giving me a great pep talk just when I needed it as well as your editorial guidance.

To Gloria Studway, Regina McNeal, Patti Lichtenhagen, Mia Grant, Joyce Grant, Susan Boler, Sonya Zeno, Monique Holsey and Shawn Stuckey for inspiring me to keep on pushing and for listening to me constantly talk about my characters and this book. I also want to thank all of you for providing me with excellent feedback and comments. Without your help, this book may have never gotten finished.

To Mary Griffin for keeping me on track during the production of this book. Friends like you are very precious and rare.

To Lisa Renee Johnson who is the president of the coolest book club on the West Coast (Sistahs on the Reading Edge) for all of your invaluable help, support and insight.

To my family, Annette and Candice thanks for putting up with all of my madness as I wrote this book.

To my agent, Sara Camilli, thank you for all of your work with helping me move this book forward. I truly appreciate all of your time and efforts.

In case I forgot anyone, which I often do, here's your opportunity to be recognized.

I would like to thank _____ for _____ because without your help I'd be _____. You're the biggest reason for my success because

_____.

Please feel free to drop me a line at earlsewell.com. Please put the title of my book in the subject line so that I know your message to me is not spam. Make sure you check out www.earlsewell.com, www.myspace.com/earlsewell, and www.aabookclubs.ning.com.

Earl Sewell

Chapter 1
Jasmine

Jasmine situated her carry-on luggage in the overhead compartment at the front of the airplane, and then sat down in her first-class seat. Once she was comfortable, she removed a book of erotic short stories from a smaller bag. It also contained a notebook for writing, her iPod and some fruit she'd purchased from a newsstand inside the airport. Jasmine momentarily glanced at the young, handsome airline pilot standing outside the doorway of the cockpit. He was partially dressed in uniform, waiting patiently to greet coach passengers who had yet to come aboard. He looked to be about twenty-eight years of age, stocky build, with full delectable lips, a mighty chest and muscular arms. He had on a short-sleeved shirt and she could see part of a tattoo, which read *Bad Boy* on the bicep muscle of his right arm.

"A cocky young man with a tattoo," she whispered to herself. The young pilot had an immaculately groomed head full of black curly hair. As she continued scrutinizing him, she was delighted when her eyes landed between his legs, and discovered a print pushing out against the fabric of his slacks.

"Young men. Always ready for action," Jasmine whispered before sweeping her tongue between her lips at the thought of what his young body would look like nude. She exhaled and closed her eyes to enjoy the intimate vision more fully in private. She imagined ripping off his shirt and pushing him down in the pilot's seat. In her mind's eye, she saw herself riding his dick as she fed him one of her breasts. The thought of the young pilot eagerly sucking her breasts and worshipping her like a mythical sex goddess caused her to feel a delightful tingle between her legs.

"Are you comfortable?" Jasmine immediately opened her eyes and tilted her head upward. The young pilot held her gaze for a moment, then smiled at her displaying a pretty set of white teeth. She paused for a second to refocus her thoughts.

"What's that mannish smile for?" Jasmine certainly didn't want him to get a sense that she was fantasizing about choking his dick to death with her strong pussy muscles. On the other hand, she couldn't help being a little flirtatious.

"Nothing, I just wanted to make sure you were comfortable," he answered as he squatted down.

"Out of all the passengers about to board this aircraft you specifically want to know if I'm okay?" Jasmine raised her eyebrow.

"That's why I'm standing here. Is there anything I can do to make you more comfortable?" The young pilot had clearly gone out of his way to accommodate any request that she may have had.

Jasmine draped her left leg over the right one and smirked. Then being unashamedly bold and straightforward, Jasmine leaned toward him and said, "I could use a foot rub. That would certainly relax me."

Glancing down at her feet, which could be easily removed from her open-toed shoes, the young pilot said, "It's your lucky day. I'm most certainly a guy who loves to take care of a woman's feet."

"Is that a fact?" Jasmine muttered, then laughed slightly.

"I'm not sure if I can accommodate that particular request right here in such a tight space, but perhaps we could make *other* arrangements." His voice was steady and confident.

Jasmine parted her lips and allowed the tip of her tongue to touch the roof of her mouth. "What a pity. Things could've gotten interesting in such a *tight* space." Jasmine glanced into his eyes before audaciously focusing them directly on his dick, which was without question, eager to meet her.

"Do you wear boxers or briefs?" Jasmine inquired although she already knew the answer.

"Excuse me?" The young pilot released an embarrassed laugh.

"Oh, don't start playing the shy and bashful role now. Your big ego walked you over here for some conversation. Now answer me. Do you like it when it's close to your body or do you like to let it hang?"

"You don't play around, do you?" Jasmine could tell he was enjoying her straightforwardness.

"You're the one who wanted to come over and play with a grown woman. I'm very frank and to the point. When I have a question, I ask it and in return I expect to receive an answer. Now tell me. Which do you prefer? Boxers or briefs?"

"I wear boxers," he answered with a flair of cockiness.

"I can tell. Perhaps you should walk your dog more often so he can raise his leg."

"I'm trying to walk him right now," the young pilot muttered.

"You don't even know my name yet." Jasmine wanted him to take a moment to think about what he was saying. "I could be a crazy and deranged man eater." She flashed her green eyes at him.

"That's a chance I'm willing to take. I've just got to know what your sexy green eyes will say to me when I'm making love to you."

Jasmine asked, "How old are you?"

"Old enough to fly this 737 Boeing jet and certainly old enough to handle other things."

Jasmine shifted her position and looked him up and down from head to toe. "I'm probably old enough to be your mother." Jasmine hoped that she'd said enough to unnerve the young Casanova.

"I've never seen my mother look at me the way you did earlier. As far as I can tell, you had something on your mind and I don't think your thoughts were very motherly."

Jasmine paused and thought about what to say next. "Okay, fair enough. I'll admit that I was ogling you a little. But as the old saying goes, there's no harm in looking."

"My name is Alex. Alex Moore. When you're ready to graduate from just looking and cross over into something more exotic, I want you to think of me. Here is my card." Alex presented her with his contact information.

Jasmine took his card and glanced at it. "You don't want to play with me. I will have your ass walking in circles and talking to yourself. I am entirely too much woman for you to handle, sweetie," Jasmine said.

"Are you sure about that? I may be younger, but that doesn't mean that I don't know what I'm doing. Trust me, I can do things to you that'll have you addicted. Hell, I just might be too much of a young man for you."

Jasmine laughed as she tucked her hair behind her ear. "You certainly talk a lot of game, but I've been playing the sport much longer. Trust me, sugar, if you were to ever get some of my sweet nectar, my man eater would most certainly school you." Jasmine winked, and then smiled at him. She had to be honest with herself. The idea of this young stud being so blatant and self-assured toyed with her hunger for excitement, adventure and the exotic.

"See, that could become an issue. You're still in school taking adult education and I'm a professor at the University of Seduction," Alex continued teasing her with his suggestive conversation. Jasmine decided to be more straightforward.

"Well, if I were to fuck you, Alex." She looked him directly in the eyes. "It would be on my terms and you'd need more than just an energetic ego and boastful words. I've heard men brag about their sexual prowess before and frankly, men who brag almost always come up short and soft."

"I'm sorry to hear about your disappointments, but that was them, not me. Do you have a number where I could reach you?" Alex stopped speaking and waited.

"No I don't. However, if I want to play around, you'll hear from me." Jasmine winked.

"Ooooh, it's like that?" Alex's tone spoke his disappointment.

"Mister Moore, you have a wonderful day," she said as she removed her iPod and put in her ear buds. The move was meant to be a clear signal that their conversation had concluded.

"It was nice meeting you, but you know I'm going to ask you to turn that off before we take off, Miss..." Alex was still trying to get her name.

"My name is Jasmine and it's time for you to move out of the way, Alex. You're causing a passenger logjam." Jasmine tilted her head in the direction of several passengers who were waiting for him to stand up so they could squeeze past him.

"You're going to call me, right?" Alex rose up. Jasmine shrugged and turned on her music. Alex smirked before stepping away toward the cockpit of the aircraft.

Jasmine peered out the window at the horizon in the distance. She'd arrived at a particular place in her life where she wasn't interested in a serious relationship. Previously, she'd had two very serious relationships, but neither one had ever materialized into marriage. One lover, a man named John Fleming who she'd met in her mid twenties and dated for three years, couldn't and wouldn't commit to her. There were far too many single women for him to play around with and the notion of settling down to raise a family was like asking him to cut off his balls and hand them to her for safe-keeping. That just wasn't going to happen.

By the time Jasmine was thirty-one, she'd met Bailey Brown through the singles dating ministry at her church. Bailey was a prosecutor who became a community activist and started a program to help first-time juvenile offenders turn their lives around. With the help of church ministers and his relationship with other professionals, Bailey was able to do some good. Offenders would come through his mentoring program and learn about more positive ways to deal with their anger, and manage the emotional issues associated with the breakdown of the family structure. Through his program, many of the young men learned how to be critical thinkers and develop leadership skills that would sustain them for a lifetime. Bailey was passionate about his work and equally passionate about Jasmine. He loved her brilliance and for their second-year anniversary, he took her on a vacation to the West Indies.

"You make my life so complete," he admitted one romantic evening when they were having dinner at an oceanfront restaurant. "And I want to marry you."

"Are you proposing to me?" Jasmine needed clarification.

"Yes, I am, but I know you're not going to make me get down on one knee to place this engagement ring on your finger."

"Yes I am," Jasmine said, not wanting to be cheated out of such a very special moment. When they returned home, Jasmine began making plans for their wedding. However, her plans came to an abrupt stop when she received news of Bailey's death. One of the misguided youth he'd been trying to help had turned against Bailey and had gunned him down in a parking lot. It took a long time for Jasmine to get over it, but with the help and support of friends and family, she found the courage and strength to keep moving forward.

Jasmine was now a forty-three-year-old, single and

successful career woman. She didn't have any children and at this particular point in her life, she'd accepted that the fantasy of the white house with the picket fence and two children wasn't going to happen.

JASMINE WAS TRAVELING TO NEW YORK to celebrate her friend Tiffany's fortieth birthday along with her sister, Lauren, and another girlfriend named Millie. Tiffany had never been to New York and was excited about spending the weekend enjoying all of the sights and festivities the city had to offer. Jasmine had journeyed to New York on a number of occasions and knew the city better than any of her girlfriends. She looked forward to all of the planned carousing—from shopping and dining to seeing *The Color Purple* on Broadway, to hitting a few clubs like Elements in downtown Manhattan and Ultra in Midtown.

As Jasmine continued to meditate, she realized all of her girlfriends were now forty-something. They'd left their thirties behind along with all of the mistakes, heartbreaks and bad decisions they'd made over the course of ten years. They were educated and successful in every part of life except love. Admittedly, Jasmine knew that at this point in her life, it would take an incredibly strong man to tame her. As a Gemini, she conceded to the astrological philosophy that two very unique and distinctive personalities lived within her. There was the brilliant character that drove her to be successful no matter what. She'd earned a PhD. in organic chemistry and worked for a small bio-tech company doing research to find a cure for diseases like Alzheimer's, HIV and cancer. She spent endless hours doing lab work, having discussions with her team of researchers, reading scores of literature on various topics important to her investigative study and waiting for results on a number of tests. Some days were more exciting than others and when her life became too boring her unpredictable, untamable, vanity-driven, free-spirited side would take over and deliver her from her own madness. Traveling to New York for four days would serve as the perfect escape her spirit craved.

An elderly couple boarded the aircraft. Jasmine briefly thought about her own parents who'd died a few years ago. Her father was a forensic scientist who worked at a crime lab until he retired and passed away suddenly in his sleep. Her mother taught high school biology for thirty years before retiring. After her father died, her mother became stricken with dementia and had to be placed in a nursing home. Jasmine worked tirelessly to find a cure, but none of the drugs she'd created worked. Her mother eventually passed away peacefully.

The airplane backed away from the gate and taxied down the runway. Before long they departed from solid ground and she was well on her way to rendezvous with everyone at LaGuardia Airport.

She looked forward to seeing Millie who was a judge

to find out more details of her divorce from her evil husband. Their marriage had been on the rocks for well over a year due to a number of reasons ranging from financial irresponsibility to infidelity. Then there was her older sister, Lauren, who worked as a DEA agent. Jasmine hadn't seen Lauren in several weeks because they'd had an argument over some silly issue that Jasmine couldn't remember. Finally, there was the birthday girl, Tiffany, who worked as a librarian at Fisk University and enjoyed an abundant amount of sex with young, virile college boys.

In order to pass the time, Jasmine decided to finish an erotic short story she'd been reading. The story was about a forty-year-old woman who had decided to take swim lessons at her local park district. That is where she'd met her young twenty-one-year-old swimming instructor, who was eager to show her his favorite stroke. Jasmine loved this particular story because she and her girlfriends were perpetually attracting younger men who were energetic, enthusiastic, and could get an instant erection at the sight of a juicy ass and succulent breasts. She opened the book, flipped through the pages and found the spot where she'd left off.

❋❋❋

My glistening dick was still inside of her. I'd made her come so hard that she was exhausted and panting. She leaned forward, resting her cheek against my own. The sweet, musky scent of our lovemaking wafted through the air of the pool house. The firmness of her body felt heavenly as I caressed her back, making long sweeping strokes up and down her spine and stopping every so often to massage her ass. She loved the way I touched her. She'd told me countless times how the thought of my smooth hands gave her goose bumps and made her wet. I pushed my dick deeper into her. Time for round two, I wanted her to sit upright and let my curved dick rub against the walls of her pussy.

"Mmmm," she cooed, and then began to pant as I guided her movements. "Shit," she whispered as she nibbled on my earlobe. "Your dick is so hard and feels so good." I felt her pussy contract, then squirt warm liquid down on the head of my Pride. I spread my fingers and threaded them through the strands of her hair.

"Damn, the way you touch makes me so weak with indescribable pleasure," she uttered. Her pussy tightened up and squeezed me with uninhibited intensity.

"Damn, baby! You drive me crazy every time you do that shit!" I said, trying to suppress the urge to let go and blast the bottom of her goddessness with hot liquid.

"Are you going to let me ride this dick the way I want to ride it? Do you promise not to move when it starts feeling too good? I want to do you right. I want you to submit to me." She met my gaze, searching my eyes for the answer instead of trusting the words that would pass through my lips. I agreed and surrendered to her will.

"Good. I want to show you just how wet my squirting pussy

can get." She skillfully raised her ass and glided her paradise upward until only the head of my manhood was inside her. She paused, contracted her pussy and held onto me in a move that affirmed she had absolute power and control over her womanhood. She sucked in air through her lips making a glorious hissing sound that matched an intensifying tightening which was making my toes curl.

"Don't move," her voice fluttered like a butterfly dancing on the wind. She once again gazed deeply into my eyes so that I could see her soul. Her back bowed, her eyes opened wider, the cave of her mouth widened and I waited to hear her cry of pleasure, teetering on the edge of sound. Time stood still. Finally, the echo of her ecstasy sang its melody. I could feel the soft, silky streams of orgasm squirting all over me. Her sweet nectar cascaded down the shaft of my manhood, around the curvature of my balls and then trickled down toward my ass.

"Damn, this dick has some power to it," she bellowed as she picked up her pace and rode me like a thoroughbred. My lover clawed her fingernails deep into my skin.

"Shit," I cried out as she changed direction and coiled her hips counter-clockwise. I craned my neck upward and swept my tongue around the bend of her breasts while simultaneously enjoying the delicacy of her beautifully erect chocolate nipples.

"Damn you!" I spanked her ass in a fit of passionate anger. She reached behind her back and toyed with my balls. I spread my legs wider and began to tremble uncontrollably.

"Oh God!" I cried out as I blasted her with successive shots of my essence.

✪✪✪

"Would you like something to drink?" A slim blonde flight attendant interrupted Jasmine.

"I'll take a cranberry juice," she answered as she began fanning herself. Reading the story had made her hot. She glanced at the door of the cockpit and thought about Alex and fucking his brains out when the plane landed.

"Is that a good book?" asked the flight attendant who had her head slightly tilted so that she could see the book cover. Jasmine held the book up so that she could see the photo of a man's chocolate ass, muscular back, and squared shoulders.

"It's a steamy one," Jasmine answered with a smile as she took a sip of the drink she'd just been given.

"Those are the best kind of novels. I love reading steamy stories."

"The photo of the man's ass is what caught my eye," Jasmine admitted.

"He does have a nice one." The flight attendant smirked before moving on to serve another passenger. Jasmine put away the book for a while and toyed with the idea of going into the cramped confines of the airplane bathroom to masturbate while fantasizing about being fucked by Alex. After reading the passage, she could most certainly attest that she was in need of man to provide her with focused concentration and deep penetration. She'd just about mustered up the courage to do it, but nixed the idea when an overweight man, with the crack of his ass exposed, made his way toward the restroom.

"Well, there goes that thought," she muttered as she reached down and removed the iPod from her tote bag. She slipped in her ear buds, reclined in her seat and listened to the smooth masculine voice of neo-soul and pop musician Seal.

Jasmine's flight arrived at the airport twenty minutes early. When she exited the aircraft, Alex was at the doorway insisting that she call him.

"Don't forget about me now."

"I don't think I could ever forget a pilot as bold as you." Jasmine said her final good-bye to him before heading down the jetway. As soon as she entered the airport, she turned on her cell phone. She'd missed a call from Millie, but immediately dialed her back.

"What's up, girl? Where are you?" Jasmine asked as she walked through the airport.

"We're all down at the baggage carousel waiting on you," Millie informed her.

"Okay, I'll be there in a moment. My plane has just arrived."

"How was your flight?" Millie inquired.

"Girl, the pilot was trying to pick me up." Jasmine laughed.

"Well, was he good looking?" Millie wanted details.

"Yes, he was a nice-looking brother and he looked like he had a big one."

"Did you get his number?" Millie kept trying to pry information out of Jasmine.

"Yeah, I got it, but I'm not going to call him," Jasmine admitted.

"Why not?"

"Girl, he was too young. He was like twenty-eight years old."

"You need to stop acting like you haven't gone there before and dated a younger guy. I do recall several conversations we've had about how much fun you had dating that guy that was like twenty-five."

"That was just a special arrangement between Steve and me. It was intimacy without intricacies. He knew his place and when I got bored with him, I told him to go find someone his own age to play with. He caught me at a weak moment." Jasmine laughed.

"Yeah right! Ever since you got some fresh young stuff, I know your ass has been dying to get some more."

"You know what. Let's just change the subject because I see you're gearing up to take this conversation to another level. What's going on with you and Frank?"

"Girl, don't even bring that fool up to me right now. I don't even want to talk about him. Right now, I just want to enjoy my time here in New York."

"That bad, aye?"

"Well, it's not good, that's for damn sure," Millie confessed.

"Okay, I'm coming towards the baggage claim area now. I'll see you in a second."

When Jasmine arrived, she greeted and hugged everyone. They were all very excited to see each other.

"Tiffany, you look fabulous," Jasmine complimented her as she gave her a big hug.

"Well, I'm not trying to look bad," she said, striking a hot pose.

"I'm serious. You look so young and energetic. How are you staying in such great shape?" Jasmine asked as she pulled her luggage from the carousel.

"By having lots of sex, honey," Tiffany joked and everyone in the group laughed.

"Hey Lauren," Jasmine said as she gave her big sister a hug and a kiss on the cheek.

"Let's not fight, okay?" Jasmine whispered in her ear.

"Okay," Lauren answered.

"Well, ladies, are we ready?" Millie asked. "I've arranged for the car service to drive us back to the hotel so we can freshen up before going out to Woodbury Common for an afternoon of shopping."

"And a whole lot of drinking." Tiffany laughed as they followed their driver out the door.

Chapter 2
Travis

Confident, Travis exited the conference room and walked down the corridor toward the elevator. He was leaving a tenure committee meeting where he'd spent most of the day presenting and defending his portfolio for permanent status. The intensity of the hearing was as bad as trying to get appointed to the Supreme Court. It was a grueling and exhausting experience, but overall he felt good about the way he'd handled himself. He'd been working at the University of Berkeley for three years as an associate professor of chemistry. He was also a part of a special research team that was investigating experimental drugs to reverse certain types of paralysis. Once he received residency status, he'd have the clout and respect that he'd been working for tirelessly. Once confirmed, he planned to use his status as leverage to become a trailblazer in his profession and perhaps one day win the Nobel Peace Prize for his research. A lofty goal, but Travis was driven to succeed at any cost. Travis envisioned having it all: social status, wealth, and the great admiration of his colleagues. He could hardly wait to get his approval letter in a few days so that he could continue pursuing his ambitions at full speed.

Travis had made arrangements to travel to New York City for a few days to meet up with his best friend, Alex. After such a stressful conference, he knew he'd need some downtime to unwind. He knew that a body massage would go a long way toward easing his stress level, so before he left he'd asked Alex if he knew of any place in Manhattan where he could treat himself to a rubdown. Alex, being the worldly person he was, recommended a place called the Asian Massage Parlor.

"Ask for a woman named MiMi," Alex had told him during their earlier conversation.

"Is she any good?"

"Dude, trust me. You're going to like MiMi," Alex had assured him.

"What does MiMi look like, man?" Travis had asked, a little suspicious of Alex's recommendation.

"MiMi is sexy. Plus, she has some skills that will make your soldier stand up."

"Man, this girl had better be on point because if she's not I'm going to kick your ass," Travis had threatened his friend.

"I'm not worried about that because you're going to thank me when MiMi is done with you."

TRAVIS ARRIVED IN NEW YORK SAFELY. Once he checked into his hotel, he got in a cab and headed to his afternoon appointment.

Travis envisioned MiMi being a young, sexy woman with a banging body who, for the right price, would be willing to toss in a blowjob. He never imagined that MiMi would be a middle-aged Asian woman, with a belly as round as a barrel and a very thick accent. She had black shoulder-length hair and she was short.

"You're MiMi?" Travis asked when she came from the back to greet him.

"Yes. I'm MiMi," she answered as she wrote something down in the appointment book that was on the countertop.

"There is not another person named MiMi here?" Travis asked, looking around.

"No. There is only one MiMi and that's me. Do you have a problem or something?" Travis sensed that if he kept asking the same question, she'd get offended.

"No. There's not a problem at all," Travis said, all the while thinking of how he was going to kill Alex.

"Good. You follow me now. I'll have you feeling as light as a feather when I'm done. You'll feel like you can walk on clouds," she said. Snickering, she escorted him to a private room where he could remove his clothes. "You just wait and see." She pointed to the room where he could change.

"I can't believe Alex played me like this," Travis muttered.

"Hurry up, so that I can work on you right away. I can already see the tension in your body. Right here in your shoulders and neck." She touched his body.

"Yeah, I'm really tense now," Travis agreed with her as he rotated his neck in an effort to loosen up the tightness of his muscles.

"A big, strong man like you needs to be relaxed, not tense. If I were your woman, I'd make sure that you were never uptight. You'd always be pleased with me because I know how to take care of a good man." She continued her snickering and flirting. Travis laughed along with her, although he didn't find MiMi to be attractive at all.

"You've ordered my specialty. The Ashiatsu Massage. Have you ever had one before?"

"I've had massages before, but not that particular kind. My friend Alex recommended that I get one."

"Airplane pilot, Alex?" she asked.

"Yes," Travis said as he entered the room. The place appeared to be very clean and the massage table looked inviting. Positioned above the table were long wooden bars.

"Oh, Alex is my special friend." She laughed like a giddy schoolgirl. "If he sent you to me, then I have to treat you *extra* special."

"No you don't," Travis assured her. He didn't know what kind of freaky shit she and Alex had done, but whatever it was, he wanted no part of it.

"Get undressed and lay down on your stomach. Drape a towel around your waist. I'll come back in a few minutes and then we'll start."

Travis did as instructed and before long MiMi returned. She turned on some soothing music that was pleasing to his ears. MiMi held true to her word and had placed Travis in a euphoric state of mind. Her touch was like an intoxicating drug that made him feel as if he were floating on a breeze.

"I'm going to make sure that I tip you very well, MiMi," Travis uttered.

"Shhhh, quiet. The best part is yet to come." MiMi didn't like to be interrupted.

She placed a light amount of warm massage oil on his back and then stood on the massage table and held onto the bars above him. Being careful not to place the full weight of her body on him, she skillfully maneuvered up and down the length of his spine with her feet. She used her big toes to massage each of the vertebrae along his backbone. Her soft feet glided along the curve of his shoulders and down the side of his arms.

Travis couldn't remember exactly when he fell asleep or how long he was out. However, when he awoke he felt revitalized and just like MiMi had said, as light as a feather. He got dressed and exited the room. He walked toward the front and found MiMi waiting.

"You were asleep for a long time," MiMi said.

"Yeah, I'm sorry about that. I usually don't fall asleep like that," Travis apologized.

"That's because you've never been touched by MiMi before. I made you feel good, aye?" She smiled at

Travis and awaited his confirmation that she'd done well. Travis looked at her differently now. When he came in, she wasn't sexually attractive to him at all. Now he wondered, if she was that good with her feet, how good was she in bed?

"You're going to come back and see me soon, right?" MiMi asked as Travis removed his wallet.

"Yeah. Hell yeah." Travis could hardly believe the words coming out of his mouth.

"Are you from New York?"

"No. I'm from California."

"Oh, that's too bad. I was hoping you'd come back to see me next week."

"Look, I'm in town for a few days. I'd love to come back again before I head home."

"Good. Let's make your appointment now? It would be a good idea." MiMi suggested a date and time that fit into his schedule. Travis tipped her well before saying good-bye.

Travis hailed a taxi and gave the instruction to drive him back to his hotel in Times Square. As soon as he was situated, he gave Alex a jingle.

"Where is your crazy ass at?" Travis blasted out his friend as soon as he answered the phone.

"I'm in a cab heading to the hotel. I just landed not too long ago. Did you go see MiMi?" he asked.

"That was some weird shit, man. She's got me feeling high like a damn satellite."

"I know. She's freaky as hell, too." Alex laughed.

"Man, please don't tell me you hit that."

"Shit, I didn't fuck MiMi. She fucked me. She was massaging me and the next thing I knew I felt her toes fondling my balls and—"

"Dawg, spare me the details," Travis said as the cab approached his hotel. "How long will it be before you get here?"

"About another twenty minutes."

"Give me a buzz when you arrive. We can go out and grab a bite to eat and then figure out what we're going to do. I was thinking about going to a comedy club."

"Cool, we can do the comedy club thing tonight because I have tickets for the basketball game tomorrow evening," Alex boasted.

"You're bullshitting."

"Now, I'm your boy. Would I bullshit you about having game tickets?" Alex almost seemed offended.

"Yeah, you would, but I believe you're telling the truth this time. Who are they playing?"

"The Chicago Bulls, baby, and I've got courtside seats, third row back from the bench. We're talking premium seats, player," Alex informed him of the sweet deal he'd gotten.

"Wait a minute. How did you get such good seats, because I know your stingy behind didn't pay for them? Usually when we go to a game, we're almost always up in the nosebleed section of the arena."

"Don't worry about how I got them. Just be glad that I'm taking your ass," Alex said.

"Don't get me wrong. I'm glad to be going; I just want to make sure you have authentic tickets." Travis moved his cell phone from one ear to the other.

"Don't worry. I didn't get them from some bozo on the street. These are real tickets."

"Cool."

"Did I mention to you about this superfine woman I met?" Travis noticed that Alex's voice was suddenly filled with excitement.

"You're always meeting some woman, Alex. But no, you didn't mention her yet."

"Her name is Jasmine, and if I had to guess, I'd say she's around forty-one or forty-two."

"How does her body look? Is she taking care of herself?" Travis asked, genuinely interested.

"Her body was tight. Nice breasts, full ass, shapely legs and a walk that says, 'I need a stallion.' I watched her as she exited the airplane and the rhythm of her strut had a sweet melody that made me want to get on my knees and sing to her. Her behind looked so good I almost ran after her just to smack it."

Travis laughed. "I've seen the type of ass you're talking about. It's the kind that has an attitude."

"Yeah, an ass in need of a serious attitude adjustment," Alex agreed with Travis' assessment.

"Jasmine has smooth caramel skin, beautiful shoulder-length hair and the most alluring set of green eyes I've ever had the pleasure of gazing into. Travis, I'm telling you, she has exotic features like the Amazonian women out of Greek mythology. She was strong-willed and intoxicating all at the same time."

"Well, did you step to her and throw some game her way? Did you get her phone number or e-mail address?" Travis wanted to know if Alex had upheld his reputation of being a ladies' man.

"You damn right I said something to her. I snuggled up to her, inhaled the sweet scent of her perfume and started speaking directly in her ear. I told her that I saw her looking at me like she wanted to eat me alive. She admitted to checking me out, but then flipped the script and started mischievously tormenting me with sexual innuendos. She was without a doubt the type of woman who liked being in control."

"Jasmine sounds like the type of woman who wants to do things on her own terms. She may be a little too much for you." Travis knew his comment would ruffle Alex's feathers.

"Man, please! I haven't met a woman yet that I couldn't have if I wanted to. That includes married women."

"What about gay women? Can your bronzed dick turn a gay woman straight?" Travis mocked Alex and his overinflated ego.

"Hell, it probably can. My penis power is potent like a motherfucker." They both laughed at the silliness of the comment. "Anyway, I gave Jasmine my number and if she calls me or we run into each other again, I'm going to have to put you down and go handle that. Damn, she looked like a goddess to me."

"Alex, stop salivating over a woman you just met and don't even know. You'll probably never see her again and if by chance you do, she's probably got a man who makes a ridiculous sum of money that your bank account can't compete with."

"Player, you know as well as I do, wealthy, well-kept women are almost always sexually frustrated. A young stud like me who can stand up in it, is what a lady like her craves. I don't want to get into a pissing contest with her husband; I just want to satisfy her unquenchable lust." Alex laughed at what he believed to be the undisputable truth.

"I'll give you that. A mature, yet sexually frustrated woman will seek out an affair not only to satisfy her thirst, but also to fulfill some wild fantasies," Travis said as the cab came to a halt in front of his hotel. "Alex, hang on, I'm at the hotel and need to pay the driver."

"Okay."

Alex remained silent while Travis went about his business of tipping the cab driver. He then walked into the lobby of the Doubletree Hotel and sat down on a comfortable chair in the lounge area.

"Are you still there?" Travis asked.

"Yeah, I'm here."

"So what else have you been up to besides chasing ass?" Travis inquired.

"I've just been doing the same old shit. Logging in long hours flying commercial jets all over the country and when I'm not flying the big jets, I'm flying a private aircraft for someone wealthy and well-connected."

"What about you? Have you stopped tripping yet? Are you ready to get back in the game? I've gotten a few secretive inquiries about you from clients on the private list. They want to know when you'll be available again."

"I haven't been on the list in three years, man. You know why I had to let that go. The woman from Rio de Janeiro overdosed on drugs in the hotel bathroom. I thought she was in there getting ready. I had no clue she'd written a suicide note before overdosing on Paco. When I discovered she was dead, I couldn't just leave her there because the police would have found me. It wasn't fun being interrogated about a woman I didn't know. I told the police I'd met her in the hotel bar for an easy one-night stand. Thank God they believed me and were able to verify that she had a history of depression."

"Yeah, that was some fucked-up shit that went down, but still, man, you've got to come back. You can't let the one incident keep you away."

"I'm not saying that it won't happen, but what will you do if for some reason you don't get tenure status?" Alex asked.

"Dude, I know I'm going to get it. I've been busting my ass too hard not to. But, if the impossible did happen,

I heard about a few leads I can look into. One of them is even in Chicago where you live."

"Okay. My father always told me to expect the unexpected and plan accordingly." Alex shared a few words of wisdom.

"Sounds like some good advice."

"No, that was sound advice. I got the good guidance from my crazy uncle, King Solomon who told me to get as much pussy as humanly possible." Travis started laughing out loud.

"You'd better hope that you don't drop off into some bad pussy one of these days."

"Hey, I'm the prince of pussy. I can tell a good one from a bad one and a juicy one from a dry one. In fact, I know all of my women by the shape of their pussy. Every time a lady calls me, a photo of her pussy pops up on my cell phone screen."

"You'd better pray that your women don't turn on you." Travis gave his friend a forewarning.

"Yeah whatever, that will never happen. Anyway, I'll talk to you when I get there."

"Cool," Travis said, then ended the call.

TRAVIS WENT BACK UP TO HIS HOTEL ROOM, removed his clothes from the suitcase and hung them up. He then found the television remote and turned it on. He briefly listened to an entertainment report about R&B singer Usher divorcing his wife and hooking up with a super fine and amazingly sexy but much older recording executive.

"Damn, these women in their forties aren't playing around when it comes to dating younger men," Travis said as he walked over to the window to see what type of city view he had. He could see hordes of tourists meandering around Times Square. He exhaled as he unbuttoned his shirt and thought about how far he'd come.

❂❂❂

Travis was blessed with a brilliant mind. By the age of sixteen, he'd graduated high school as valedictorian with a perfect four-point-zero grade-point average. He received an academic scholarship and in the fall of that same year, he attended the University of California at Berkeley. By the time Travis was eighteen, he was a junior in college. It was at that time he'd met Alex, who was also eighteen, an incoming freshman and his new roommate. Alex was from Chicago and was attending Berkeley on a football scholarship.

Alex was a very self-centered and egotistical guy, who enjoyed boasting about his sexual prowess, but especially about receiving his pilot's license before his driver's license. Getting his pilot certification was easier for him because his grandfather and dad were airmen themselves. His family owned an aviation academy in

Illinois and possessed a modest fleet of Cessna aircraft.

Alex was a decent student, but only when he needed to be, which was generally a few weeks before final exams. The rest of the time he partied, played football and quenched his unyielding thirst for women. Alex made it his personal mission to get Travis to loosen up and enjoy his time in college.

"Come on, man. You need to stop playing with your chemistry set and come to our victory party. The football team just won the conference title and there is going to be a massive celebration. There will be enough tits and ass for everyone."

"You go on and have a good time. I need to study," Travis had said to him without so much as looking up from his books.

"What kind of guy are you? How could you not want to party and chase girls? Are you gay or something?" Alex had asked.

"Hell no!" Travis had said, instantly offended.

"You ever think about dudes or try to be with one?" Alex had continued his inquiry as he moved closer to him.

"I can assure you that I've never had any such thoughts." Travis had slammed his fist on this textbook. He was getting frustrated with Alex and his petty conversation.

"Okay, no need to get your underwear in a bunch. But look, there is a good chance that I'll be bringing a girl in here tonight, so when I do you're going to need to step out while I do my thing."

"I am not getting out of my bed in the middle of the night so you can bang some chickenhead."

"Suit yourself, Travis, because I'm going to do her whether you're in the room or not. I'm just trying to save you the aggravation of feeling left out."

"Don't do me any favors," Travis had remarked with a nasty attitude.

"What's the problem, dude? You're a nice-looking brother. A little nerdy, but it's not like you've got bad skin or poor hygiene. Girls will fall all over you, if you'd just open your mouth and speak."

"I'm not like that. My parents told me that I had to come here and get an education, not party. They expect me to be at the top of my class and that takes dedication, determination, and sacrifice." Travis had firmly stood his ground.

"Getting to know women and fucking are also a part of being educated," Alex had countered.

"Whatever, Alex. Just go and have a good time." Travis hadn't felt like speaking to him anymore.

"Okay, Steve Urkel. Have fun playing with yourself," Alex had said before grabbing his leather bomber jacket and heading out.

Over the course of his junior year, Travis had inadvertently walked in on Alex having sex on a number of occasions—once during a threesome and another time when he was banging the professor of his Asian-American studies class.

One afternoon, when there was nothing particularly

interesting going on around campus, Alex had offered to take Travis for a bite to eat at a nearby fast-food restaurant.

"Come on, Einstein." He had collapsed the screen on Travis' laptop. "Even you have to take a break to eat."

"Alex, I've got a lot of work to do, man. I don't have time to eat." Travis had opened up his laptop once again. Alex had tried to close it but Travis had swatted his hand away. He was irritated by the interruption.

"I'm treating, okay. I have money and plenty of it," Alex had offered. Travis had paused for a second and then changed his mind.

"Well, if you're treating, I'm eating." Travis finally had agreed to take a break.

"Come on, let's get out of here. Open up that window first. It smells a little funky in here."

"Dude, the funk is from your smelly-ass football shoes. You need to donate those son-a-bitches to science because there has to be a new type of fungus growing in them."

"Well, guess what, genius. If you figure it out and create a cure, you'd probably make millions of dollars. And when you do, I most certainly want my share of the profits." Alex had laughed as he had walked out of the room.

When they had arrived at their destination, they were seated in a booth seat near a window. They had looked over the menu, made their selections and informed the waiter.

"So I'm curious," Travis had asked.

"About what?" Alex had removed his straw from its paper wrapping and had stuck it into his glass of water.

"How does a guy who's as young as you get so many girls and not have any drama?"

"Because I'm a pimp." Alex had laughed at his own comment.

"You are not a pimp. I'm serious. I mean, you've got girls coming and going and I just don't get it."

"You're envious, right?" A sly grin had spread across Alex's lips. Travis had leaned back in his seat and had given him a condescending glance.

"I may be a little green about it," Travis had admitted. "So what's your secret?"

"There is none and trust me, I do have drama. I just know how to manage my women."

"Manage your women. You make it sound as if you're herding cattle." Travis had fiddled with his silverware.

"Call it what you want, but for as long as I can remember, girls have always been drawn to me."

"My, aren't we conceited?" Alex and his ego at times had gotten on Travis' nerves.

"Hey, I'm being honest with you. The men in my family have always been able to pull women. That's just the way it is. Ever since I was little boy in kindergarten I had girls bringing me extra food. Hell, if I pouted a certain way, I could even get what I wanted out of my teacher. By the time I was in junior high school, I had girls fighting over me. Shit, when I was a freshman in high school, I'd gotten between more legs than a lot of the senior guys."

"How do you know what to say? Or better yet, who taught you what to say?" Travis had asked.

"Now that's a very interesting question. I'd say my biggest influence came from my uncle, King Solomon."

"King Solomon?" Travis had laughed at the name. "What kind of name is that?"

"His real name was Sal, but everyone called him King Solomon because he had a harem of women and his pockets were always filled with money from his gambling winnings. He was as brawny as Luther Vandross and was fond of dressing sharply. I was spending time with him the summer before I entered high school. It was during those weeks with him that I learned a lot about life, gambling and women. He asked me if I'd been with a girl yet and I said no.

"He asked me how far I'd gotten with a girl and I said third base, but it was more like second base. He asked me what happened and I told him that the girl kept fighting me off when I tried to pull off her panties. Then he said, 'You have to find one who is ripe. The quiet girls will give it up quicker,' he said. And I was like, 'for real?' Uncle Solomon gave me a bunch of tips on what to say, and how to play the game. Hell, I just listened and took notes and if I ran into a snag, I called him up."

"So when did you lose your virginity?" Travis had

asked just as their food had arrived. They'd both ordered the special—a triple cheeseburger loaded with three types of cheeses, mushrooms along with French fries and coleslaw.

"I lost it when I was fifteen," Alex had said as he bit into his burger.

"Fifteen, come on, you're shitting me, right?" Travis had asked.

"No."

"Damn." Travis couldn't imagine having sex at that age.

"And get this, the woman who cracked my first nut was much older than me."

"How much older?"

"She was a grown-ass woman." Alex had paused. "You remember that movie that came out a while ago called *The Inkwell* starring Larenz Tate?"

"Yeah, I remember it. It's the one where the married woman has sex with—wait a minute… You lost your virginity to an older, married woman?" Travis had asked, finally making the connection.

"Damn right, I did," Alex had said, "and that shit was the fucking bomb!"

"Can't she go to jail for that?" Travis had scratched his head.

"Who was going to fucking tell? I damn sure wasn't and I knew for a fact she wasn't. Hell, her husband was never around; he was always traveling on some business trip. I was walking home from football practice one day and she asked if I could help carry some storage boxes from the house to the garage. I said sure. Once that was done, I was all sweaty, so she asked if I wanted to come in for a cold drink. I didn't think anything of it and followed her back inside the house. She had on some tight shorts and when she bent over to get my drink from the refrigerator, her chocolate ass cheeks bubbled out. At that moment, everything King Solomon told me came into play. I knew she was teasing me to see how I'd react.

"I started telling her how good she looked and if I was her man, she'd never be lonely. She laughed because she thought I was too young to know anything about having a woman. I told her that I knew enough about women to understand that they need their man to pay more attention to them. She then decided to make herself a cocktail and after a few drinks, my fingers were exploring her juicy pussy. She cracked my nuts and my entire world changed."

"How?" Travis had placed his elbows on the table and had leaned forward.

"Well, for starters, my confidence level in everything skyrocketed. She showed me everything: where a clit was, how to eat her pussy, suck on her breasts and even taught me the rhythm of the stroke. I'll tell you, Travis, there is no melody sweeter than the sound a woman makes when your dick is inside of her."

"What does it sound like?" Travis had asked curiously.

"It depends on the woman. Some shout and others cry or whimper. They make all kinds of sounds that you won't hear unless you're deep inside stroking the walls of her pussy with your dick."

"So what happened to her?" Travis had continued to probe.

"She moved. Her husband got a job in another state. She told me to go blow some young girl's mind with what she'd taught me."

"Did you keep up with her? Did she give you her phone number or anything?"

"No. I wasn't in love with her, Travis. I understood the nature of our relationship. I wasn't trying to marry her. I wanted to have sex and the trade-off for her centered around the feeling of being desired—an element that had gotten lost in her marriage."

"So is that how you get the women? You make them feel truly desired?"

"It depends on the woman. Some women already know they're hot while others have reservations about their own beauty. Some women just want to fuck while others are looking for you to put a ring on their finger. Those are the ones I run away from."

"So what type of woman do you like better, older or younger?"

"It's funny you should bring that up." Alex had repositioned himself in his seat. "Because something weird happened recently that I want to talk to you about."

"How weird?"

"Well, how can I put this…" Alex had leaned closer to Travis and had begun to whisper. "You know that I nailed one of my professors, right?"

"Yeah."

"Well, she introduced me to this secret society."

"What kind of society?" Travis had asked.

"A secret one; I just told you that," Alex had whispered.

"What in the hell…you're not making any sense." Travis had looked at Alex perplexed as he'd scratched the stubble on his chin.

"It sounds pretty straightforward, don't you think?"

"Okay." Travis had paused in thought for a moment. "So she put your information on this list, or profile or whatever; what does that mean?"

"Here is how it works. There are career women out there who don't have time for a family or a relationship, but enjoy having uncommitted sex, especially with young men. If they initiate contact with you, they'll send you a text message with the name of a hotel and a time to be there. You go to the hotel and wait in the bar area alone. The initiator will find you by looking for a handkerchief that you're supposed to place on your leg. If the initiator likes what she sees, she'll make contact. If not, she'll send you a text message saying *no thanks.*

"That sounds insane!" Travis had gazed at Alex as if

he'd lost his mind, but another part of him was very intrigued.

Alex had grinned. "I know, but it's so much fun. You don't have to worry about calling her up the next day, or sending her flowers, or even remembering her birthday. It's an arrangement to fuck off some frustrations and that's it."

"Have you done this already?" Travis had asked.

"Damn right I have and I love it."

Travis had finished his food and thought about what Alex had just told him. He wanted to tell him how bizarre this society was, but he couldn't. Hanging around Alex allowed an untamed part of him to come alive. He surreptitiously wished he were as experienced as Alex. He'd grown a little weary of being a virgin as well as focusing only on his studies.

"Why do you have that odd look on your face, Travis? What are you thinking about?"

"I don't know. I mean… Do you think you could get me on the list?" Alex had laughed out loud.

"I don't think you'd be able to handle it," Alex had said earnestly as he slowly shook his head.

"I can handle myself. I've done some things in the past."

"Like what? Looked at a porn site?" Alex had continued to mock him, which only aggravated and made Travis more determined to prove himself.

"I want to get on the list, Alex. I'm not playing."

"You're serious, aren't you?" Alex had stopped laughing.

"Hell yes. I want to do it."

"I don't know, Travis. I haven't really been doing this that long and I'm not sure I can get you in."

"Don't bullshit me, Alex." Travis wasn't going to allow Alex to disregard his request.

"Okay, man. Have it your way. I'll see what I can do."

A FEW DAYS LATER, Alex had informed Travis that he was able to get him on the list. Wanting to look more mature than his years, Travis had used an emergency credit card with an eight-thousand-dollar limit that his parents had given him. He had purchased several expensive suits and shoes. Within a month, he had received a text message asking if he was available for a rendezvous at the Doubletree Hotel in Berkeley. Nervous, but determined to step outside of his comfort zone and into a double life, Travis had agreed to the meeting.

When he had arrived, he had taken a seat on a brown leather sofa in the waiting area and had picked up a copy of a daily newspaper nearby. He had placed a red handkerchief on his left leg so the person would be able to spot him. A short time later, a stunningly beautiful, middle-aged woman of mixed heritage with a fit body stood before him and had asked, "Did you receive a text message earlier today?" Her British accent was steady, calm, and direct. Travis, on the other hand, was extremely anxious. It had taken him a moment to find his voice.

"Yes. I did get your message." He nervously had folded up his newspaper.

"Then let's go. Follow me," she had said. They had walked over to the elevators and had stepped inside. She had pressed the tenth-floor button and had stood behind him.

"Ummm, I've never done this before," Travis had said. "What's your name?"

"You know that question is against the rules." She was firm with him.

"That's right. I'm sorry, I forgot."

"Someone did explain the rules, didn't they?" she had asked, placing a hand on his right shoulder.

"Yeah, I know the rules. I'm just a little edgy, is all."

"I hope that doesn't mean you're going to have performance issues." She had stepped closer to him and had placed her hands on his behind, then had squeezed. Travis flinched nervously as she stepped around to face him.

"Oh, no. Not at all, trust me, I don't have any trouble getting hard." Travis had laughed nervously as he had wiped sweat from his forehead.

"You're a virgin, aren't you?" She had smiled naughtily at him.

"No I'm not." Travis had denied it.

"Yes, you are. There is no need to lie about it. Every-

thing about your manner says inexperienced virgin."
Travis had remained silent because he didn't want to
blow it.

"It's okay. I have a soft spot for bashful boys. In fact,
I'll probably enjoy giving you your first real orgasm.
It's kind of empowering, spreading open the pillars of
my paradise to a young man ready to graduate into full
masculinity."

"I promise I won't mess this up for you."

"I know you won't. Because I'm going to take the
time to show you all of the miracles and wonders of a
woman's body. Consider it a gift from a stranger."

The following morning, Travis had awakened to
find himself all alone in bed. His British lover was
gone. On the nightstand, she'd left a note for him that
read: *Thank you for a pleasurable evening. Remember what
I've taught you.*

Travis never saw the British woman again, but she
opened up an entirely new world for him. Alex was
right. After the experience, his confidence level skyrocketed. Travis, being the perfectionist that he was,
spent countless hours reading literature on the art of
making love. With his newfound skills and interest, he
embraced his new lifestyle and his love for mature,
intelligent, and sexy women. Then after the incident with
the woman from Rio, he realized that his hedonistic
indulgences were keeping him from fulfilling much
more ambitious goals.

After college Travis went on to graduate school but Alex's life took a different turn. He was on track to go pro, and even had the Philadelphia Eagles highly interested in him. But then all types of false allegations surfaced and Alex's name was mentioned. Even though Alex was cleared, it weakened his chances of playing professional football. Travis asked Alex what happened but at that time, his wound was too raw and Alex was too emotional to discuss it. One year after he'd graduated from college, Alex was invited to attend a football camp for the Dallas Cowboys, but wasn't able to secure a spot on the team.

Chapter 3
Jasmine

The following morning Jasmine awoke feeling a little jetlagged from traveling across a time zone. Although the time difference was only an hour, she still felt as if she needed more sleep. She glanced over at a digital clock sitting on the nightstand and focused her vision on the time.

"Shit, it's already eight-thirty. I'm supposed to be in the lobby to meet everyone by nine o'clock." She huffed before tossing back the sheets and sitting upright. She reached for the remote, aimed it at the television and pressed the power button. She flipped the stations until she found the Weather Channel.

"Ninety-five degrees and sunny; it's going to be a hot and sticky one. My hair is going to end up looking messy if we hang out in the hot sun all day shopping high-end stores in Manhattan. That's Tiffany for you though."

The girl certainly qualifies as having champagne taste and a beer-belly budget. She loves to tell everyone how much she's paid for merchandise, even if she's paid too much for it.

She believes telling someone the price makes it seem more valuable than it actually is. Jasmine grumbled at Tiffany's values as she rose to her feet and went into the bathroom.

After an invigorating shower and face time in front of the mirror, Jasmine exited the bathroom and unzipped her suitcase in search of something to wear.

"Okay, I want to look fabulous, but I don't want to upstage Tiffany because she's put on a few extra pounds. She's gone from a healthy size ten to a robust fourteen." Jasmine began laughing at her impolite comment. "Be nice, Jasmine. Tiffany is celebrating her birthday and you shouldn't be so critical," she said to herself.

Jasmine finally decided on wearing her denim capris, her brown leather sling-back sandals and a simple top. No sooner than she'd put on her clothes and began squirting on some of her Cool Water perfume, her cell phone rang. She looked at the caller ID. It was Tiffany.

"Happy birthday, darling," Jasmine answered.

"Thank you! I'm just too damn sexy and fine at forty. Where are you? We're waiting on you." Her voice was jovial and full of life.

"Beauty takes time, honey. I'll be there in a moment." Jasmine laughed.

"Well, beauty had better get her narrow ass on down here before she gets left." Tiffany was trying to sound tough, but Jasmine knew her friends wouldn't leave without her.

"I'll be there in a moment. I'm walking out the door now," Jasmine informed her as she slid her key card into her pocket and grabbed her purse.

When Jasmine arrived in the lobby, Millie was trying to convince Tiffany to grab something to eat in Times Square.

"I don't want to eat in Times Square. I want to go up to Harlem and eat at Amy Ruth's Restaurant."

"But Tiffany, you know all of that soul food cooking isn't good for you," Millie reminded her.

"Millie, stop arguing with her. She's got her mouth all set to eat at Amy Ruth's and we should just go. It's her birthday and it's what she wants to do," argued Lauren who was trying to diffuse the situation before it blew up into a shouting match.

"Hey, I'm really looking out for her. I want to make sure she sees another birthday. Don't you think I'm doing the right thing, Jasmine?" Millie said, not willing to back down.

"Oh no you don't. I'm not co-signing that check with you, Millie. If that's what Tiffany wants to do, we shouldn't be trying to change her mind."

"Thank you, Jasmine," Tiffany said as she started moving toward the exit.

"Okay, I'll go along with the will of the group. But when we're all sitting around the waiting room while she's having open heart surgery, I'm not going to say a word."

"Millie, that's not nice," Lauren said. "What's wrong with you? Why are you acting so snippy?"

"Forget it." Millie dropped the subject and her attitude.

"Amy Ruth's, here we come," Jasmine bellowed as they all exited the hotel.

When they arrived at Amy Ruth's, everyone ordered the type of food they had a taste for.

"Oh my goodness, it is so great to be here with you guys. I feel like the chicks from *Sex and the City*," Tiffany said as she took a bite of her waffle.

"Oh yeah, and what character would I be?" asked Millie.

"Miranda," everyone said on queue.

"And I would be like Carrie. Mild-mannered, yet always analyzing everything and looking for under-standing," admitted Tiffany.

"So that leaves Samantha and Charlotte," Jasmine said as she glanced at her sister, Lauren. "Neither one of us is like those two."

"Damn, is that thunder and lightning I hear?" Tiffany looked out of the window.

"And what's that supposed to mean?" Jasmine asked as she took a sip of orange juice.

"Girl, you know that you have some Samantha-like tendencies." Millie busted her girlfriend out.

"I am nowhere near as promiscuous as Samantha." Jasmine didn't like the comparison.

"No, but you damn sure flirt with men like her," said her sister, Lauren.

"She would know better than any of us. She's lived with you most of her life," Millie said.

"So I guess that means you're Charlotte, the sensitive and prissy rich girl who secretly likes kinky sex," Jasmine shot back at Lauren.

"I think that pretty much sums me up." Lauren continued to laugh.

"Hey, do you guys realize that we are all now in our forties, unmarried, well, with the exception of Millie, and we don't have any children."

"I'm so thankful that I don't have children. It's entirely too hard to juggle a demanding career and change a diaper," Millie chimed.

"With the amount of money you make, Millie, you can get a nanny to do that," Lauren said.

"Do you really want a nanny to raise your child?" Tiffany asked. "I mean, doesn't that take away from the mother experience?"

"I guess that's why none of us ever became mothers because that's an experience we didn't want," Millie said.

"Well, I don't agree with that, Millie. I really wanted to have children at one point. I wanted to be a mom and take the kids to the zoo and water park. I think I would've been a good mother."

"Well, I know one thing is for sure, it's too late now because I'm entering menopause." Lauren leaned back and threaded her fingers though her hair.

"You guys know what this means, right?" Tiffany asked.

"No, what does it mean?" Jasmine played along.

"It means that we're Cougars. We're women who aren't afraid to date younger men and who refuse to be judged by what other people think. We make no apologies for our lifestyle, we know what we want and we're not afraid to go get it. We're healthy, radiant, desirable, and financially secure," she said excitedly.

Lauren frowned. "Why do we have to be called Cougars? Why can't we just refer to ourselves in the way you just described? Cougars sounds so predatory, like we're desperate women who'll jump the first hard dick that happens to come swinging along," Lauren said.

"I kind of like the name," Tiffany laughed. "It's sort of empowering if you ask me and now that I am a Cougar, I'm much more comfortable in my skin. Plus after sex I can look over and say, 'Don't you need to be somewhere right now?'"

"I like dating younger guys, but thirty-three is my cut-off." Lauren repositioned herself in her seat.

"You don't know what you're missing," Tiffany said, emphasizing the word *missing*.

"Ooo, Tiffany, how low did you go, girl?" Jasmine laughed and teased her.

"Let me tell you. I love my job. Being on a college campus filled with young men who constantly flirt with me and tell me how good I look just excites the hell out of me."

"Uh-huh. But girlfriend, how low did you go?" Millie now wanted to know.

"Twenty-one," Tiffany boldly admitted.

"You had sex with a twenty-one-year-old boy?" Lauren spoke louder than she intended to. Some of the orange juice she was drinking went down the wrong pipe and she began coughing. She gathered herself. "That's borderline cradle robbing."

"He wasn't a boy when I got done with him and I didn't rob the cradle; I rocked it until the legs broke off." Tiffany laughed through her words.

"Well, hell, girl, what was it like?" Jasmine asked.

"Honey, he was all energy and he didn't run out of gas. Just stayed hard and that's the way I like it. I was so sore the next day, but I felt good."

"I'm sorry, that's just too young for me. That's entirely too much teaching," Lauren said.

"I like teaching them about life, and, honey, he took to coochie like a squirrel to a tree. Once I showed him what to do, he stayed on it without complaining." Tiffany raised her hand above her head and clapped twice.

"That's what I'm talking about," Jasmine chimed in. "I like it when they don't complain and just do the job."

"Okay, I didn't want to bring this up, but I'm having an affair," Millie blurted.

"What?" everyone exclaimed.

"I always knew you were a slut," Lauren joked.

"Honey, I knew you and Mr. Egotistical Prick were

having trouble, but not to the point of you having an affair."

"Who is the guy?" Tiffany asked.

Millie paused for a long moment and debated whether or not she wanted to spill her little secret. "He's an intern," Millie reluctantly admitted.

"Well, how good is he in bed?" Jasmine asked.

Millie gave her a mannish glare. "Unbelievable. I haven't had a fully erect dick inside of me for so long. Glen, my egotistical husband, suffers from erectile dysfunction, and he can't take Viagra because of his heart problems."

"So you've been walking around sexually fuck-straighted," Jasmine concluded.

"That's putting it mildly. I mean the vibrators just weren't cutting it."

"Well, you shouldn't feel bad about it. It happens to the best of us. Just have your fun and move on."

"It's a little more complicated than that," Millie continued.

"Do tell, is he married, too?" asked Tiffany.

"No, but I am under investigation."

"Investigation for what?" Lauren asked.

"Somehow, someway, the disciplinary commission is investigating me for allegedly fixing court cases."

"You've been fixing court cases?" Lauren's voice was filled with horror.

"Hell no! Someone is trying to make it seem that way,

and if the media gets wind of it, I'm afraid some ambitious journalist will start snooping around and uncover my affair."

"Well, let's just hope that doesn't happen. And if it does, fuck them. They don't have any right to judge you. Who do you think is behind this smear campaign?" Jasmine said, continuing her inquiry.

"I have no clue," Millie said.

"If you want, I could call in a favor and see what I can find out for you," Lauren offered.

"Thanks love, but right now I just want to take a wait-and-see approach."

"Well, you know that I'm here for you if you need me." Tiffany placed her hand on top of Millie's.

"Thank you." There was a short moment of silence, then Millie spoke again. "Let's talk about something else. What's going on with you, Jasmine?"

"Nothing, just working and coming home every day."

"Whatever happened to the young twenty-five-year-old guy you were seeing?"

"Steve? Oh, I let him go. He had too many mother issues," Jasmine grudgingly admitted. "But the airline pilot on my flight was cute and very flirtatious. However, he wasn't really my type."

"I don't know why you ladies want to mess around with babies in their twenties. I'm telling you, come up to the dirty thirties. By the time a man hits thirty, he should have matured," said Lauren.

"What are you talking about, Lauren?" Tiffany glanced at her as if she were from another planet. "I've dated men who were fifty and still acted like a child. You can't gauge maturity by age only. You can find a young man who is very mature and articulate. I truly believe that age is just a number and I'm open to loving anyone who loves and treats me good."

"Girl, you need to call a spade a spade. You like college boys because they make you feel young," Jasmine said.

"And what's wrong with that?" Tiffany wanted Jasmine to explain her comment.

"Nothing is wrong with it. I think it's wonderful."

"Well, I don't know about you guys but I am stuffed," Lauren confessed.

"Yeah, I need to walk some of this food off. Are you guys about set? We've got a busy day. We've got to do some more shopping and then it's off to a nightclub. Come on and stop acting like old ladies. We're going to paint this town red and party all night long!" Tiffany popped her fingers and did a little dance move.

Chapter 4
Travis

Travis had on his favorite black silk, short-sleeved woven sport shirt, a pair of loose-fitting Sean John jeans and his favorite pair of casual duck-billed shoes. He and Alex had just gotten out of a cab and were walking toward the entrance of Madison Square Garden. Alex and his lustful nature were constantly on the prowl for a new sexual conquest and New York City was filled with beautiful women, young and mature from all walks of life.

"How are you doing, baby? You know you're wearing that dress," he said to a pretty Middle Eastern woman who paid him no attention.

"Have you ever had a woman from the Middle East?" Alex asked as they stepped inside.

"No, I can't say that I have," Travis answered as he read the signs for the direction to walk.

"I hear that they're good in bed." Alex flipped his wrist to look at his watch.

"I'm sure they are," Travis said as he continued.

"Why are you in such a funk? I thought this was going

to be a fun trip and you were going to loosen up a bit. At least that's what you told me you were going to do." Travis could tell right away that Alex was going to be extremely annoyed if he didn't behave in a hedonistic manner.

"I'm cool, man; I just have a lot on my mind."

"The only thing you truly need to have on your mind is hooking up with a fine babe who can help you relieve some stress. That's why I sent you to see MiMi. She must be losing her damn touch."

Travis laughed. "MiMi was truly something else, and she hasn't lost her touch. I'm having a lot of issues with my current boss. There is a lot of political bullshit happening, and I have a feeling they're gunning for me. Before I came down, I checked my e-mails and I had a nasty gram."

"See, that's your problem. You don't know how to leave work at the office. You're one of those driven bastards who has to work twenty-four-hours, seven days a week. You'd better take it easy before you lose all of your hair, gain a gut and complicated health issues. I mean, seriously. We're young, handsome, college-educated men. We have an abundance of women from a variety of ethnic backgrounds to select from: ladies who are young or marvelously mature and freaky as hell. What more could a guy ask for?"

"Alex, my ambitions go beyond sexual conquests. For ten years I've been on the list. I've had my fun, but now it's time for me to get serious. I want to win the

Nobel Prize for being a brilliant chemist who creates a cure for something like cancer. Do you know how wealthy I'd be if I found a cure? I'd be like fucking Bill Gates, so goddamn wealthy it's too ridiculous for words. Damn, sometimes I wish I had his brain and created Microsoft."

"Dude, this is about as good as it gets for us. Unless you're a professional athlete, actor or singer, life isn't going to get any sweeter for you in this country."

"I don't believe that." Travis flat out refused to allow Alex to blow the light out on his dream.

"I know you don't and I'm not trying to be a dream killer, but on the real, you need to be thankful for what you have. You have a PhD. in organic chemistry. You're a doctor and by society's standards, you're one of the elites in this country."

"Hell, anyone with an opportunity, a little bit of will and a lot of desire can do what I've done. I don't want to just be good, man. I want the world to know my name. Like Steve Jobs, or Robert Jarvik, the inventor of the artificial heart, or even Dr. Ben Carson. I want to be an inventor and innovator who changes the world."

"You sound like you're going to become some obsessed nut-sack who ends up in the mental hospital talking to a padded wall." Alex spoke truthfully about the way he felt.

"I doubt that I'll go insane." Travis disregarded his statement.

"I don't know about that, dawg. Sometimes you can

get so focused that you just tune the fuck out. I've seen you do that shit and it's not pretty."

"That's just the nature of my work." Travis defended his sometimes altruistic behavior.

"That's why you need a friend like me. Someone to help you realize that all work and no play will make you a dull boy."

Travis smirked at the simplicity and the truthfulness of the statement.

"Speaking of individuals doing extreme shit, are you still flying people like Hatcher McKean around? They're known underworld kingpins, but if they need to book a private flight somewhere, they call you. What's up with that shit?"

Alex glanced around as if he were suddenly paranoid. "Shhhh! What the fuck is wrong with you, man? Don't go blurting shit like that."

"I was just asking a question."

Alex began to whisper. "I fly all kinds of people around on commercial and private airlines. I'm just a damn pilot making a few extra dollars. What they do to make money is their business. I don't ask questions. Do you understand where I'm coming from?"

"Just answer me this. Are they the ones responsible for getting you such good seats? I mean, even if you're making cash on the side, to get such choice seats is very expensive."

"Don't worry about how I got the tickets, Travis. Let's just enjoy the game and have fun, agreed?"

Alex stopped walking, then extended his hand so they could agree to just have some fun.

"Cool," Travis conceded and gave him a brotherly handshake and a pat on the back.

"Stop being so damn nosey." Alex got in the last word as they continued on their way.

THE GAME WAS FAST PACED AND EXCITING. At half time the Bulls were down by twenty points. They fought their way back into the game and with only seconds left on the clock found themselves ahead by two points. The capacity of the crowd had risen to their feet, and roared to an earsplitting level. The Knicks tossed the ball inbound, hustled up the court and at the very last moment put up a three-point shot that sailed through the hoop.

"Damn it! Son of a bitch!" Alex howled. "Why didn't the damn defender do his fucking job? There is no way the Knicks should have had an unobstructed view of the basket!"

"Calm down, man." Travis knew that Alex didn't take loss in any form well. His competitive nature, if left unchecked, had gotten him into a few fistfights over the years. Travis immediately saw that this part of his personality hadn't changed with maturity.

Travis watched as Alex curled the knuckles on his right hand, then held up his left palm and punched it a few times. "Damn! I had money on this game."

"One day you'll get enough of gambling your paychecks away," Travis said as he slapped the back of Alex's right shoulder a few times.

"I don't gamble my paychecks away." Travis saw a disgusted look formed on Alex's face as the team headed to the locker room.

"Come on, there is nothing you can do about it now, crybaby," Travis said, wanting Alex to start moving toward the door.

"They need to do a better job drafting high-quality players." Travis listened as Alex continued to gripe. His favorite teams were the Chicago Bulls and the Chicago Bears, and he followed them both religiously.

"Keep it moving, Alex. You're in my way and I've got to hit the bathroom before I bust wide open," Travis said.

"I can't wait to get online and blog about how they gave this game away," Alex said.

"Will you stop your bitching and move?" Travis snapped at him like a whip cracking against the air.

Alex finally complied and began moving toward the exit.

By the time the two were back on the street, Alex was still raw about the loss. Although Travis tried to change the subject, Alex wanted to relive that lost shot over and over again. Travis hailed a cab and told the driver to take them back to the hotel.

"Did the Knicks win?" asked the driver as the cab bolted out into the flow of traffic.

"Yeah," answered Travis.

"Those are my boys. They're going to win it all this year," said the driver.

Travis glanced over at Alex and saw that his ears were filled with sore loser steam.

"We're Bulls fans," Travis announced so the driver would shut up before Alex choked him to death.

An hour later, Travis was standing in the lobby of the hotel. He'd just come back down from his room where he'd changed clothes and freshened up. He had on an all-white linen suit, with an olive-green Bahamas Joe silk shirt and stylish Gucci shoes.

"Can I get you a cab, sir?" asked the doorman as he moved toward the exit.

"No thanks," Travis answered as he removed his cell phone and checked to see if he had any messages. Seeing that he had none, he put it away and found a spot to sit and wait on Alex. He hoped he was done licking his wounds.

"Are you ready to go?" Alex finally showed up looking debonair in his black slacks, crisp purple shirt and sport jacket.

"Yeah, I'm ready. Where are we headed again?" Travis asked.

"I told you, to this spot where all of the sexy hot Cougars hang out. I'm feeling depressed and I need the company of a radiant woman to cheer me up."

"I feel you on that one. Do you know what I like

about dating Cougars?" asked Travis as he stood up and headed toward the hotel exit.

"The fact that they like to fuck all of the time," Alex said, believing that he'd answered Travis's question.

"Yeah that, and the fact that they're so easygoing. They always smile and don't stir up a lot of drama like some women our age."

"Oh, I can tell you right now, I can't stand chicken-heads."

"Or ghetto girls," Travis added as a cab pulled up. They got in and Alex told the driver where to go. At that moment, Alex's cell phone rang. When he opened it, Travis saw the name, which appeared in bold letters on the caller ID. It was Hatcher McKean.

"I've got to take this, so be quiet." Alex pushed his index fingers against his lips.

"Dude, whatever you're doing for him—" Alex cut Travis off.

"Will you just chill and let me handle some business." Alex contemptuously glared at his friend, just before answering his phone.

Chapter 5
Jasmine

Jasmine, Lauren, Tiffany and Millie had just exited a Broadway theater. They'd seen *The Color Purple*, starring *American Idol* icon Fantasia. They were all buzzing with energy and excitement as they stepped out onto the overcrowded and noisy streets of New York City.

"Fantasia did such a wonderful job," Jasmine spoke loud enough for everyone to hear her. Tiffany raised her hand and hailed a cab. Shortly thereafter, an empty cab pulled over. Once they were situated inside, Tiffany gave the driver the address to the Rooftop Lounge. Fifteen minutes later they arrived at their destination. After Millie paid their fare, they entered the building and took the elevator up.

The swank club was filled with the sounds of laughter and multiple conversations. Women were wearing their most expensive designer shoes and clingy, cleavage-boosting dresses. Several people were taking photos with their cell phones while waitresses fetched them more cocktails. Some were eating while others stood around the brick railing and took in the spectacular view of the city. Positioned in a designated corner was a DJ playing a smooth jazz song by Chris Botti.

"Wow, how did you find this place, Tiffany?" Millie asked.

"My oversexed neighbor told me about it," she explained as they claimed an empty table. "She's fifty years old and says that she's having the most amazing sex life with a guy who is thirty-one that she met here."

"Shit, I'm not mad at her. I could use some amazing sex right about now," Jasmine said, laughing.

"Neither am I," Tiffany added as she smoothed out the fabric of her dress.

"I feel as if I'm away from everything up here," Lauren stated as she admired the New York skyline.

"Well, a city like New York doesn't have much land, so it makes sense to build a club like this on a rooftop. It's so pretty up here," Jasmine said.

"I'm glad it's not cold up here," Millie chimed in as she picked up a drink menu.

"Yeah, it's surprisingly warm now that you mention it," Jasmine agreed.

"There are some nice-looking men up in here," Tiffany said, releasing a playful growl as she scanned the parameters of the club.

"We're not going to have to put a leash on you, are we?" Millie asked jokingly as she rummaged through her small purse.

"Girl, please! It's my birthday weekend and I plan to

enjoy it to the fullest. Besides, whatever happens in New York City…" Tiffany paused for emphasis.

"Stays in New York City," everyone said in unison, then began laughing obnoxiously.

"It looks like they have a nice selection of martinis. They have a chocolate martini, candy apple, pineapple, dirty blond and a white chocolate one," said Lauren.

"Now that white chocolate martini sounds really good," Millie admitted. At that moment a waitress came over.

"White chocolate martinis for everyone," Lauren said to the waitress. "The first drink is on me, ladies."

"Well, I don't want that. I want pineapple. What about you, Tiffany? Did you want to change your order?" Jasmine asked.

"Nope," she answered as she focused her attention on two fine gentlemen who'd just arrived. "Would you look at the fine men who just walked in?" Tiffany nodded her head in the direction of the men.

"You've got to be kidding me," Jasmine blurted.

"What's wrong with them?" Tiffany didn't understand why Jasmine sounded so disenchanted.

"The one on the right is the airline pilot I was telling you guys about earlier." Jasmine turned her back, hoping Alex wouldn't see her.

"He's cute," Tiffany said.

"He's very cocky," Jasmine explained.

"There's nothing wrong with a man who has confidence." Tiffany continued to watch Alex and Travis as they walked toward the other side of the club.

As the evening moved forward, the ladies enjoyed their drinks, discussions and sisterhood. Several young men approached them during the course of the evening for flirtatious chatter and a chance to tell the ladies how beautiful they looked. Tiffany, Lauren, Jasmine, and Millie all loved the attention they were receiving. When one handsome young man learned that Tiffany was celebrating her birthday, he shared with her that he was commemorating his twenty-fourth birthday.

"Can I get a birthday kiss on the cheek from all of you beautiful ladies?" he asked. None of them saw any problem with his request and endearingly kissed him on the cheek. The young man then howled and told them how much he loved them. It was obvious that he'd had too much to drink, but he was very easygoing, vibrant and fun-loving.

"Excuse me, I need to head off to the ladies room," Jasmine said as she pushed back her seat and rose to her feet.

"Hang on, I'll go with you," Tiffany said, rising to her feet to follow Jasmine.

"Are you having a good time?" Jasmine asked as she and her friend walked through the crowd.

"The best time of my life. I love you guys so much," Tiffany said. "I'm so blessed to have girlfriends like you guys."

"The feeling's mutual, love," Jasmine said as she looped her arm around Tiffany's waist.

Once they freshened up, Tiffany and Jasmine headed back to their table. As they approached, Jasmine stopped cold in her tracks.

"Oh Lord, it's the airline pilot. He's made his way to our table," Jasmine said.

"I see."

"I'm going to put in an order for some food at the bar. Do you want anything?" Jasmine asked.

"Just get a platter that has a sample of everything. I'll eat off of that."

"Okay, I'll be over in a second."

Jasmine turned to the left and headed directly for the bar. There was a handsome man leaning his back against the mahogany structure. Jasmine couldn't help but add up his designer white suit and shoes.

"Excuse me. Can I get right there?" Jasmine asked.

"Oh, I'm sorry."

"Thank you." Jasmine tried to get the attention of all three bartenders several times, but without success.

"Jesus, what do I have to do in order to get some service around here?" Jasmine griped.

"What? No one is helping you?" asked the man standing next to her.

"No. It's like I'm invisible or something."

"Hang on." The man stepped away and then returned with a waitress.

"Would you be so kind as to take her order?" said the handsome man.

Pleasantly surprised, Jasmine gave the waitress her order and said she'd wait there for it.

"Thank you," Jasmine said to the kind stranger.

"No problem. My name is Travis, by the way."

"I'm Jasmine."

"That's a pretty name. My friend was telling me that he'd recently met someone named Jasmine."

"It's a pretty common name so I'm not surprised by that."

"Do you like this place?" Travis asked, looking directly into her amazingly hypnotic green eyes.

"It's nice. It's my first time ever coming here. What about you? Is this a popular spot?"

"This is my first time here as well." Travis leaned in closer, and spoke purposefully in her ear so she could hear him. "I flew in from California to meet up with a buddy of mine. Every few months we pick a city to hang out in."

"New York is a great city to visit. I don't know if I'd like living here though," Jasmine admitted.

"Oh, you're not from the Big Apple?"

"No. My girlfriends and I flew in to celebrate a birthday."

"Is it your birthday? Because if it is I'm going to have to sing 'Happy Birthday' to you," Travis asked, fully prepared to sing.

"No, it's not my birthday." Jasmine laughed. She studied Travis more thoroughly. He had smooth brown skin, a prominent jaw line and a boyish face. He was without a doubt a charmer, but there was something extra about Travis. It was his eyes; they seemed to speak before any words passed through his lips.

"You have lovely eyes," Travis complimented her.

"Funny, I was just thinking the same thing about you." Jasmine raised her right eyebrow.

"What's that supposed to mean?" Travis asked.

"Nothing. Other than the fact we're both sizing each other up at the same time." Jasmine rested her elbow on the countertop.

"So what part of California are you from?" Jasmine decided to give Travis more of her attention.

"Berkeley."

"I've never been there," Jasmine said.

"You should come sometime. It's a great town and has the best seafood in the world," Travis proudly stated. "What about you? Where are you from?"

"Chicago," Jasmine said dryly. "I'm not looking forward to the upcoming winter months."

"I don't see how people in Chicago survive such cold winters. Sometimes I'll catch a glimpse of a report saying that it's like one-hundred degrees below zero."

Jasmine laughed. "Honey, it doesn't get that cold. Exposed human skin wouldn't survive in such extreme temperatures."

"I know, I'm just giving you a hard time."

"Now why do you want to give me a hard time? You hardly even know me." Jasmine wanted their conversation to continue. There was something about his spirit that she was drawn to.

"It's just a figure of speech," Travis explained.

"You mean to tell me you don't want to give me anything that's hard?"

"Oh. See now you want to play with me." Travis gave her a sly glance. "But if I were to give you any part of me, it would be more than just the hard parts." Travis winked.

"If that's the case, I'd also better make sure I give you something you can feel."

"Well, a skilled lover knows how to move around in tight places," Travis said as he got the attention of the bartender.

"If I didn't know any better, I'd swear you were teasing me." Jasmine gazed directly into his eyes.

"I don't tease, baby. I seduce." Travis met her gaze with his own.

"I've heard it all before, Travis," Jasmine said, enjoying the mystery of him perusing her for an intimate encounter.

"You see, that's the thing with certain guys. They talk a lot of bullshit, but when it comes down to performing they can't last more than two seconds." Travis popped his fingers twice for emphasis. "Dudes will have a premature orgasm and talk about how that has never happened before or it was a slip-up because it felt so good."

"Sounds like you're speaking from experience," Jasmine said, playing the devil's advocate.

"Every man at some point in his sexual life will run across a woman that may be a little too much for him to handle. However, I believe it's a guy's responsibility to learn how to work his shit. He needs to have a very intimate relationship with himself so that he learns to delay gratification."

"What are you, a sexologist or something?"

"Close, but not exactly. Let's just say I've studied the subjects of intimacy and arousal thoroughly."

"Is that a fact?" Jasmine was now more curious than ever.

"Come closer," Travis requested. Jasmine obliged by leaning toward him. Travis placed the fingertips of his left hand on her hips and whispered in her ear. "I'm more like an experience you'll savor and crave. I'm like a delicious treat you'll adore snuggling up with while wearing your favorite pajamas. I will have your appetite longing for me in a way you've never thought possible. I will take you to the stratosphere and have you inhaling the pillows just so that my masculine scent can dance around in your head." Travis paused and read her body language as she digested what he'd just said. When he saw her shoulder rise up to meet her ear as if she were being tickled, he knew that Jasmine was very interested in him. "That's the kind of lover I can be to you."

"How many women have you said that bullshit to?" Jasmine wasn't about to fall for the string of crap he'd rehearsed.

"I haven't been walking around whispering lies in the ears of women. However, if you'd like me to lie, I can accommodate your request." Travis noticed the waitress returning with Jasmine's order.

"Your food is here." He nodded his head in the direction of the approaching waitress.

"So Travis, do you think you're the type of man who can blow my mind?" Jasmine asked as the thought of taking him back to her hotel room and fucking him until he begged for mercy entered her mind.

"No, I'm not that guy. I am the man who has the potential to stimulate your mind and perhaps make you a happier woman."

"And how would you go about doing that?" Jasmine asked as she paid the waitress and set her food on the bar.

"By listening and paying attention to you. By never walking on your love or taking you for granted. I'd build a bridge of trust and understanding that could never be destroyed or dismantled. I'll treat you better than you'd treat yourself."

"I will admit that sounds very nice, even romantic," Jasmine said as she picked up her food.

"Well, Travis, it was nice meeting you." Jasmine shook his hand with her free one.

"It was nice meeting you as well." Travis held onto her hand and swept his thumb across the back of her hand.

"Jasmine!" Alex walked up and interrupted the moment. He finished off the drink he had in his hand and set the empty glass on the bar. "It's me, Alex, the pilot. Don't you remember who I am?"

"Dude, give me a minute here." Travis kept Alex from toppling on top of Jasmine. Travis didn't appreciate the disruption and was letting Alex know it.

"Oh no, Travis. I saw her first, man. You know the rule. You don't go after the same girl your best friend has a hard dick for." Alex, his ego, and competitive nature were pissing Travis off.

"Are you guys involved in some type of competition to see how many women you can bed or something?" Jasmine sensed that she was the prize of some boyish scheme.

"No. It's nothing like that." Travis immediately denied her assumption.

Alex couldn't maintain an erect posture. "I didn't ever think I'd run into you again. What's up, baby? Are we going to do the do or what?" He slurred his words, his eyes were glassy and he refused to listen to reason. It was clear that he was intoxicated and needed to call it a night.

"Alex, why don't you have a seat?" Travis said.

"Hell no! I don't want to sit down." Alex grabbed his crotch. "I want to give her some of this." Alex tried to push up against Jasmine, but Travis prevented him from doing so.

"You need to get him out of here. Obviously he's had one too many. I hope he isn't flying tonight."

"I've flown drunk before. It's not a big deal," Alex boasted as he stumbled backward and knocked over a few cocktail glasses sitting on the bar. The sound of shattering glass made heads turn.

"Oh shit. I fucked up. I'll pick up the broken glass." Alex stooped down, lost his balance and toppled over.

"Why the fuck did you push me down, Travis?" Alex asked with a confused look on his face, falsely accusing his friend.

"Let me help you up," Travis said as he helped him to his feet.

"I've never seen him get this hammered before," Travis said apologetically.

"Sure," Jasmine said before turning to leave.

"Hey, can I get your phone number?" Travis asked.

"No."

"How about an e-mail address?"

"At this point, honey, I'm not even willing to give you a smoke signal." Jasmine walked away.

"Why do the pretty ones always have to be coldhearted bitches?" Alex asked.

"You're lucky that you have a friend like me because any other guy would have disowned your ass."

"Hey, man. She wasn't worth it any motherfucking way." The alcohol allowed Alex to make statements that would lead to an ass kicking if he were alone.

"Have a seat," Travis told Alex, who sat on the bar stool and slumped over. Travis got the attention of the bartender once again and ordered a cup of coffee for his friend.

Chapter 6
Travis

Travis awoke to the sound of heavy rainfall from a thunderstorm system passing through the Bay Area. He turned over in his bed and hugged the pillow tighter, hoping to get a few more minutes of sleep before getting up to start his day. Just as he was about to drift back to sleep, his alarm clock began buzzing and playing loud music.

"Damn!" Travis griped as he opened his eyes. His immediate thought was to hit the off button and go back to sleep. However, that wasn't an option, because if he had, he'd most certainly oversleep, especially with the lulling melody of raindrops present. He willed himself to sit upright in his bed. After taking a long stretch, he rose to his feet and lazily moved over to the balcony window in his bedroom. He drew back the chocolate drapes, slid the glass door open and stepped outside. He took a deep breath and inhaled the scent of the morning rain.

"Come on, Travis. You need to shake off the damn jetlag and get your ass in gear," he spoke to himself. He stretched his body out some more before heading back inside. He went into the basement where the workout room was located, flipped on the light switch, and plugged his iPod into his bookshelf stereo system. Travis selected his favorite workout songs, turned up the volume, then began running on the treadmill. Afterward he did a chest and back weightlifting routine using his Bowflex Home Gym.

After a great workout, a long shower, and face time in front of the mirror, Travis got dressed, then went to the kitchen to eat breakfast. He cooked himself some egg whites, two slices of turkey bacon, and an English muffin. Once his food was ready, he grabbed the television remote and turned on the small television situated on the granite countertop. The weatherman said the storm would be gone, but later in the afternoon the temperature would rise into the nineties.

"Another hot and sticky one," Travis mumbled as he sat at the small table in the kitchen. He glanced out of a nearby window and noticed a few tree branches floating in the pool. He made a mental note to remove them before he left for work.

Travis loved his house. It was actually his parents' house, but they'd moved a while ago to a retirement home in Hawaii. The house had four bedrooms, a formal dining room, two large family rooms, three bathrooms and a large backyard with an in-ground swimming pool. The house was paid for and his parents allowed him to stay as long as he maintained it. Although the arrangement was excellent, the thought of purchasing the house from his parents had crossed his mind several times.

After he finished with breakfast, Travis checked all of the windows and doors to make sure they were locked and headed off to work at the university. As he was driving he received a phone call.

"What's up, fool?" Travis said to Alex.

"Nothing, ass wipe, what are you doing?" Alex fired back with an equal amount of sarcasm.

"Just heading to work. Where are you? Back home or in another city?"

"I'm still in Chicago, but I'm headed to the airport now. By this afternoon I'll be in Omaha, Nebraska."

"Omaha sounds like a fun place." Travis laughed with an air of cynicism.

"Omaha is actually a great town."

"Well, one thing is for sure. Out here in Berkeley we don't ever hear anything good or bad about Nebraska." Travis was surprised by Alex's apparent fondness for the city. "Look, I know you didn't call me up to make small talk about Omaha. So what's up?"

"That chick, Jasmine. Are you sure you didn't get her phone number?" Alex asked yet again.

"Dude, I don't believe you just asked me that question. This is like the hundredth time already."

"I'm just making sure." Alex acted as if he didn't understand what the problem was.

"That lady is gone. She wasn't interested in you. Now get over it and move on."

"How do you know? Did she say she wasn't interested?"

"If I didn't know any better, I'd swear you were turning into some deranged stalker. The whacked-out part is, you're stalking a person you hardly even know."

"I'm not a stalker, there was just something about her that…I don't know…I just want to know everything about her."

"Look, for the last time, Alex. She didn't say anything about you until you brought your drunk-ass over and fucked up my chances with her. We had a good flow going until you gave her the impression that we had some type of secret bet going on."

"I wasn't that drunk." Alex downplayed that part of the night.

"The hell if you weren't, Alex. You were only two sips away from being totally wasted and vomiting all over yourself. You're lucky that I'm your boy and took care of your punk ass."

"Whatever, Travis. It's a good thing I came over when I did because a woman like Jasmine needs a man who'll devote all of his attention and time to her and not to his chemistry set," Alex joked, but Travis heard an undercurrent of suspicion and jealousy in his voice.

"Well, if she's too much for me, then she's damn sure too much for your ass." Travis stood firm on his opinion.

"Whatever, man. When you find her phone number, you just make sure you give it to me."

"I don't understand how you can be this infatuated with someone you barely know. It sounds to me like you're slipping, man. You may be trying to settle down and find true love."

"You know damn well I don't believe in all of that sappy stuff. I'm a stick-and-move kind of man. I can't be tied down."

"That's what your mouth says, but your behavior and your constant inquiry about this woman is a little over the top, don't you think?" Travis asked as he stopped at a traffic light.

"Maybe she'll call me. I did give her my phone number," Alex remembered.

"There you go; she'll call you to tell you to leave her the hell alone because by then I will have had her ankles in my hands and her toes pointed toward the ceiling." Travis couldn't quell the urge to play a mental mind game with his friend.

"Fuck you, Travis."

"No, motherfucker, fuck you," Travis fired back.

"Look, on the serious note, did you get your tenure like you wanted?"

"I haven't heard yet. I thought I'd have something in my mailbox by now, but I don't. I'm sure I got it. I'm not worried about it," Travis said.

"I can see you now, working in the lab, cloning shit. Just don't get too carried away and re-create Frankenstein, or that acid-bleeding creature from the movie *Aliens* or some other biomedical fuck-up that's highly aggressive and likes to kill." Alex laughed.

"Dude, I'm not some mad scientist."

"Sure you're not," Alex said mockingly. "Well, that's what I was calling about. Let me know once everything is official so I can come out there and celebrate with you."

"Will do. Later." Travis and Alex said their good-byes before ending the call.

After arriving on campus, Travis walked into his office, powered up his computer and began finishing up his PowerPoint presentation "Solving Synthesis Problems in Organic Chemistry." The class he taught was designed to assist students in developing the essential skills required in problem synthesis problems as well as cover a variety of related issues such as retro-synthesis and other fundamental concepts. He enjoyed teaching, but he was truly much more interested in the lab work he was involved with. He was doing promising research on spinal cord injuries and hoped to develop a formula that stimulated nerve repair.

Travis had just finished up his lecture and was shouting out the reading assignment as students exited.

"Read chapters six and seven on alkenes and alkynes," he said. Once everyone was gone, he locked up the lecture hall and headed over to the lab.

WHEN HE ARRIVED HOME LATER IN THE EVENING, the letter he was waiting on was in his mailbox. Once he was inside he walked over to the sofa table and placed his briefcase and keys there. He then sat down on the sofa and opened the letter and began reading aloud.

Dear Professor Adams,

The Tenure Review Board has completed its deliberations concerning your interest in Permanent Status at the University of California at Berkeley. Several well-qualified candidates applied for the position. Although your credentials are exceptional, the panel has made its selection. We wish to thank you for your hard work and wish you the very best in your future endeavors.

"I don't believe this bullshit!" Travis crumbled the letter and flung it to the other side of the room. "Those lowdown dirty bastards!" Travis roared like an angry grizzly bear. He was so livid that he squatted down, lifted the sofa and flipped it over.

"Those motherfuckers!" He hated losing and abhorred being overlooked. Evil and wicked thoughts entered Travis's mind. He believed that some type of personal retribution was in order. A voice in his head told him to head out to the shed, grab his baseball bat and go bash in the heads of everyone on the review panel for placing an enormous pothole on his road to greatness.

Chapter 7
Jasmine

It was Friday evening and Jasmine was in her office working late, still playing catch-up after she'd returned from vacation on Monday. She loathed that no one could do her work in her absence, but she'd come to terms with the fact that, at times, managing her workflow was similar to wrestling a crocodile. Jasmine felt overwhelmed most of the time because there was always some experiment that needed to be monitored, new studies to be analyzed or some meeting she had to attend.

At 11:45 p.m. she decided to call it quits for the night. She'd worked herself near exhaustion and her body kept telling her it was time for her to get some rest. Jasmine was thankful her house was only fifteen minutes away. She shut down her computer, grabbed her purse, and headed out the door. She walked down the brightly lit but desolate corridor toward the security guard station.

"Hello, Sam." She caught the security guard snoozing with his feet propped on the countertop. When he heard her voice, he nearly tipped over in his seat as he tried to sit upright.

"Hey, Miss Jasmine. I didn't realize that anyone was still here. Almost everyone is gone by this time on Friday," he said apologetically while sweeping away breadcrumbs from a partially eaten submarine sandwich from his shirt.

"That's because you didn't do your rounds like you were supposed to, Sam. A killer could've been back there slicing me up and you wouldn't have heard a thing."

"I'm sorry about that. It won't happen again, I promise. I was just tired." Sam was a young guy who'd just turned twenty-years old. He favored the iconic rapper Snoop Dogg and liked to boast of how one day he was going to be a big star.

"Why are you so tired, Sam?" Jasmine asked out of nosiness.

"I was at my family reunion earlier today and I guess I'm just kind of worn out," he answered honestly.

"I understand how those family reunions can be." Jasmine smirked at him before walking toward the glass exit doors.

"Make sure you watch me get into my car safely, Sam. Don't let anyone grab me."

"Shit, you'd better hope that I don't grab your fine, sexy ass," he muttered.

Jasmine heard every word he'd mumbled. She looked over her shoulder disapprovingly and glared at him. "What did you just say?"

"Nothing. Don't worry. If anyone tries anything, I've got something for them." Sam removed his night-stick and slapped it in the palm of his hand a few times. "You have a good night and drive safely," Sam said.

THE FOLLOWING MORNING Jasmine drove to the gym for her yoga class. She was waiting on Lauren to arrive, but as usual she was running late. Jasmine entered the room where the class was held. The space was as large as a dance studio and had floor-to-ceiling mirrors on three of the walls. The usual Saturday morning bunch was there along with a few new faces. In total there were about twenty people in the class. Jasmine began spreading out her yoga mat on the blond wood floor, keeping in mind to save some space for Lauren.

"Okay ladies, we're going to get started in a few minutes," announced Harrison, the young instructor. Jasmine glanced up at him and admired his body, which was a thing of pure beauty. Harrison had on a pair of black loose-fitting gym shorts and a snug-fitting tank top that accented his muscular shoulders and sizable biceps. The sexual thoughts running freely in Jasmine's mind were simply scandalous. She imagined herself with her legs locked around his waist with her back against one of the mirrored walls. He was fucking her while she looked at their reflection in another mirror. She could see herself biting his neck and clawing her fingernails into his back.

"Girl, you're not saying a word, but I can hear everything your eyes are saying." Lauren finally showed up.

"How old do you think he is? About thirty, right?" Jasmine asked as Lauren placed her yoga mat next to hers.

"You know damn well that Harrison is nowhere near thirty, Jasmine. I'd say he's twenty-two at best."

"Are you sure?" Jasmine asked, half wanting him to be a little bit older.

"Look at his face. You can tell he's young." Lauren was trying to point out the obvious truth.

"It's not his face I'm interested in. Look at his deliciously tight ass. I wonder how his dick hangs." Jasmine was dying to know.

"I have no clue." Lauren glanced at Harrison. "Shit, now you've got me wondering what he's working with."

Jasmine sucked air through her teeth. "Shit, I'd screw his young ass all night long and keep his face buried between my thighs," Jasmine said as she watched him place a compact disc in the player.

"You need some dick and in a bad way," Lauren said as she stood on her mat.

"Tell me something I don't know," Jasmine joked. "I'm going to fuck him though."

"Well, stand in line, girlfriend, because you're not the only one who wants a piece of that. I'm sure every woman in here is longing for a round in the sack with him."

Jasmine huffed. "I don't care about these bitches in

here. I'm not trying to marry him. I just want to play with him for a little while and teach him about life."

"You're going to mess around and break his heart," Lauren said.

"I doubt that. I'm just going to show him a thing or two." Jasmine laughed as yet another wicked thought flashed across her mind.

"You are a mess, Jasmine."

"Nah, I'm just a free spirit. I'm a liberated and sexually unconstrained woman who is only doing what men have been doing since the dawn of time. I'm just getting my freak on." Jasmine laughed yet again.

"Speaking of freaky, you won't believe what I did last night," Lauren whispered.

"Did you do something really nasty?" Jasmine's attention was now focused on her sister.

"Girl, *nasty* isn't the word for it. What I did is illegal in all fifty states," Lauren confessed.

"Yeah right, you're too reserved and mild mannered. Besides, you don't have the guts to step outside of your comfort zone."

"You don't know me like you think you do. Trust me, I was way out of my comfort zone. LeMar and I drove downtown to the boat harbor near Soldier Field."

"He's the young guy you've been seeing, right?" Jasmine asked.

"He's not that young; he's in his thirties," Lauren said.

"And you're forty-six and thirteen years older than

him, which makes you a Cougar whether you want to admit it or not."

"Whatever, all I know is that sex with him is fucking liberating," Lauren said as Harrison instructed everyone to begin doing light warm-up exercises. "He brought along some marijuana for us to smoke while we strolled along the lakefront and admired the luxury houseboats."

"But you don't smoke," Jasmine said, utterly surprised by what Lauren was telling her.

"Well, I did the other night—well, that morning actually because it was around two-thirty a.m."

"But why?" Jasmine asked, trying to understand her motive.

"Dumb animal curiosity, I suppose. The dumber the shit sounded, the more excited I was about doing it," Lauren answered honestly.

"Okay, so how dumb did you get?"

"I had no idea that weed could make me so fucking hot. I mean I knew I was high, but I liked it and all I wanted to do was fuck. So LeMar comes up with the dumb-ass idea of sneaking onto one of the empty houseboats."

"No you didn't!" Jasmine tried to keep her voice low, but it was becoming increasingly difficult.

"Girl, I don't even remember how we got on the boat. All I know is that it was exciting as hell being at the stern of the boat with my skirt above my hips and my ass in the air."

"Which part is the stern?" Jasmine asked because she couldn't remember.

"The back of it."

"Okay, go on," Jasmine said.

"It was just wild, that's all. I felt as if I were living on the edge," Lauren said as Harrison instructed everyone to do jumping jacks.

"I do believe LeMar has turned you out." Jasmine gave her sister a knowing glance.

"No he hasn't."

"That's what your mouth says, but I know better." Jasmine continued to follow Harrison's instructions.

EARLY AFTERNOON ON SUNDAY, Jasmine got up early and took care of some house cleaning chores she'd been neglecting. She dragged her unpacked suitcase down to the laundry room and began unpacking the clothes she'd taken to New York. During the process of checking her blue jean pants pocket, she came across the business card that Alex had given to her. She looked at it and laughed.

"I will not be calling you," she said as she ripped up his card and tossed the pieces into a nearby trashcan. She went back upstairs into her kitchen, grabbed a note pad from a drawer and began making a shopping list. She then put on a pair of jeans and her favorite button-down shirt and headed out to a nearby grocery store.

Jasmine meandered from aisle to aisle picking up the items she needed. When she arrived at the checkout counter the line was long. To kill time she checked her cell phone for messages.

"Hey, how are you?" Jasmine glanced up and saw Harrison standing next to her. She placed her phone back inside her purse.

"Well, hey, handsome. What are you doing here?" Jasmine perked up. Her boring and mundane chores were about to get interesting.

"Just picking up some personal stuff. What about you?" he asked.

"I'm doing the same thing," she admitted as she undressed him with her eyes.

"So do you like the yoga class?" he asked with a hint of bashfulness in his voice.

"You have no idea how much I like it. You're so strong and flexible and I'm all tight." Jasmine accented the word "tight" so that he'd pick up the hint that she was flirting with him.

Harrison laughed. "Where exactly are you 'tight' at?" he asked.

Jasmine glided her hand seductively down her side and around the bow of her hips. "I'm tight all over, but my hips are extra tense. Maybe you can help stretch them out, really, really wide." Jasmine looked deeply into his eyes so that he could see every naughty thought she had.

Harrison licked his lips and the moment Jasmine saw his succulent tongue, she wanted it in her mouth. "So what are you saying? You want a private session?"

"Come here." Jasmine wiggled her index finger so that he'd lean in closer. She wanted to make absolutely certain that he heard what she was about to tell him. Once he drew closer, she pressed her cheek against his. She liked the coarse feel of his razor stubble against her soft skin. She cradled the back of his head and whispered, "I want an intimate session with just you and me stretching and exploring each other. I want you to spread open your legs so that I can lick your balls and suck all of the juice out of that delicious-looking cock of yours. Have I made myself clear?" Jasmine let her last sentence linger in midair and awaited a response.

"Yes." Harrison laughed nervously.

"Did that make your dick hard?" Jasmine asked, wanting him to volley back and forth with seductive chatter. But Harrison was young and hadn't yet perfected that part of his seduction techniques, so Jasmine had to help him along a little.

"Very much so." Harrison tried to pull away, but Jasmine wouldn't release him. Instead she stepped a little closer, and without concern for who might be looking, she slid her hand down and squeezed his pride.

"I want simple and uncomplicated sex from you." She continued to pour her seductive words into his ear. Harrison flinched as goose bumps formed on his skin.

He finally pulled away from her and took a few deep breaths to gather himself.

"Give me your contact number, Harrison," Jasmine demanded as she took her cell phone out again. Harrison gave her his number.

"You know… If you've got time, I know of a place we can go that's not too far from here," Harrison said. The uncertain look on his face still suggested that he was somewhat fearful of being rejected, as if she didn't really mean everything she'd said.

"Really? You want me that badly?" Jasmine asked.

"Hell yes!" He flashed his boyish and charming smile.

"Then you'll need loads of stamina. Is that something you have?" She knew the answer to her question, but she enjoyed watching his eyes dart from left to right as he searched for the perfect answer to her inquiry.

"Yes." He swallowed hard and then leaned forward to whisper in her ear. "I'm always hard."

"Wonderful. Later this afternoon I'm going to call you. At that time you can tell me where you are and I'll come to you."

"Okay. That'll give me plenty of time to take care of a few arrangements," Harrison said.

"I'll see you later." Jasmine winked at him.

As PROMISED, JASMINE CALLED HARRISON and he gave her the address to a popular spa that offered private rooms for couples. She packed a small bag filled with one of her most revealing lingerie pieces.

When she arrived, Harrison was waiting for her in the lobby. When he saw her, he smiled gleefully, then took her by the hand and escorted her back to the suite he'd secured. It was immediately apparent to Jasmine that he was rather familiar with the place by his thorough knowledge of the multiple corridors. The spa suite he'd rented out for the day was beautifully decorated and featured a heart-shaped whirlpool, two massage tables and a king-sized bed. A popular melody by Snoop Dogg called "Sensual Seduction" was playing. Jasmine couldn't stand the rapper, but for some reason she didn't mind the fact that this particular song was playing. The lighting was ideal, not too bright and not too dark.

"This is nice," Jasmine said, impressed with the place.

"I thought you'd like it here." Harrison locked the door and approached her from behind. Her pulled her into him and began kissing the back of her neck.

"My, you're certainly ready for some action." Jasmine could feel his erection pressing against her ass.

"I have wanted you for a long time," he whispered as he continued to shower her with kisses.

"Really? Why didn't you say anything?" Jasmine tilted her neck to the left and then slowly swung her chin toward her right shoulder so that she could hear every word clearly.

"I was afraid to and besides, I had no idea of what to say. So I just sat back and admired you. Sometimes I'd purposely stand behind you when you were doing the downward dog movement and fantasize about fucking you in that position."

"If you keep talking like that, I just might let you do it. But I believe in what is good for the goose is good for the gander. I want you to get in the downward dog position with your palms flat on the floor, your legs spread apart and your ass in the air so that I can put your balls in my mouth."

"That sounds so hot. I've never had anyone to talk to me like that before."

"That's because I know what I want," Jasmine said. "Now take off your clothes and go get in the shower. I'll join you there in a moment," Jasmine instructed.

Harrison slowly undressed in front of her so she could see his body. His tight white briefs barely kept his dick restrained.

"Damn, you look fantastically sexy." Jasmine liked his athletic body. He had a wide chest, muscular arms, a sexy and well-developed midsection and a long dick that stood at attention.

"Don't take too long," Harrison said before he stepped away.

"I won't," Jasmine assured him. Jasmine removed her street clothes and slipped into a sexy purple sequined and sheer net baby doll dress and her matching G-string. When she heard the water hissing from the shower, she decided to let Harrison see what she had on. The material on her outfit was very light and she didn't care if it got wet. Jasmine stood in the doorway of the bathroom, observing him as he washed his body. The way the water cascaded down his chocolate skin was too sexy for words. Harrison finally noticed her watching him.

"Damn!" he said and quickly turned off the water.

When he stepped out, Jasmine focused her attention on his erect cock. He had a fair amount of pubic hair, which she'd address with him at a later time. His dick, however, was swollen and pointing directly at her, eager to take her on and satisfy her lust.

Jasmine stepped forward and lowered herself to her knees. She placed her right hand around his dick, raised it up toward his bellybutton. She placed the padded part of her thumb on the long vein at the base of his cock, just before his balls. She pressed gently while stroking it up and down until the head of his dick was oozing with pre-cum.

"Oh God!" Harrison said as he reached down and threaded his fingers through her hair. "Oh, that feels so damn good. You have no idea how much I want this."

Jasmine stopped for a moment and glanced up at him.

"Are you going to fuck me good?"

"Yes, I promise," Harrison cried out as Jasmine went back to work. Jasmine opened her mouth as wide as the sky and took in his dick until she gagged on it. She then pulled it halfway out of her mouth, then sucked and stroked it, savoring the taste of his essence. Harrison's knees buckled and her experience immediately warned her that if she kept going, he was going to blast all of his hot liquid in her mouth. She kissed the head of it a few times for good measure before rising to her feet.

"Your turn. Get down on your knees," Jasmine said as she took a shoulder-wide stance. Then she peeled back the fabric of her G-string, squeezed her ass cheeks and pushed her pelvis forward.

Harrison made wild and untrained flicking motions with his tongue. "Slower, baby," she instructed him and like an obedient student he did as she commanded.

"Put your hands on my ass and squeeze it hard." Harrison followed her every instruction.

"Right there. Don't move. That's my spot. Loop your tongue around in slow circles." Once again Harrison complied.

"Oh that's it, baby." Jasmine clutched a fist full of his hair and pulled it while simultaneously fucking his face with her hot pussy.

"Keep going. Keep going. Keep going," she repeated over and over again. She raised her right leg and draped it over his shoulder and down his back.

"Put your finger inside me." Jasmine was feeling a great orgasm stirring deep within her belly. Finally, she reached the point of no return and exploded.

"Was that good?" Harrison wanted confirmation that he'd satisfied her.

"Yes. That was nice." Jasmine applauded him for a

job well done. She then led him to the bed, pushed him down and grabbed a condom she'd placed on the nearby nightstand.

"Hurry up and put it on," she told him as she removed her sexy lingerie. Harrison positioned himself on his back and stroked his own cock a few times to make sure the condom was on securely.

She straddled him and guided herself down on his Pride. Once he was inside of her, she rotated her hips in a clockwise motion, thrusting her hips hard every time her hips swung past twelve. She was making sure his delicious cock rubbed every wall of her Goddess. Her breasts stood proudly, her chocolate nipples were erect and waiting for Harrison to pinch and squeeze them. When he didn't pay her tits any attention, she glanced down and saw that his eyes were gleaming with absolute amazement. He looked as if it was the very first time he'd ever felt the warm folds of a woman, but she knew that wasn't accurate. Then the revelation hit her. He'd probably never been fucked by a mature woman and more than likely spent an enormous amount of time begging silly young girls to let him have a go at it.

"Is this your first time with a grown woman?" Jasmine asked. She and her ego just had to know.

"I've been with girls before," Harrison answered.

"That's not what I asked you." Jasmine gripped his dick with her pussy muscle.

"Yes." He sighed. "I had no idea it could feel this good. You know how to move so well." A twinge of excitement coursed through Jasmine's body when he told her that.

"Well then, I think it's about time you learned how to really fuck."

"Am I doing something wrong?"

Jasmine could hear the fear of failure in Harrison's voice.

"You're doing fine, but let me show you how to really use that magnificently flexible body of yours." Jasmine stood up.

"What do you want me to do?" Harrison asked, ready to do whatever she commanded.

"Sit up. Place the soles of your feet flat on the bed. Now place your hands next to your hips and rise up into table pose. Squeeze your ass cheeks and hold there."

"Now you're the instructor." Harrison laughed nervously.

"Yes I am. I can hardly believe that you haven't done it in every imaginable position possible."

"I've always wanted to but never—"

"Shhh, there is no need to give me an explanation. All I want you to do is keep your dick hard." While still holding the position, Jasmine straddled him, then turned her back to him and lowered herself down until his cock was deep inside her. In her reverse cowgirl position, she rode him hard and enjoyed a wonderful orgasm. She got into the missionary position and placed the back of her knees on his shoulders. Harrison pumped her wild and frantically. He pushed her legs aside and lowered himself on her, panting heavily in her ear. She could hear his orgasm about to erupt, so she sprawled her legs out wide for him. It only took seconds for him to moan in her ear as if his orgasm was the most exquisite one he'd ever experienced. Their bodies were slick with a mixture of sweat and sex juices. Harrison had collapsed on top of her, so she pushed him off.

"I'm sorry, I didn't mean to fall flat on you like that," Harrison apologized as he tried to catch his breath. Jasmine sat up in the bed. Her Goddess was only partially satisfied and was ready for round two.

"Let's go take a shower. I'm not done with you yet," Jasmine said as she rose to her feet and walked toward the bathroom.

Chapter 8
Travis

Travis had just finished his morning workout. He'd taken a shower and then stood in front of a mirror in his bedroom adjusting his necktie. The end of the school semester had finally arrived, and with it, the closing phase of his job at the university. After the shock of being rejected for tenure status wore off, he picked himself up, dusted his bruised ego off and updated his portfolio. He'd forwarded it to a number of prospective employers, but thus far he had not received any return phone calls. After he ate breakfast Travis grabbed a few storage boxes and placed them on the back seat of his car before driving to work.

There were only two minutes left for his students to complete their final exams. Once their time was up, he'd collect their papers and grade them over the weekend. He'd then calculate the students' grades and post them. After he completed that task he could say with absolute certainty that he was unemployed.

"Okay, guys, your time is up," Travis announced. "Leave your exams right here on the podium as you exit."

Once all of the students turned in their work, Travis collected their papers, stuffed them in his briefcase and headed toward the lab to pick up a few personal items. On his way he picked up the storage boxes from his car. When he arrived at the lab, he saw Carol, one of his colleagues walking in the door. Carol was a petite woman in her early fifties. She had sandy-brown, shoulder-length hair and pale skin that was in need of some sun. She was married to a hotshot lawyer and had two children, a fifteen-year-old and a nineteen-year-old. Carol was a real sweetheart and a mentor to Travis.

"Hello, Carol," Travis greeted her.

She smiled at him sweetly. "Hey, Travis. You're carrying boxes. Today must be your last day," she deduced.

"Yeah, this is it. I'm at the end of the road. I came here to pick up a few things," Travis said as he held the door open for her. "Thank you for all that you've done for me here. I really appreciate you taking me under your wing."

"Oh Travis, I knew you were special the moment I first saw you in my advanced chemistry class. I saw nothing but fire and determination in your eyes. I knew you possessed the mind of a genius from our very first encounter. It really pissed me off when I heard about your rejection letter. I hope you realize that their decision probably wasn't based on your skills and leaned more towards politics," Carol said encouragingly.

"Yeah, I've come to terms with all of that. The best I can do is move forward and achieve something magnificent like winning the Nobel Prize in chemistry, and show those snobby elitist bastards the error of their judgment. I got a pretty shitty deal, because there was no one more qualified than me," Travis said as they entered the lab facility and walked down a corridor toward the lab.

"So what are you going to do? Do you have any interviews lined up?" Carol asked, genuinely concerned. Over the past three years they'd worked closely with each other and had established a great rapport.

"I've got nothing right now. But I'll keep my ears open. I'm supremely confident someone out there will appreciate my exceptional abilities."

"Did you plan on taking some time for yourself? Perhaps you should consider flying out to Hawaii to see your folks? I'm sure they'd love to see you."

"Nah, I don't want to do that right now. My goal is to get back to work and dazzle the scientific community. I'm going to focus on getting back in the saddle. I may have been bucked off the horse, but I'm a tough cowboy," Travis said as he was about to enter the lab and end his conversation with Carol.

"Hang on a second, Travis. Would you be willing to travel to a different state for a job?"

"I'll go anywhere as long as it's not Antarctica," Travis joked.

"What about Chicago? It's cold there, but not nearly as cold as the North Pole."

"I like Chi-town. My best friend lives there." Travis

folded his arms across his chest, then eyed her inquisitively. "Why do you ask?"

"Do you have a minute to stop down in my office?" Carol asked.

"Absolutely." Travis followed her toward her office. Once inside, Travis took a seat and Carol closed the door. She walked behind her desk and sat down, then opened up a drawer on her desk and pulled out a blue file folder.

"Take a look at this," she said, handing him the file.

Travis opened it up and read aloud the narrative about Headroom Pharmaceuticals and qualifications for a position as a chemist. "*Headroom Pharmaceuticals develops, manufactures, and markets products that save and sustain the lives of people with hemophilia, immune disorders, infectious diseases, kidney disease, and other medical conditions. Okay, blah blah blah, looking for an organic chemist with three to five years of experience in analytical development and validations for pharmaceutical development. Qualified candidate will participate in the development of new pharmaceutical products and the support of existing products.*"

"Well, what do you think?" she asked.

Travis stopped reading and glanced up at Carol. "This sounds exactly like the type work I love doing."

"When I read it, I immediately thought of you. That position has your name written all over it, Travis." Carol leaned forward and united her fingers into a praying position and then rested her elbows on her desk.

Travis continued to read the documents before him. "I would agree with that. Can I keep this information? I'll reach out to the human resources person at the company and start the process of applying," Travis said, closing the folder.

"If I could get you an interview, would you consider moving to Chicago to take the job?" Carol asked, wanting to know if Travis was serious or only mildly interested.

"Of course I would. This sounds like the type of work that would give me the type of opportunity I've been searching for," Travis said, enthused about the prospect.

"I know the president of the company. She and I went to school together and she's the godmother of my eldest daughter. I'll give her a jingle and see what can be done in terms of getting the process started."

"Carol, that's the best news I've heard in some time. This is so nice of you." Travis spoke with sincerity.

"I can probably get your foot in the door, but it's up to you to land the job."

"I guarantee you this, Carol. I will outshine any other applicant if you give me the chance to," Travis said self-assuredly.

"You had better, because with a recommendation coming from me, you will have to prove that you're the best of the best."

"I'm even better than the best," Travis said with an arrogant sensibility.

He hung around Carol's office a bit longer and talked about a variety of topics ranging from her kids to the politics at the university.

A FEW WEEKS LATER, Travis finally got the phone call from Headroom Pharmaceuticals he'd been waiting for. As soon as he got all of the details, he phoned Carol to thank her once again. He then immediately made plans to fly to Chicago. He got online and secured his airline reservation. He was about to make lodging arrangements, but then decided to save a little money by crashing at Alex's condo. He phoned Alex to find out if it would be too much of an inconvenience if he spent a few nights at his place.

"Of course it isn't. You know that you can stay with me anytime," Alex said.

"I just wanted to make sure. I didn't know if you secretly turned in your player's card and were shacking with someone," Travis teased him.

"Man, please! I'm never settling down." Alex laughed. "When are you coming to town?"

"I'll be there on the twenty-third, but it's not for an interview. That's the last part of the process. First, I have to give a seminar on my research."

"Aww shit, I was afraid you were going to say that day," Alex grumbled.

"What, do you have something going on that week?"

"No, it's not that. I'll be out of the country the week you're here," Alex explained.

"Oh, where are you going?" Travis inquired.

"South America."

"I take it that it's a private flight for those mobsters you're playing around with. Alex, I worry about you playing with fire like that. How are you able to get time off from your regular job to do that on the side?"

"Don't worry about me or how I do what I do. I'm just flying the damn plane. I don't ask questions and I don't get involved. All I do is provide a service."

"I'm just saying. Hanging around those types of people can lead to deadly consequences," Travis reminded Alex of the obvious.

"Well, for the amount of money I get for my service, it's a chance I'm willing to take."

"Okay. Don't say I didn't warn you." Travis made his final comment on the matter.

"Point well taken. I'm going to FedEx you a key to my place," Alex said, changing the subject. "You can take a cab from the airport to my house. I'll leave plenty of food in the refrigerator and you can also eat out if you'd like. There are plenty of places around to dine."

"Sounds like a plan to me." Travis got up from his computer and walked into the family room. He picked up the remote and turned on the TV, then pressed mute.

"Cool. I'll ship the extra keys in a day or so. Call me once you get them," Alex said.

"I will. So, what else has been going on?"

"The usual, man. Just flying all over the place and fighting the jet lag."

"How is your dad doing?"

"He's okay. He's hooked on Viagra though. He said it's the greatest pill that man has ever invented. Hell, I have to admit, I even use it from time to time."

"You have to be careful taking that. In fact, if you don't have to, you shouldn't use Viagra because it happens to have a spillover effect. It blocks PDE-5, but it also has an effect on PDE-6."

"Okay, you just talked way over my damn head with all of the PD shit. You need to just speak plain English. You've got to remember that simple motherfuckers like me don't know what the hell you're talking about."

"Okay, let me break this down for you. PDE-6 is used in the cone cells in the retina, so Viagra can have an effect on color vision. Some people who take Viagra notice a change in the way they perceive green and blue colors, or they see the world in a blur for several hours. Since you're a pilot you really shouldn't take that stuff, especially within twelve hours of a flight. Lots of young guys who take Viagra recreationally may not realize that they can become dependent on it. In other words, they can't get it up without taking the pill and I know you don't want that to happen."

"Hell motherfucking no I don't want that to happen. The only thing I heard about the pill was that you can't get an erection that lasts too long and so far that's never happened to me," Alex said.

"Dude, Viagra can fuck you up if you're not careful.

You could develop headaches. In some men, Viagra opens up arteries in the brain's lining and causes excess pressure. It can also cause a heart attack. Matter of fact, heart attacks are one reason why Viagra is a prescription drug rather than an over-the-counter drug like aspirin."

"Well, if the pill can fuck you up like that, why even put the shit on the market?" Alex asked.

"Because, regardless of the risks, consumers are willing to pay through the nose for it," Travis said with brutal honesty.

"You see, it's mad scientists like you who design these drugs and get people all hooked. Do you realize that in some respects, your profession is probably worse than a mobster who sells drugs because chemists are the people who design the shit to begin with." There was a long moment of silence.

"You know, I've never looked at it that way. I've always felt as if my profession was about finding cures and helping people live longer. I never thought about the darker side of the industry."

"Yeah, your profession most certainly does have a darker side. You know it's been rumored that the HIV virus was engineered in a lab to kill black people," Alex said, absolutely convinced of this.

"Alex, that's not true." Travis dismissed Alex's strongly held belief.

"Okay, hotshot. Hang with me for a second here

while I attempt to help you take off your blinders. What lab did they engineer marijuana in?"

"Marijuana wasn't engineered in a lab. It's a plant." Travis laughed.

"Exactly. It's a natural part of the earth. Now, where does crack cocaine grow?"

"You can't grow cocaine; it has to be made."

"And who came up with the idea to make it?" Alex let his question linger in the air.

"It was probably designed by a chemist," Travis reluctantly admitted.

"Exactly. Just like all kinds of other biomedical germs like the flu virus. I swear to you, man, insane scientists are in labs creating a new strain every year just to make money off of the public. And you know what? The government scientists know about it. They have labs underground where they do secret experiments on animals and people. I'll bet you they're even quietly cloning humans."

"Alex, don't you think you're reaching with that one? The government doesn't have any hidden labs, and they're definitely not conducting any unregulated experiments on people or cloning humans."

"You ever heard of the Tuskegee Study? The government injected black men with syphilis between 1932 and 1972. Now I know you heard about that shit?" Alex was certain he'd made his point.

"Of course I've heard of the study, but you've got it

twisted. The government never injected the men with syphilis; the men already had the infection. When the study began in 1932, the standard medical treatments for syphilis were toxic. Part of the study goal was to determine if patients were better off not being treated with such toxic remedies. Researchers wanted to understand each stage of the disease in hopes of developing a suitable treatment. The tragic part happened when penicillin became the standard treatment and the men were never given the drug."

"Okay, you're getting all technical on me, but regardless…you can never say that the government has never experimented on people before."

"No, I can't say that," Travis admitted.

"You can be so straight-laced sometimes, Travis. I'm just trying to get you to understand the bigger picture."

"Point well taken, Alex."

"So, if you get this job are you going to be making more money?" Alex asked.

"I should be or at least that's the goal. I don't want to sponge off my parents forever. A man has got to cut his own path in life."

"Amen to that, brother. Look, I've got to run. I'll give you a buzz later," Alex said, sounding suddenly rushed.

"Okay. Talk you later." Travis hung up the phone.

Chapter 9
Jasmine

Jasmine and her team of scientists walked into the small auditorium at her workplace. She placed her notepad on the seat. In the corner of the room on a separate piece of furniture there was a breakfast buffet with bagels, pastries, fresh fruit, coffee and a selection of juices. She picked up a plate and placed a small vine of grapes on it, then grabbed one of the miniature bottles of orange juice. Just as she sat down, more members of the executive management team and employees entered. The president of the company, Helen Holmes, decided to approach Jasmine before she could take her seat.

"Good morning," Helen greeted Jasmine with the customary pleasantry and a smile that never fully formed.

"Good morning. It's good to see you," Jasmine answered.

"Be sure to come by my office, let's say around one this afternoon. I have a few things I'd like to discuss with you."

"Sure. I'm looking forward to it," Jasmine said as she

headed back to her seat. Once she was situated, Monica, a member of her team, leaned toward Jasmine and whispered, "What do you think this surprise meeting is about?"

"I have no idea. Helen wants to see me in her office later on today though." Jasmine plucked a grape and ate it.

Helen was a driven woman in her fifties. Her hair had turned silver instead of gray. She had blue eyes and pale white skin with rosy cheeks and thin lips. She was a straight-no-chaser kind of person who didn't calibrate her words when speaking. Jasmine had learned how to speak her language early on. Helen wasn't one for casual conversation; she was into formulas, calculations and had killer business savvy. She never married nor had any children, only a goddaughter who lived in California, but whom she was very fond of. She rarely took a day off and if she did, it was generally to take care of some task or household chore that required her attention or direct supervision. Helen could be so uptight at times that many of the women gossiped about how a big dick, a good fuck and a strong orgasm would do her crotchety disposition a world of good. The company was Helen's life; started by her great-grandfather in the 1940s and had remained in the family ever since. Helen and her slightly older brother took over when their father passed away ten years earlier.

"Okay, everyone have a seat so that we can get started."

Helen stood at the podium and waited for the modest number of employees to get settled. "As you know, the primary purpose of this company has been engaged in the discovery, development and commercialization of drugs in the areas of infection, cancer, respiratory disease and other areas of medicine. Sometime ago—I can't remember exactly when because it's been so long—I gave Jasmine Sallie and her team the task of developing a new antibiotic for the treatment of respiratory tract infections. She and her team worked tirelessly to develop a new formula. From the discovery stage to the preclinical trials, and in every phase thereafter, Jasmine has made this product a reality. We are now at the brink of commercialization for this medicine, and I am both excited and confident that it will soon be available for use by practitioners around the globe. So I'd like everyone on Jasmine's team to please stand up and be recognized by your peers."

A large smile formed on Jasmine's face as she and her team rose to their feet and listened to the applause of their colleagues.

"Thank you, Jasmine, and every member on your team for a job well done. Jasmine's team isn't the only group that is worthy of adoration. Jim Williams and his team were charged with developing a new drug to help battle pneumonia. He and his team have also worked tirelessly to develop a formula. I am happy to announce that his new drug has just passed a critical

Phase Three test. Let's give Jim and his team a big round of applause," Helen said.

Jasmine, along with everyone else, rose to their feet and clapped. As she sat back down, she felt her cell phone vibrating. She removed it from her hip holster to see who was calling.

It was Harrison. Jasmine ignored his phone call. A few seconds later, she felt her phone vibrate again. This time Harrison had sent her a text message: *I need to see you. Please!* Jasmine exhaled a disgruntled sigh before shutting off her phone. She'd have to deal with Harrison later.

Jasmine listened as Helen gave everyone a status report on the direction of the company. Then the director of sales and the director of marketing gave updates as well. An hour later the meeting ended. Jasmine went back to her office and shut her door for some privacy. She powered her phone back on and noticed that Harrison had phoned her several more times. She was about to return his phone call, but couldn't because of an incoming call from Tiffany.

"Just the woman I need to speak to," Jasmine answered.

"Are you sure? Because I haven't heard a single word from you since you told me about that young yoga instructor. I was calling to see if he's allowed you to come up for air yet?" Tiffany laughed.

"Girl, I let him go," Jasmine said as she plugged in her earpiece.

"You let him go? Damn, that didn't last long. What happened?"

"It's a long story," Jasmine said.

"I've got time. I'm on my lunch break."

"You mean to tell me you don't have some young guy trying to sweep you off of your feet?"

Jasmine chuckled as she walked over to her office window and glanced at the few gray clouds in the sky. She wondered if the area was going to receive some much-needed rain.

"Nah, not today. I'm hiding out. You know my shit attracts young men like bees to honey. I've got that sweet, sticky stuff they just can't seem to get enough of. The minute I'm spotted on the floor, the young guys flock to me, and the other librarians have a problem with that. But that's another issue that we'll discuss at a later time." Tiffany coughed, then cleared her throat. "Seriously though, what's been going on with you?"

"A lot," Jasmine replied.

"Nothing tragic, I hope."

"No. Everything is going well at work; it's my love life that's gotten kind of twisted around," Jasmine answered honestly. She began to think about ways to help Harrison get over her.

"How did it get twisted around? I thought you liked this Harrison guy."

"Yeah, but just for a friendly fuck. He got a little confused about the nature of our relationship. Plus, I was getting tired of him," Jasmine admitted.

"What did he get confused about?"

"Well, first of all, let me start by saying that I totally forgot how young he was. I called him up one night when I was leaving work late. I was on fire and wanted it in a very bad way. Now mind you, he's never been to my place, and every time we've hooked up he's always gotten a room. So I'm thinking, hey, I'll just come by your place this time so you don't have to spend extra money. Then he says to me, 'Okay, let me make sure my mamma is asleep though.'"

"Oh my God!" Tiffany gasped and then started laughing.

"'Oh my God' is an understatement. Reality slapped me hard that night. I never even thought about where he lived because he always talked about home as if he had an apartment."

"Well, did he recently move back home or something?" Tiffany asked.

"Hell no! He lives in the basement of his mother's house."

"So did you go over there for some sneaky, quiet sex, or did you take him back home with you?" Tiffany joked.

"Neither. I told him that I wasn't coming. He offered to drive over to my place, and when I told him no, he got upset with me because as he put it, I was playing with his emotions."

"Don't tell me he started falling in love with you." Tiffany eagerly awaited Jasmine's answer.

"Girl, yes! He started whining about how he thought about me all of the time and how he wanted to always be near me. He said that he'd never felt that way about anyone before, and he wanted to do whatever it took to make me happy and to make our relationship work. He even said he was ready to move out of his mother's house and into mine."

"Oh shit. It sounds like you blew his damn mind."

"Well, you know, a sister does have some killer skills."

Jasmine and Tiffany both joked about her comment.

"But that's so sad, yet kind of flattering that he wants more out of the relationship."

"Tiffany, you know as well as I do that it wouldn't work with someone that young. He doesn't have enough life experience on him yet. And I'll be the first to admit that being with him did make me feel very young and carefree."

"So what happened next?" Tiffany asked.

"I took a few deep breaths, thought about it for like half a second and told him that it was time for him to move on. I suggested that he find a young girl and blow her mind with what I've taught him."

"How did he take that?"

"He acted as if I were crushing his heart," Jasmine said.

"That is so precious," Tiffany said with a sentimental tone.

"I knew that he was in over his head with me from the jump start. The first time we did it, he had this look of amazement on his face. I knew then it was the best pussy he'd ever had."

"Sounds like you opened his nose up wide," Tiffany said.

"Yeah I did. He admitted that I was the first mature woman he'd ever been with and he never knew that it could be so good. Anyway, now he won't stop calling me and I may have to change my damn phone number. So I wanted to ask you, have you ever had one of your boy toys get a little too hooked?"

"I can honestly say no, that hasn't happened," Tiffany answered. "It's pretty much a foregone conclusion that we're just having fun. In fact, I tell the young men flat out I'm a Cougar who likes to play. College guys understand that and take it for what it is: A mutual agreement to have intimacy without intricacies. But it sounds like your friend is totally sprung."

"Well, I've sprung his ass in another direction and the hell away from me," Jasmine said with all seriousness. "So have you heard from Millie?"

"Yeah, I talked to her the other day. I'm surprised she hasn't called you and filled you in on all of her drama."

"Did something happen?" Jasmine asked.

"Shit, a whole lot has happened, she—"

"Oh shit!" Jasmine interrupted Tiffany. "Girl, I've

been on this phone with you for too long. I have to rush off to a meeting with my boss. I'll call you back later."

"Okay," Tiffany said, fully understanding Jasmine's urgent departure.

Jasmine grabbed her ink pen and writing pad and rushed out of her office. She decided to run up the two flights of stairs to Helen's office instead of waiting for an elevator. When Helen's assistant saw Jasmine approach her desk, she hung up the phone.

"I was just about to call you," the assistant said.

"Sorry about that. Is she waiting for me?" Jasmine asked.

"Yes. Just go on in."

Jasmine walked into Helen's office and found her sitting at her desk reading documents.

"There you are. I thought you'd forgotten about me," Helen said as she got up and closed her office door for more privacy.

"No, I didn't forget. Time just got away from me, that's all," Jasmine explained.

"That's because you enjoy what you do and time seems to fly when you've found your passion." Helen sat back down at her desk.

"I want to thank you for recognizing my team and the work we've done," Jasmine said as she clicked her ink pen and prepared to take notes.

"There is no need for that. This meeting is more informal. I have two things I'd like to discuss with you."

"Okay." Jasmine listened attentively.

"As you know, we have an open chemist position that we need to fill. I've received a number of inquiries and selected the resumes of four applicants." Helen handed Jasmine a folder filled with the background information on the candidates. Jasmine took a moment and glanced at the contents of the folder.

"One guy is from Berkeley. They have an excellent chemistry program out there," Jasmine said as she flipped the page and looked at another person's qualifications.

"It's funny you should mention that one. He comes highly recommended from a close friend who teaches there. However, he doesn't have as many years in the field, but if he passes the grade and we discover he's the best pick of the crop, I want you to assign him to your team."

"Oh really," Jasmine said, trying not to sound surprised.

"Yes. Whichever candidate is hired, I want them to work under your direct supervision. I believe that you have a certain flare for nurturing young talent. You have a unique gift for bringing out the best in a person. I also want you on the hiring committee."

"When do I start?" Jasmine asked.

"The process will start next week. I'll have my assistant forward the schedule to you. I believe the first person will be the woman from GlaxoSmithKline. She's scheduled to present a seminar on the research she's been doing."

"Great, I'll make sure that I clear my calendar." Jasmine felt good about being included in the process.

"There's something else. A rather special project I want you to begin working on. It's a rather complex idea, but I want to see if you and your team can come up with a pill that will do for women what Viagra has done for men with erectile troubles. I want you to create an aphrodisiac for women."

"An aphrodisiac for women?" Jasmine repeated what she'd heard just for clarification.

"Yes, I know. It's an idea that's very cutting edge. However, if we can come up with a compound that has the ability to unlock the mystery of arousal in women, it would be something so revolutionary, so groundbreaking and radical that the scientific community would have to salute us for our innovation. Our investors would love it because it would be a blockbuster pill that industrialized nations would purchase in large quantities."

"Research on this is going to be a risky business, don't you think? I mean, shouldn't we be working on finding cures for more life-threatening illnesses?" Jasmine asked.

Helen smirked and leaned back in her chair.

"Jasmine, finding a cure is one thing, but creating a pill for someone with a chronic problem is another. For example, let's take asthma. There is no cure for it, only an abundance of medications designed to relieve the symptoms. We're living in challenging times. The landscape is littered with small biotech companies who aren't paying for patents or royalties. They're just rolling generic drugs off of a conveyor belt and putting up only a small amount of money to cover the cost of distribution and marketing to the public. You and I both know that the drugs they're selling in the market-place today are at least fifteen years old. There has been no real breakthrough in anything since the invention of penicillin. It's going to take small biotech companies like ours to do the real innovative work because the big boys are too antiquated, strictly structured and too regulated to do anything meaningful." Helen stood up and walked over to her window and pulled back the drapes. "Do you know that there are millions of women out there who can't achieve an orgasm?"

"I've heard stories, but I've never thought much of it," Jasmine answered honestly and thought about discussing it with her girlfriends at some point, "That's because all of the focus has always been on men. They knew that with age the very essence of their manhood would fade away. When they happened to stumble on Viagra, it immediately became a successful pill that men wanted. However, they were only thinking of themselves and not women. They figured an erect cock was all a woman needed. But as you and I know, that's only a small part of the equation. Wouldn't you agree?"

Helen turned to meet Jasmine's gaze. "Yes," she answered as she listened intently.

"If science can develop something that a woman can take which stimulates arousal to the highest degree, we'd change the way men and women relate to each other and we'd own the patent to it."

"Creating something like that, would, without a doubt be very pioneering," Jasmine said as her mind began to think of a good place to start.

"Yes it would, and if created, it would provide us with the money-making pill the company could make billions off of. I wish I had thought about doing this earlier in life, because I don't want to have to wait fifteen years to see it hit the market."

"Well, I guess I'd better start thinking of the best way to approach this." Jasmine said.

"Yes, you should, but I want you to start on this *after* we've gone through the hiring process. I also need you to keep me apprised of your progress once you've started."

Helen nodded her head in a gesture to let Jasmine know she was more than serious about the project.

"Okay," Jasmine said.

"That will be all. I have a meeting with a senator I must prepare for. Damn blood-sucking politicians," Helen murmured under her breath.

Jasmine then stood up to leave.

"Oh, and Jasmine… Great job on the creation of the antibiotic. Hopefully it will change the way doctors treat respiratory infections. Our investors were pleased."

"Thanks," Jasmine said and then exited her office.

Chapter 10
Travis

Travis arrived at Chicago's Midway Airport on a balmy afternoon. He walked off of the aircraft and began heading toward the baggage claim area. He stopped briefly at the concession shop to pick up a newspaper, then continued onward toward the baggage claim area. Once he retrieved his luggage, he headed outside where he hailed a cab and gave the driver the address to Alex's downtown condo. As he rode along, Travis picked up the newspaper and began reading an article about the pharmaceutical industry that had caught his eye. A local female senator named Yolanda Cobb was up for reelection and there was a commentary about her going around soliciting campaign contributions from local pharmaceutical companies, one of which he had an interview with. He read the article with interest and intrigue, primarily because Senator Cobb was also reported to have close ties to pharmaceutical regulators.

This has scandal written all over it. But then again Illinois is known for shady politicians, Travis thought to himself. He turned the page and saw an article about the impeachment of the Illinois state governor for trying to sell a senate seat.

A SHORT TIME LATER, the cab pulled in front of Alex's house. Travis paid the driver, grabbed his luggage and headed inside. Alex lived in the South Loop area of Chicago in a residential community called Central Station. The development looked out on Grant Park, the Museum Campus and Soldier Field Football Stadium. The Chicago Lakefront, Buckingham Fountain, and Navy Pier were all within walking distance or just a short cab ride. Travis used the key that Alex had sent to him earlier to gain entrance.

"Hello," Travis called out just to make sure Alex didn't have a change of plans and was still at home. After hearing no response and glancing around he knew that his friend was indeed out of town.

Alex had a flare for art. He liked to collect unique items such as tribal masks, glass figurines, and sea shells whenever he traveled someplace exotic. The decor of his home reflected his unique sensibilities, but it wasn't over the top. He had beautiful hardwood floors throughout his unit and a see-through glass stairway that allowed the downstairs and upstairs areas to interrelate. Travis pulled his suitcases into the spare bedroom, then went into the kitchen where he'd found a Post-It note from Alex that read: *My home is your home. Best of luck on your interview.*

Travis set the note on the countertop and opened up the refrigerator. He grabbed himself a beer, twisted off the cap, and took several long gulps until he finished off the bottle.

"Damn, that was good," he said aloud. He went back into the bedroom and retrieved his laptop, then sat down at the kitchen table, booted it up and went over his presentation notes for his seminar in the morning.

WHEN TRAVIS ARRIVED AT THE BIOTECH FIRM, he was escorted into an auditorium where there were several people waiting on him. He shook hands with everyone on the committee and thanked them for the opportunity. Travis was nervous and anxious, but eager to get started. After a little setup time, he began his presentation which he delivered masterfully. Next, he had taken a few questions from the committee and was thanked for his time.

By the time Travis had made it back to Alex's place, he received a phone call from the biotech company much sooner than he'd expected. He thought it'd take at least several days for them to call him back, however, he was scheduled for a formal interview in two days. Travis spent the next forty-eight hours really doing more research on the company so that he'd be able to answer questions intelligently.

When he returned for the interview, he was placed in a special conference room. He'd anticipated a single interview by multiple people, but was surprised when a woman entered the room.

"Hello, Mr. Adams," greeted a stunningly beautiful woman with a set of alluring eyes that looked very familiar to him.

"Hello." Travis stood up to shake her hand. "I'm sorry, but I didn't catch your name."

"My name is Jasmine." She smiled before taking a seat. For the life of him Travis couldn't pinpoint why she looked so familiar.

"That was quite an impressive presentation you gave yesterday," Jasmine said as she threaded her fingers together into a prayer position and placed them on the tabletop.

"Would you like something to drink before we get started? Coffee, tea, or water?"

"No, I'm fine. Thanks for asking."

"Okay then," Jasmine said as she opened up a folder with a form inside that she planned to fill out during the interview process. Travis kept gazing at Jasmine and her features, trying desperately to search his memory of when and where he'd seen her. Even now her voice was starting to sound so familiar.

"I'm going to begin by telling you a little bit about me," Jasmine said.

"Yes, please do."

"I'm one of the head researchers here. I have my own team and we've been doing research on a variety of drugs."

"Yes, I've learned that you and your team are about

to get a new antibiotic approved for the marketplace. Congratulations," Travis said.

"I see you've done your homework." Jasmine smiled.

"I'm very good at researching things." Travis laughed.

"So I see," Jasmine commented.

The interview was scheduled to last one hour, but ended up taking an hour and a half. By the time Travis left he felt confident, but didn't want to jump up for joy just yet; he knew from experience that nothing was guaranteed.

On Friday evening Travis decided to head over to a mix-and-mingle gathering hosted by a company called Blackfitandsingle.com taking place at the Shedd Aquarium Museum. He'd heard an advertisement about the event on the radio and thought it would be an excellent way to unwind after his grueling interview process. He put on his black pinstripe business suit and a nice shirt without a tie. He hailed a cab so he wouldn't have to walk. When he arrived, the place was crowded with people who appeared to have just gotten off from work. Travis really wasn't on the prowl; he just wanted a drink and a little casual conversation. After navigating his way through the crowd, he finally found the bar. He ordered a beer and then stepped out onto the terrace where it was much cooler. There was a magnificent view of Lake Michigan and the Chicago skyline. Travis leaned forward and rested his elbows on the concrete railing and watched as lovers strolled hand in hand along the path below him.

"If I didn't know any better, I'd say you were following me." Travis slowly craned his head to the right to see if the voice was speaking to him.

"Ms. Sallie, wow, this is a surprise. How are you doing?" Travis stood with a more erect posture.

"Oh, come on now. You don't have to be so formal. The interview is over. You can call me Jasmine," she said as she took a small sip of her wine.

"Okay." Travis smiled.

"I saw you when you walked in," Jasmine said, glancing at his fit body. "That's a very nice suit."

Travis tugged at his jacket. "Thanks, I'm a sucker for tailored suits."

"You don't remember me, do you?" Jasmine leaned her hip against the concrete banister.

"You know, I was trying hard to place where we'd met, but I still haven't figured it out."

"For a man who makes a living doing research, I would have never thought that trying to recall where we'd met would be such a puzzle to you." Jasmine took another sip of her wine.

"You know this is killing me, right?" Travis said.

"I'll let you off the hook this time since we've only really met once and rather briefly at that. We met in New York a few months ago."

Travis snapped his fingers. "That's right! You were there celebrating your girlfriend's birthday."

"Yes I was, but I had no idea that I was engaged in a

conversation with such an intelligent young man. I thought you and your friend were playing some childish game."

"My friend Alex was drunk. He has the hots for you, to put it frankly. Whatever you said to him during your flight to New York has piqued his curiosity about you," Travis said, taking a gulp of his beer.

"I was only flirting with him a little. He really isn't my type," Jasmine admitted.

"So I guess that means you're not married," Travis concluded.

"No. I've never been married."

"Kids?" Travis asked.

"No children either. I was engaged once to a wonderful man. I loved him very dearly, but sadly he passed away."

"Oh, I'm sorry to hear that."

"Shit happens, you know. Some things that take place are just beyond our control."

"Isn't that the truth," Travis agreed. "So, how do you think I did? Will I get the job?"

Jasmine smiled, then handed her empty wineglass to one of the waiters who was passing by. "I can't discuss that with you, Mr. Adams," she said firmly.

"Hey, I had to ask." Travis shrugged.

"I understand." Jasmine paused for a long moment. "So tell me about you."

"You already know everything about me," Travis said.

"That's the professional side of you. I'm talking about the personal side. Any children?"

"God no. I'm not the fatherly type," Travis admitted.

"Oh, I'm sure you'd make a great father. You just have to find the right young woman."

"That probably won't happen anytime soon." Travis waved his hands totally discounting Jasmine's theory.

"You don't have to be modest. You're a handsome young man. I'm sure that you have plenty of young ladies stalking you."

"You see, that's the thing. I've never really dated women my age. I prefer to date women who are older."

"Is that a fact?" Jasmine raised her eyebrow.

"A fact that can be scientifically proven." Travis smirked.

"You are a witty one." Jasmine liked his easygoing manner. Jasmine looked him up and down, then said, "This may sound a little bold, but are you seeing anyone in particular at this time?"

"Why do you want to know?" Travis asked.

"It's just a question."

"Let me ask you a question. Have you ever dated anyone as young as me?" Travis looked directly into her eyes. He was once again enjoying a flirtatious conversation with her.

"I prefer dating men your age," Jasmine said.

Travis turned and rested his elbows on the concrete banister. "Can I get you another drink?" he asked, thinking that he was going to have Jasmine tonight.

"No. In fact, I'm about to go home," she said.

"But you just got here."

"I was here before you, remember?"

"Yeah, but I was enjoying your company. You just can't walk away and leave me like this."

"Sure I can. I'm positive your friend, Alex is lurking around somewhere."

"He's not here. He's out of town," Travis said.

"Well, tell him I said hello the next time you see him." Jasmine smiled pleasantly at him once more, then walked away.

"Wait a minute." Travis trailed behind her. "Will you at least let me walk you to your car?"

"Sure, if you'd like to, but it's not necessary," Jasmine assured him.

"No, I really want to. So where do you live?" he asked.

"Not too far from here. It should only take me about thirty minutes to get home. Especially now that traffic has died down some."

"This may sound a little off the wall, but I'd like to see you again. Even if I don't land the position, I wouldn't mind having lunch or dinner or even just a cup of coffee with you," Travis said as he walked down the stairs of the museum.

"Why?" Jasmine asked, deciding that she'd allow him to chase her for the moment.

"Well, for starters, I think you're hot. You look fantastic."

"So you only want me for my hot body?"

Travis smiled. "No, no. I want to get to know you better as well." Travis cleared up his intentions.

"Shit, I was hoping you only wanted to have kinky sex," Jasmine said. They had finally reached her vehicle. She opened her car door and got inside. She fired up the ignition, and then rolled down her window.

"You don't know the things that I could do to you, Jasmine," Travis said, glancing at her lustfully.

"Oh, no, my dear. You have no idea how I'd rock your world." Jasmine winked at Travis and then began to pull off.

"So you're going to just leave me like this? Standing in the middle of a parking lot?"

"Go back inside and have a good time. I'm sure there are plenty of Cougars in there who'd love to play with you tonight." Jasmine pressed the accelerator and zoomed off.

Chapter 11
Jasmine

On Saturday morning, Jasmine awoke to the sound of her cell phone ringing. She turned over in bed, placed a pillow over her head and tried to get more sleep. The phone stopped ringing, but then started right back up. Annoyed, Jasmine reached over to turn the phone off, but saw that Harrison was once again calling her.

"Oh Jesus, Harrison. Grow the fuck up and leave me alone!" Jasmine uttered as the phone once again stopped. A few seconds later, it began ringing again.

"I see right now that I'm going to have to change my damn phone number." Jasmine debated whether or not to answer the phone. She thought she'd made herself perfectly clear, but Harrison was obviously having trouble moving on. Jasmine decided that she needed to be a little more forceful with him, so he'd understand that she wanted all of the phone calls and text messages to stop.

"Hello," she answered.

"Hey!" Harrison sounded excited.

"What do you want, Harrison? You woke me up," Jasmine said curtly.

"You haven't been coming to yoga class. I just wanted to make sure you were okay."

"I'm fine," Jasmine said.

"Will you be coming back?" he asked.

"I don't think that's a good idea, Harrison. At least not right now."

"Why not?" he asked innocently.

"Look. We had fun and now it's over. It's time for you to get on with your life and stop worrying about me."

"How can you switch from hot to cold like that?"

"Harrison, you're making this more complicated than it has to be. I wanted to fuck you, so I did. Now I'm done fucking you. Just forget about me." Jasmine was trying her best to let him down easy.

"It's so hard though. I still want to be with you," Harrison whined like a snotty-nosed boy.

"Harrison, this is going to sound really mean, and you'll probably think I'm a real bitch afterwards, but I'm doing it for your own good. Stop fucking calling me!"

Jasmine hung up the phone. She placed her forearm on her forehead and exhaled, fully anticipating a return phone call, but to her delight he didn't call back.

"Thank goodness. Maybe he's finally gotten the message through his thick head." Jasmine hated to let go of the comfort of her bed, but now she was wide awake and thirsting for a cup of coffee.

After freshening up in the bathroom, she walked downstairs to her kitchen and cooked breakfast. She went into her office, sat at her desk and began going through all of her mail which had piled up. She paid her bills, did some filing and then checked her Facebook page. She was surprised to see a friend request from Travis Adams. Jasmine smirked, then denied his request. She knew that he'd be receiving an offer for the position on Monday and didn't want to start a relationship with him, especially since they'd be working together. That was one of her rules. She didn't date guys she worked with. Although she had to admit that she was very attracted to him.

Just as Jasmine was about to move on and check her e-mail account, she heard her doorbell chime.

"That ain't nobody but Lauren. She's the only person who comes over totally unannounced." Jasmine got up from her seat and went to answer the door. Sure enough her sister was standing there wearing her DEA jacket, bulletproof vest and gun belt. She was also driving a blue Crown Victoria squad car. Jasmine opened the door.

"What are you doing here? Shouldn't you be at work?" Jasmine asked.

"Yeah, but I don't have to report in for another two hours. I have a task force meeting later on today. We're raiding a medical marijuana dispensary."

"Oh, one of those places that administers marijuana

legally to patients, right?" Jasmine had a very clear idea of what Lauren was talking about but wanted to confirm it.

"Yes. It appears as if there have been violations of federal and state laws. Girl, it's rough out there. Just two days ago we raided a home that was turned into a crystal meth factory, right in the middle of suburbia. It's a damn shame."

"Who was making it? The homeowners?" Jasmine asked as she led Lauren into the family room.

"No. The house was a foreclosure. The suspects took over the house, but we believe that there are also either bank employees or real estate agents involved. Someone had to provide these criminals with a list of addresses as potential sites to set up their operation."

"Wow," Jasmine said as she sat down.

"It's getting worse and worse out there. People who've lost their jobs, livelihood, and hope are turning to either using drugs or selling them. It's a real mess."

"It sounds like it," Jasmine agreed.

"I didn't stop by to talk about my job though. I came by to ask your thoughts about what happened with Millie," Lauren said.

"What do you mean what happened with Millie?" Jasmine was confused.

"You didn't hear? Millie didn't call you to talk about it?" Lauren was truly surprised.

"No. I haven't heard from Millie. I did talk to Tiffany

and she was trying to tell me something, but I had to run off to a meeting."

"Well, listen to this mess."

"I'm all ears." Jasmine leaned in toward Lauren.

"Millie's lover came to her house to confront her husband."

"What!" Jasmine shouted.

"You heard me. The young lawyer she was messing with called out her husband and they got into a fistfight on the front lawn of Millie's house."

"You've got to be fucking kidding me."

"I'm not lying."

"Well, who won the fight?" Jasmine asked out of curiosity.

"Millie's husband got his ass kicked from what I understand, and the police arrested Millie's lover."

"Oh shit. Why did the lover go to Millie's house in the first place? How did he even know where she lived?"

"Sounds like Millie had brought that man to her house before. Anyway, Millie's husband found out about the affair she was having and he lost it."

"What do you mean, 'he lost it'?"

"He hit Millie," Lauren explained.

"Oh, that fool has really lost his mind! It sounds like we need to catch a flight out there to help Millie deal with this. He shouldn't be putting his damned hands on her."

"I know that's how I feel as well but there is more. You're not going to believe this part."

"Oh Lord." Jasmine paused, then waited for Lauren to give her the final detail.

"Millie's husband was also having an affair with the young intern's mother." Jasmine's mouth opened as wide as the sky. She was completely speechless, blown away by this news.

"How in the hell did that happen?" Jasmine asked.

"Girl, your guess is as good as mine, but Millie and her husband were screwing two different members of the same damn family."

"Ooo, that sounds messy as hell. No wonder I haven't heard from Millie. She's got a big pot of shit stirring." Jasmine tried to imagine what her girlfriend must have been going through. "Have you talked with Millie at all?"

"I called and left a message. I told her that you and I were ready, willing and able to come out there and see about her. She shot me a text message back saying that she had him locked up for hitting her and that she was fine."

"Has the media gotten wind of all of that? You know she was under investigation," Jasmine reminded her.

"I don't know. That's a good question. I do know that Millie's husband is also pressing assault charges against the lover in addition to having to defend his own case."

"Damn!" Jasmine said as she and Lauren moved over to a nearby sofa and sat. "I'm going to give her a call today to find out how she's doing. It sounds as if her life is in a chaotic tailspin."

"Well, if you get through to her, let her know that we're here if she needs us. But you know how Millie is. She won't ask for help even when she needs it the most."

"I know but this is different and I intend to make sure she understands that she has friends who care about her and are on her side." Jasmine coughed a few times and then continued, "Not to change the subject, but did I tell you that Harrison, the yoga instructor, turned out to be a damn stalker?"

"A stalker? What are you talking about? Is he following you around or something?"

"No, he just has a difficult time understanding that all I wanted to do was fuck him. He tried to turn a good fuck into a meaningful relationship," Jasmine joked.

"Goodness, Jasmine! You didn't have to break the boy's heart."

"Honey, he hasn't been a boy in some time." Jasmine rose up to turn on the stereo. The sultry voice of Jazmine Sullivan came through the speakers.

"So what's going on with you and your friend?" Jasmine asked.

"Everything is going well. No complaints here," Lauren said.

"Well, we're about to hire a young, sexy chemist named Travis Adams," Jasmine said, putting on a wicked grin.

"Oh yeah. Is he a new fish you have on your hook?" Lauren asked.

"Nah, although he was eager to jump on the line. He told me that he only dates older women, then tried to undress me with his eyes on the sly." Jasmine laughed.

"How old is he?" Lauren asked.

"Twenty-eight."

"That's not a bad age. He should have gone through enough relationships by now to have a little more life experience under his belt."

"Oh honey, he appears to have an abundant amount of experience under his belt. I can tell by how confident he was. He thought he was going to bed me last night when I ran into him at a social function."

"Well, you know the rule. You shouldn't fuck a coworker," Lauren said.

"Aren't you being a little hypocritical seeing as how you're doing just that?"

"As Daddy was so fond of pointing out: Do as I say, not as I do." Lauren laughed and then made a move toward the door.

"He did say that all of the time, didn't he?" Jasmine reflected for a moment. "Make sure you call me after your raid. You know how I worry about you."

"I will," Lauren said and hugged her sister.

"Be safe," Jasmine said. She walked Lauren toward the Crown Victoria, and watched her get in and drive off.

Chapter 12
Travis

Travis received a handsome offer for the position at Headroom Pharmaceuticals which he gladly accepted. He worked out the details of his start date so that he could have enough time to return home, contact his parents and take care of all the details associated with moving out of the house.

With Alex's help he was able to locate a decent two-bedroom apartment in the Wrigleyville neighborhood just north of downtown Chicago. His apartment was directly across the street from Wrigley Field, which was the home of the Chicago Cubs baseball team. His vintage apartment building had rooftop seating so that he could enjoy a game during the season without ever really having to leave home. Sports bars ruled the area, which suited Travis just fine because he figured that it would provide him with plenty of opportunities to unwind when life got a little too stressful. His new neighborhood also had excellent restaurants that ranged from Chicago-style to upscale full-service restaurants.

It was a bit of an adjustment to move from a spacious house to the more compact confines of an apartment.

He also had to get used to parking his car on the over-crowded streets of Chicago. Travis figured that after twelve months on the job he'd have a better sense of whether or not he was going to stay or decide to move on. If he elected to stay, he'd then begin the search for a home.

TRAVIS WAS IN HIS APARTMENT UNPACKING the last of the boxes he'd shipped from California. He'd just opened a container with an assortment of items including an old photo album. He decided to take a moment to flip through the photos and saw one of him and Alex when they were undergraduate students. The photo was ten years old and was taken shortly after a game in the bleachers of the football stadium. Alex was holding up his finger indicating that he was number one and Travis was standing behind him with two fingers held up directly behind his head. Travis laughed at the silly photo. His cell phone vibrated, indicating that he'd just received a text message. He pulled out his phone and read it.

"In your neck of the woods. Stopping by 2 C U." The text was from Alex. Travis responded and then went back to viewing his photo album. The next photo was of him walking across the stage getting his PhD.

"God, I was so wasted that day because I'd been out the night before fucking a woman from Australia who was visiting the United States for the first time. She had a voracious appetite for black men. I almost didn't make it to graduation because she drained me before I left," he muttered to himself as he thought about all of the wild times he'd had. At that moment he heard his doorbell buzz. He went to glance out the window to see who was downstairs. He raised the window and leaned slightly forward.

"Alex?" Travis called to him.

"What's up, pimp? Are you going to open the door or just leave me standing out here?"

"Hang on," Travis said as he went to buzz his friend in. It took Alex a few moments to hustle up to the second floor.

"What's going on?" he asked as he entered the apartment and shut the door.

"I'm still unpacking," he said as he walked toward the dining room where the boxes were stored.

"I thought I'd drop in to see how you were doing. I still can't believe you actually live here in Chicago now."

"Neither can I." Travis huffed as he handed Alex the photo album he was looking through. "There is an old photo of us in there."

"Oh shit," Alex howled. "We were so young then."

"We're still young. We haven't even crossed over into our thirties yet," Travis reminded him.

"But we were still teenagers when this picture was taken. We had a shit load of fun in college, didn't we?"

"Yeah we did, but you had a lot more fun than I did as I recall." Travis continued to empty the box.

"Shit, I'm still having a blast. I love my carefree bachelor lifestyle. I honestly don't see how a person can get married and just settle down with one woman. That shit would drive me crazy." Alex couldn't see the possibility of falling in love at all. Emotionally unconnected sex was all he was after.

"You say that now, but I think eventually we'll settle down with someone," Travis said to ruffle his feathers.

"Not me. Can't do it, won't do it and absolutely refuse to do it." Alex was unyielding and wasn't going to change his mind.

"I heard that," Travis agreed.

He glanced at Alex for a moment and noticed some bruises on his neck.

"What happened to your neck?" Travis pulled his shirt collar so he could see more clearly. "Damn, those bruises are all over your chest and shoulders. Did you get into a fight or something?"

"Dude, that's what I came by to tell you, I hooked up with this Cougar last night—wild and passionate. She kept biting the shit out of me whenever she had an orgasm."

"Damn, didn't that shit hurt?" Travis winced.

"Hell no, at least not at the time. The woman was new to the list and I was her first. She was tall. I mean really, really tall. Her curvaceous mahogany legs were long enough to drop kick a brother into the middle of next week. She told me that she was from Miami and that she'd never been with a gigolo before."

"You're not a gigolo though." Travis laughed.

"Yes I am. I let the ladies know that I'm a trained gigolo with exceptional skills. Shit, I don't fuck around. I'm giving these ladies what they want and providing an excellent service."

"Okay, I see your point." Travis backed down.

"Anyway she says to me: 'Start by eating my pussy.' I was like cool, no problem. Man, I must have licked her snatch for a good forty minutes. She squirted cum juice all over my face and lips. She was so wet that I had to ask her how long it had been."

"What did she say?"

"She said it's been over a year. Right then I knew that it was going to be an all-night job. I popped a Viagra, put on my rubber glove and let her ride cowgirl style. Her pussy had a fucking death grip. I mean she was squeezing my shit like she was trying to strangle it. I bust a nut so big I felt like she was a damn vampire sucking out my blood. All I wanted to do was take a nap after my release."

"Oh, don't tell me you pulled the old, 'give me a minute' line?" Travis laughed.

"Hell no, I was still hard and we fucked in every position imaginable. I was hitting the back of her pussy like a fighter punching a bag. That's when all of the biting started. She got animalistic on my ass."

"I can tell." Travis smirked as he glanced at the love bites once more.

"Anyway, when I left her, my nuts were tender but

she was satisfied. How is the new job going?" Alex asked, switching the subject.

"So far so good. My first week hasn't been too bad. I spent the majority of my time reading."

"Do you like your boss?" Alex asked.

"My boss and I get along just fine," Travis said.

"Good, I'm happy for you, man. I'm glad things are working out. Why don't you take a break from all of this unpacking and let me treat you to lunch."

"That sounds like a plan to me. Let me grab my wallet," Travis said as he walked toward his bedroom.

"What's your boss's name?" Alex spoke loud enough for Travis to hear him.

"Sallie." Travis gave Jasmine's last name.

"How does she look? Would you bang her if you had the chance?" Alex asked.

"There is no doubt about it. She's a thoroughbred and I'd love to be her jockey," Travis returned. He picked up his keys from a nearby countertop and walked toward the door.

"So are you going to put the moves on her or what?" Alex asked, curious about Travis's intentions.

"I've thought about it, but right now I'm really focused on doing a good job," Travis admitted.

"Oh boy, here we go. You're about to go into the nutty professor mode again. Although it would be cool if you could create a formula like they did in the movie. I'd have you tweak it a little bit so that I'd be irresistible to women. If you could do that, I'd buy a supply of that by the barrel."

"Man, come on and stop fantasizing about being the Casanova of the twenty-first century," Travis said as they walked out.

Chapter 13
Jasmine

Jasmine arrived at her office at 6:30 a.m. so that she could begin her research on the project that Helen had given to her. It was going to be a huge task coming up with an aphrodisiac for women and she knew it. When she walked into the lobby, she was greeted by Sam, the young security guard.

"Good morning, Sam. I noticed another car out in the parking lot. Has someone else come in?"

"Yup. It's not often that someone arrives at work so early in the morning," Sam said as he rose to his feet and folded his arms across his chest.

"Really. Who's here?" Jasmine asked.

"That new guy, Travis. He came in around four a.m. Said that he wants to hit the ground running. Either that guy is super dedicated to his work or he has no life at all outside of work."

"Hmm, interesting." Jasmine pondered over her thoughts as she glanced back at Travis's black sedan.

"You're not pulling a double shift are you, Sam?" Jasmine asked, turning her attention back to him.

"No, ma'am. I'll be leaving in another thirty minutes. I can't wait to get home and get some sleep. Working the night shift isn't easy."

"Good for you. If I don't see you again, enjoy your day." Jasmine nodded her head and continued on. Once she got upstairs, she used her access keycard to gain entrance into the lab. She wanted to know what Travis was doing. She walked around the lab and searched for him as she passed the beakers, microscopes, conveyor belts where experimental pills were produced, supplies, computers and various tanks of chemicals. She then entered a section of the lab where the live test subjects such as mice and rabbits which were bred for experimentation were caged. When she didn't find him there, she continued to search for him as well as call out his name.

Jasmine searched every corner of the lab but did not find him. She now stood outside the workshop door of the on-staff machinist wondering where he could be. Then the thought struck her. "He's probably in the restroom," she whispered. Jasmine exited the lab area and walked across a long corridor to where the offices were located. When she opened the door, she saw Travis standing in the aisle wearing a white lab coat and reading a document.

"There you are," she said.

The sound of her voice startled him. "Damn. You scared the crap out of me," Travis said, placing his hand over his heart. "I didn't think anyone would be here this early."

"I think you just won the company award for showing up to work extra early," Jasmine said as she approached him. "What are you reading?"

"The results of lubricant for post-menopausal women. It's rather interesting," Travis admitted.

"Did you finish reading the other material that I gave you? There is a reason that I gave you so much." Jasmine wanted to make sure he wasn't cutting any corners.

"Yes, I've read it all. I read the lion's share of it here and took the rest of it home. I finished up Sunday afternoon."

"You don't screw around, do you?" Jasmine asked, very impressed by his work ethic.

"Not when it comes to my work. I live and breathe for this stuff. I love the challenge and mystery of it. When I met with Helen and she explained her desire to do groundbreaking work in the area of female sexual dysfunction, I'll be the first to admit I was intrigued and eager to begin so that we could get something in the pipeline."

"Let's not rush something into the pipeline that's going to fail." Jasmine liked his enthusiasm for the task at hand, but wanted him to explore all possibilities.

"Trust me, I don't want to fail. I want to succeed more than anything. Helen said that if we can create something that's clinically proven safe and effective, we could enhance the lives of people all across the globe. That's the kind of work I want to do and that's the sort of thing that will make the scientific community stand up and applaud our work."

"Sounds as if you have big ambitions," Jasmine said.

"Yes I do," Travis answered.

"Tell you what. Why don't we get together for a meeting on Friday around nine a.m. Gather up as much information as you can throughout the week and I'll do the same. Then we'll put our heads together and work on this."

Travis's gusto was infectious and had somehow reignited Jasmine's passion for her work.

"You go it," Travis said with slight smile and then continued with his reading.

BY WEDNESDAY EVENING, Jasmine decided she'd go home at 5 p.m. instead of working past her regular hours. She was exhausted and needed to catch up on her rest. As soon as she entered the house, she walked over to her sofa and plopped down. She pulled off her shoes and wiggled her toes which were aching from being confined in her shoes.

"Oh, what I wouldn't do for a foot rub right now," she said aloud as she reached for the television remote. After flicking through the channels and finding absolutely nothing worthwhile to watch, she decided to run herself a hot bath. Twenty minutes later, her tired body from the neck down was completely submerged in water. As the warm water began to relax her, she thought about Travis. Over the past few weeks, he hadn't made any more advances toward her. He'd been completely professional and had behaved as if he didn't want her when she knew for a fact he did. On the one hand, Jasmine admired his cool demeanor and self-control; he wasn't all over her. She would have hated to pull him into her office and give him the *inappropriate behavior* speech. Then, on the other hand, it annoyed her that he hadn't made any type of advance, not even a wink of an eye on the slick tip. Jasmine had a love-hate relationship with her scatter-brained logic and the indecisiveness of her wishes.

"Well, girl," she spoke to herself. "The best thing you can do right now is masturbate and use your mind to imagine what it would be like to have some of Travis." Jasmine closed her eyes, took several deep breaths and relaxed. She imagined herself somewhere far away from the stress and anxiety of her career.

Jasmine walked along a tropical beach in a white sun-dress, wearing no underwear and enjoying the tickle of a breeze as it flowed between her thighs like a tranquil river. The sand warmed her bare feet as she moved toward the shoreline and stood still, allowing the rushing tide to bathe her feet. She admired the beauty of the horizon and its heavenly glow. As she continued on her stroll, she saw the silhouette of a man approaching. It was Travis, shirtless and wearing white linen pants that were rolled up to his calf muscles. Travis pulled the drawstring on his slacks and stopped. He took them off and tossed them aside on the sand. His dick, now free of its fabric prison, dangled between his legs and bounced as he continued to walk toward her. Jasmine couldn't wait to get to him. She couldn't wait to feel the silkiness of his dick in the palm of her hand.

Jasmine's body began to ache. Her pussy contracted and caused her to take several more deep breaths. She ran her fingertips over her breasts making small circles around her nipples.

"Oh, Travis." she spoke his name as she spread her thighs and slid her fingers down to her Goddess. She toyed with herself, inserting her fingers inside of herself while concentrating on the fantasy unfolding in her mind. *Travis had reached her now. They embraced and kissed each other passionately. The succulent flavor of his tongue was like no other she'd ever experienced. His hands were positioned on her ass, squeezing and caressing her.*

"I want you to fuck me doggie style," Jasmine said as she lowered herself to her hands and knees. *Travis knelt behind her, then slowly guided his long cock inside of her.*

"Pound me, baby," she said after a few minutes of him gently thrusting his body against hers. Eager to please, Travis did just that. He pounded her hard and spanked her ass. Jasmine continually clutched the grains of the warm sand, allowing the granules to seep through her fingers. The sound *of the powerful waves crashing against the shore in perfect rhythm along with the deep strokes Travis was giving her made her feel breathless. Travis pushed himself deeper and deeper inside of her. She felt herself explode on his hard shaft.*

Jasmine slowed the pace of her fingers circling her clitoris. She enjoyed the euphoric moment that her masturbation session had provided. "Damn, I wonder if he's really that good in bed?" she said aloud as she repositioned her body and prepared to get out of the tub. Once she toweled off, she went into her bedroom, opened up her underwear drawer and removed her vibrator.

"Come on," she spoke to it. "I'm hornier than an inmate who's just gotten out of prison. I'm going to give you a workout tonight."

FRIDAY MORNING PROMPTLY AT 9 A.M., Travis knocked on Jasmine's office door. She was on the phone speaking to Helen, but waved Travis inside and motioned for him to take a seat at her conference table. She finished up her phone call, then jotted down a few notes so she wouldn't forget what Helen needed her to do.

"Is it a bad time?" Travis asked. "I could come back."

"No. This is still a good time," Jasmine said as she searched her messy desk for the research information she'd gathered. Once she located it, she joined Travis at the conference table.

"Okay." Jasmine exhaled as she scooted her chair

closer to the table. "Why don't you go first and let me know what you've found so far."

"Sure. As you know, the properties in Viagra are designed to increase blood flow to the genitals. The drug works well for many men who suffer with impotence or erectile dysfunction because it's considered a physical condition rather than an emotional problem."

"Still, increased blood flow to the genitals of women can work as well, especially if a woman is suffering from vaginal dryness," Jasmine chimed in.

"Absolutely, but female sexual dysfunction is characterized by a lack of desire, arousal, and orgasm. Lack of sexual craving is the chief complaint among women, affecting about one-third of them at some point in their life."

"That, of course means that we'll somehow have to address the emotional component of the problem. That's going to be especially challenging among women who have had very negative sexual experiences." Jasmine began taking notes. She loved being engaged in the critical thinking process because during the course of conversation and debate, great progress could be made.

"Unlike men, the most important sex organ for women is between the ears. Once a man achieves an erection he's pretty much set for the most part. A man can have emotionally detached sex with very little difficulty. Women, on the other hand, need a purpose. They need to feel connected to their partner."

"That's not entirely accurate," Jasmine interrupted Travis.

"Sure it is." Travis was certain his theory was correct.

"Women can have emotionally unattached sex, too. It just depends on where she is in her life," Jasmine explained.

"How so?" Travis leaned back in his seat and placed the index finger of his right hand on his temple.

"Let's say you have a careerwoman who's had her fair share of relationships. She arrives at a point in her life where it's too painful to allow herself to get emotionally attached to someone, but she still has the need and desire for the type of penetration her toys can't provide. So she decides to seek out casual relationships, which she knows are only going to last a short period of time."

"You sound like one of the clients from the list." Travis didn't mean to speak what was on his mind.

"What list?" Jasmine asked, confused.

Travis chuckled to stall for time while he thought of a quick lie. He most certainly didn't want to explain his own personal sexual history to her. "It was a foreign film I once saw," he explained. "It was about women who were into casual dating. I didn't mean to bring it up."

"Oh, I see." Jasmine wrote down a few more notes and then continued to share her thoughts. "Sexual dysfunction for women can also be triggered by family concerns such as child care, illness, stress or job worries."

"Let's not forget fatigue and depression. Those are major factors that can inhibit a woman's desire."

"Okay. So in the grand scheme of things, what are we really looking for here?" Jasmine asked a rhetorical question.

"I think we're saying a number of things. Number one, female sexual dysfunction seems to be psychologically rather than physically rooted. Two, what the genitals are doing may play a less important role in how a woman defines her sexual arousal; and three, can we make an aphrodisiac that addresses all of this and make women want to have sex all the time." They both glanced at each other and smiled. "All she has to do is hit forty and then nature will take over," Jasmine joked.

"Okay, so maturity also plays a role in all of this," Travis said, not skipping a beat or losing his train of thought.

Jasmine was a little disappointed that he didn't play into the little cat-and-mouse trap she'd set for him. She studied him as he wrote down some notes, fully concentrating and completely focused. It was then that she realized Travis was like a statue.

"The next thing we should probably take a look at is some non-prescription stuff that's already on the market. I meant to pull some information, but I didn't get a chance to. So why don't we schedule another meeting for next Tuesday?" Jasmine suggested.

"There is no need to do that. I pulled a pretty extensive list of products that have unsubstantiated claims." Travis pulled out several sheets of paper that were stapled together. "I made a copy for you," he said as he handed it to her.

"You're good," Jasmine praised him.

"Good isn't enough for me. I want to be above and beyond that." Travis's arrogance and ego had reared their heads.

"Yes. I know you've mentioned that before." Jasmine paused to take a look at what he'd given to her.

"I highlighted a few interesting ones like this one here." Travis reached across the table and pointed to what he wanted her to look at. "Kyrian claims to have been clinically tested and proven to increase the female sexual experience. However, when I read the literature on it, I didn't see anything that suggested that they had a control group. Then there is this cream here, which says that if a woman applies it to her genital area it will increase sexual desire."

Jasmine drew a line through the product name. "I know for a fact that product has been pulled off of store shelves. There were reported cases that the product damaged the soft tissue of the labia," Jasmine explained.

"Okay, I must have inadvertently overlooked the recall data on that."

"No, you didn't overlook it. The news about it was just circulated this morning. That was one of the topics that Helen and I were discussing when you walked in."

"Oh okay, I thought I was slipping there for a minute." Travis breathed a sigh of relief.

"What else do you have?" Jasmine asked, wanting Travis to continue.

"There is DHEP which is a male hormone produced by the adrenal gland and ovaries and converted to testosterone and estrogen. DHEP depletes with age, but can be purchased over the counter in supplement form. I read in one small study published in a medical journal that women who took fifty mg of DHEP daily noticed a significant increase in sexual interest. But the drug has several drawbacks because of its potential for heart attacks and breast cancer and masculine side effects such as facial hair."

"I don't like that one. The risks are far too great. When we produce something, I don't want the side effects to lead to death or cancer. We wouldn't be doing the public any big favors by putting something like that on the market," Jasmine said conclusively.

"No matter what we create, the potential risks for side effects will always be a concern. There is just no way around that true fact. I think we should continue to look at as much data as we can and then start creating a pill and experimenting," Travis argued.

"Trust me, I get that part, Travis. I've been doing this kind of work for more than fifteen years. I want us to take our time with this and play it safe. I don't want to put something in a pipeline that's going to fail. One step at a time. I like to do things by the book, understood?"

"Yeah, I hear you." Travis said, with a hint of impatience in his voice.

Jasmine tilted her head slightly. "Come on now, Travis. You know this isn't an exact science, and it takes years of research and testing before a product is approved for the market."

"I understand that and I'm sorry if I seem a little agitated or aggressive. I suppose that I want my moment in the spotlight to arrive sooner rather than later."

"Don't sell your brilliance to a pawnshop of chemistry for a short-lived moment in the spotlight. Trust me when I say it's not all that it's cracked up to be." Jasmine gave him a few words of wisdom.

"I'll remember that," Travis said with a smile.

"Good," Jasmine said as she looked at her watch. "Jesus. It's twelve-thirty p.m. I can't believe we've been at this for three-and-a-half hours."

"That doesn't surprise me. Sometimes I'm so engrossed in my work that an entire week can go by." Travis laughed nervously.

"That's happened to me from time to time as well. Do you want to go someplace and grab lunch? We can continue our discussion over a meal," Jasmine suggested.

"Yeah, that sounds good."

"Great, I know a wonderful place not too far away." Jasmine and Travis both rose to their feet. As Travis walked out, Jasmine noticed that he had a cocky swagger.

"Damn, he has a sexy-ass walk," muttered the temptress within her. "When I get around to fucking his cocky ass, it's going to be pure pleasure."

Chapter 14
Travis

Early on Saturday morning, Travis got out of bed and decided to head over to the lakefront for a brisk morning jog. As he shuffled along the running path with the bicyclists, skateboarders, and other fitness fanatics, he thought about Jasmine. He had to admit that his boy Alex was right. Jasmine was fantastically sexy in a way that many older women seemed to have perfected. She had a type of seductiveness about her that he was attracted to. Whenever he saw her walking in the office, his dick got hard at the sight of her ass pushing out against the fabric of the skirts she was so fond of wearing. Whenever this feeling came over him, he wanted to approach her from behind, place his hard dick between her ass cheeks and say to her, "Squeeze." He desperately wanted to have her chocolate legs wrapped around him, but not at the risk of losing his livelihood. He was lusting for her; there was no question about it. Travis just wasn't exactly sure how she'd react if he made advances toward her now that she was his boss.

After running two miles and fantasizing about Jasmine giving him a blow job and then blasting her mouth with a healthy amount of his essence, Travis turned around and headed back to his apartment. When he arrived back home, he showered, changed into his most comfortable pair of blue jeans and then headed out to run a few errands. He had to drop clothes off at the dry cleaners, do a little grocery shopping and take his car in for an oil change. By 1 p.m. he'd taken care of what needed to be done and returned home. When he entered his apartment again, he was greeted by a stack of boxes that still needed to be unpacked.

"Ugh, I'll get to that later," Travis griped. He wanted to take some time to really explore the city. Since his arrival, he hadn't really done much. He thought it would be cool to perhaps hit a few shopping malls to pick up some fresh workout gear, grab a bite to eat and possibly catch an early evening movie. He decided to phone Alex to see if he was up for hanging out.

Travis got his answering machine. "Yo, this is gigolo Alex. Your pleasure is my business. I'm not in right now, but leave a message and I'll get back to you to schedule an appointment for some personal satisfaction."

"What the hell kind of message is that?" Travis laughed. "Boy, you need to take that crazy shit off of your voicemail. Anyway, this is Travis calling to see if you wanted to hang out, but I guess you're out of town. Call me when you get a chance," Travis said and then hung up.

"If I sit in this apartment, I'm going to go crazy," he spoke to himself. *This is my life in a nutshell. No kids, no woman, and no drama. All I do is work late hours and come home just to rest and start over again. Damn, man, you need some type of excitement in your life. You're starting to act like an old cantankerous man.*

Travis wasn't one to sit around idly and lick his wounds of self pity, even though by the standard of many, he had a wonderful life. He went into his bedroom and flicked on the television just in time to catch an episode of *Family Guy*. He had a few chuckles off of his favorite character, Stewie. When the program ended, he cut off the television and realized that the only thing he truly wanted to do was head to the lab and work on creating the aphrodisiac.

When he arrived at the lab, he was greeted by Sam, the security guard.

"You can't get enough of this place, can you?" the young security guard asked as he placed a clipboard and an ink pen in front of him. "I need you to sign in."

"Looks that way, doesn't it?" Travis said, laughing over his words as he wrote his name.

"You and I are the only two people here," Sam said.

"Is it usually quiet around here on Saturdays?" Travis asked.

"Pretty much. Every now and again someone will drop by just to pick up something they forgot."

"Well, you'll probably be seeing much more of me on the weekends."

"Okay. How long do you plan on staying?" the guard asked.

"I probably won't leave until late." Travis smiled slightly and continued on his way.

He went into an area of the facility where a number of books on chemistry were shelved. He pulled several down and went back to his office. He opened them up, pulled a writing pad from his desk drawer and began jotting down notes. He'd been working nonstop for well over three hours when he was startled by a knock at his door. When he looked up, he saw Jasmine. She looked fantastic in her straight-leg jeans, brown low-heeled shoes and dark-brown poplin shirt. Her hair was styled perfectly and the red lipstick she had on made him want to feel and savor her taste. She leaned against the frame of his office door with her arms folded across her chest.

"You're a real workaholic. But you probably already know that." Jasmine inhaled deeply, then released her breath slowly.

"I can't help that. I've always been this way. I'm very disciplined," Travis said, sitting upright and tapping the eraser side of his pencil on a page of one of the open books.

"Have you even stopped to get something to eat?" Jasmine asked. What she really wanted to do was eat him. His intelligence was just as seductive to her as his physique.

"No, I haven't. I'll get around to it soon enough. I wanted to present you with some possibilities when we meet next week," he explained.

"You don't have to try and impress me, you know," Jasmine said.

"But I want to," Travis said, trying to create a ripple in the waters of his desire for her.

"You're just spinning your wheels. I'm already impressed with you."

Travis chuckled, trying to downplay the fact that she didn't catch his drift. He paused for a long moment to access whether or not he should risk being more bold and straightforward.

"Why are you toying with me?" Jasmine took a courageous leap forward.

"What do you mean?" Travis asked, wanting to make absolutely certain that they were on the same page.

"Are you really going to sit there and make me spell it out for you? You know what I mean."

"So I take it that it's no accident that you're here on a Saturday looking like a million bucks." Travis allowed her to see him undress her with his eyes.

"What, this old outfit? It's been in my closet for ages. Do you really like it?" Jasmine stood erect, then slowly turned around so that he could see all of her.

Travis could feel an erection building up from deep within. He brushed his fingertips across his lips as he thought about his next move. "You don't want to engage in that type of recreation with me, Jasmine. I'm too much for you to handle."

"There you go again talking shit that you know you can't back up." Jasmine moved toward him and stood in front of his desk. "Are you trying to flirt with me, Mr. Adams?"

"No. I'm trying to fuck you, Ms. Sallie," Travis fired back.

"Well, that's a good thing because I have an insatiable appetite for young, strong, and cocky guys like yourself. Honey, I'm a grown-ass woman who'll take you to levels of pleasure that you can't even read about."

"Oh, now see, you don't know me, Jasmine. You talk a good game, but you'll be singing a different tune when I have your knees pinned to your ears."

Jasmine smirked at the thought of that. She felt herself getting turned on in much the same way as she had when they first met in New York. "Well, if you have the knowledge, skill and expertise to make this pussy sing a different tune, then I need to forewarn you."

"About what?" Travis rose from his desk and walked around the front of it. He rested his behind against the desk and spread his legs apart. He wanted Jasmine to step between them so that he could glide his hand around the curvature of her ass.

"I will eat you alive, Travis. I will make your toes curl and your body quake. I will blow your mind sky high," Jasmine said as she stepped between his legs.

Travis raised his arms and made a motion to caress her ass, but Jasmine grabbed both of his wrists. She leaned forward and pressed her knee against his Pride. She slid her cheek across his and stopped when her lips touched his ear.

"If we go here, we must be discreet. No open displays of affection in the office. No disrespecting each other and no one—I mean *no one* but us will know about our little secret. This arrangement isn't about love. It's about mutual satisfaction. If you can't handle those terms of engagement, then we'll pretend this conversation never took place. Have I made myself clear?"

Travis tilted his lips upward to her earlobe. "I may seem like a spunky, energetic and inexperienced cub to you, but trust me, baby, on the inside I'm a grizzly bear who knows how to make a green-eyed cougar like you growl with unimaginable satisfaction. I can handle your terms; just make sure you keep your emotions in check."

"Then bring it," Jasmine said as she stepped away and looked at him with her seductive green eyes.

"Close the door then," Travis said.

"Oh no, baby, nothing is going to happen in this office. Besides, I want some foreplay. I have tickets to a Frankie Beverly and Maze concert tonight. You need to go home and prepare for it," Jasmine said.

Travis was about to ask for additional details when his cell phone rang.

"Go ahead, answer your phone. There is no need to dodge your phone calls."

"It's not like that. I don't even know who this is. The number is blocked," Travis said as he picked up the call, fully expecting to get someone who'd dialed the wrong number.

"Hello?" Travis answered, wanting to end the call as quickly as possible.

"Travis, it's me, Alex."

"Alex? Whose phone are you calling from and why do you have the number blocked?" Travis asked.

"Travis, listen. I'm in trouble."

"Trouble? What kind of trouble? What's up with all of that noise I hear in the background?"

"I need a huge favor from you, man." Travis turned his back to Jasmine for a little more privacy.

"What's going on, player?" Travis could sense the urgency in Alex's voice.

"I'm in jail, man."

"Jail? What the fuck did you do to wind up in jail?"

"I'll explain it to you later. I just need you to come and bail me out of this hell hole?"

"How much is your bail?" Travis asked.

"Twenty-five hundred dollars," Alex said.

"Twenty-five hundred dollars?" Travis spoke through clenched teeth.

"I'll get it back to you. I promise. Just come and get me out of here, dawg," Alex pleaded.

"Okay, what police station are you at?"

"The one on Seventeenth and State Street," Alex said. "Hurry up, man. There are some crazy folks up in here."

"Okay, I'll be there soon," Travis said and hung up the phone.

"That didn't sound too good," Jasmine said.

Travis stood with a perplexed look on his face. "No it wasn't. You remember my friend, Alex, right?"

"Yeah, the pilot," Jasmine said.

"Well, he's gotten into some type of trouble and has been arrested. He needs me to come bail him out of jail."

"Wow. Does he get into trouble often?" Jasmine asked.

"No. I've known him for ten years and nothing like this has ever happened."

"You should go. We can hang out some other time," Jasmine said, genuinely concerned.

"He's like a brother to me," Travis said as he scribbled his cell phone number down on a piece of paper. "Here's my number. Give me a call so that I'll have yours. I'll call you back as soon as I get a chance," Travis said and walked out. As he rushed down the hallway he stopped, turned around and rushed back to Jasmine. He pulled her back inside his office, shut the door, and kissed her passionately.

"I just had to know what your lips tasted like," Travis said.

"You just broke one of the rules. No open displays of affection at work," Jasmine reminded him.

"It takes two to tango, Jasmine. You're just as guilty as I am."

"That may be, but we can't allow this sort of thing to happen here." She smeared away her red lipstick from his lips. "Go see about your friend. I'll be around."

Travis kissed her forehead, then turned and rushed out the door.

Chapter 15
Jasmine

After Travis left the office, she called him as promised so that he'd have her cell phone number. He didn't call her back until after 8 p.m., but by that time she was at a concert with her sister, Lauren, enjoying herself. She told Travis to give her a call the next day and they'd talk then.

Late Sunday afternoon, Jasmine was lounging around her house wearing black silk pajama shorts and a matching camisole. She'd rented a movie, *The Curious Case of Benjamin Button*, and looked forward to seeing what all of the hype was about. She removed a slice of sinfully delicious chocolate cake she'd picked up from a nearby bakery from the cake plate on her kitchen table. She walked into her family room, placed the disc in the player, grabbed her favorite throw and then started the movie. An hour later, Jasmine was completely engrossed in the film and didn't want any interruptions unless someone was gravely ill. Just as the movie was reaching its climax, she heard her cell phone ringing on the nightstand in her bedroom. She was going to pause the movie to see who was calling her, but she decided to return the call later. At the conclusion of the movie, she was nearly in tears.

"That was such a great movie," she said as she got up and took her dirty dishes into the kitchen. She glanced at the black cordless phone on the kitchen countertop and decided to give Tiffany a buzz.

"What's going on, diva?" Tiffany asked. Jasmine could tell by the excitement in her voice that Tiffany was in a great mood.

"Just calling to see how you were doing and to find out what's the four-one-one on everything," Jasmine teased her.

"Girl, let me tell you what I went and did." Tiffany started laughing.

"Oh Lord, let me sit down," Jasmine said as she extended the phone cord over to her kitchen table.

"You're not going to believe this crazy shit," Tiffany said matter- of-factly.

"Lay it on me, girl. What happened?" Jasmine was dying to know.

"I had sex with two guys," Tiffany blurted.

"Wait, you mean you're seeing two guys at the same time?" Jasmine asked.

"No silly, I fucked two guys at the same time. I had a threesome."

"No you didn't!" Jasmine's voice rose to an earsplitting level.

"Yes I did! And they were twin brothers!" Tiffany said unashamedly.

"Oh my God! How in the hell did you manage to pull that one off? I mean, how could you do two brothers?"

"Just like that." Tiffany popped her fingers. "They seduced me and goddamn it, I'm glad that they did, because they found the right freak for the job." Tiffany laughed uncontrollably, then cried out, "Woo woo woo. That shit was good to me!"

"Okay, heifer, give me the details," Jasmine said.

"Girl, I'm not even sure how the shit happened, it just sort of did," Tiffany explained.

"Were they students at the university?"

"Yes, music majors with a set of voices that have the power to make any woman's panties soaking wet. Tommy and Bobby are only twenty-one, but their singing voices are more mature than their years. Girl, I'm telling you... I didn't know their voices were so powerful."

"Their voices had a boom to them like Luther Vandross...Cisco...and Tyrese?" Jasmine asked, looking for a clearer description.

"Yes. The kind of voices that can make you cry in church, give you goose bumps at a concert, and make you scream until you lose your voice. Tommy and Bobby are still trying to find themselves, so to speak. They're church boys who I think have been sheltered a lot and lived with very strict parents. Now that they're in college and have more independence, they're learning very quickly about the world and the people in it. As they mature they are going to be a pair of heart-breakers."

"Do you think they'll ever be famous?" Jasmine asked.

"Oh yeah, especially to an audience that can appreciate true talent and gifted voices."

"Okay, so get to the good part." Jasmine was eager to learn how she had ended up having both of the young men at the same time.

"Okay, so what had happened is this: The theater department was presenting a variety show. Tommy and Bobby were asked to sing some well-known love ballads. So they would come into the library and look through our music catalog. I suggested some great love songs and even suggested they look at a documentary film on great male vocalists. To make a long story short, they really got into the project and learned a lot about how to put on a great act. Because as you know, singing in front of an audience is never easy."

"Did you show them a few dance moves, too?" Jasmine laughed.

"Girl, I didn't have to. They worked all of that out."

"Okay, I was just teasing you. Go on," Jasmine said.

"So, they came to me one afternoon and asked if I'd come to the theater so they could perform for me, and get my honest opinion. Initially I said no because I figured they'd do just fine. But then Tommy, the taller one, begged and pleaded with me. The next thing I knew, both of them were insistent about me coming. It was then I realized they truly valued my opinion. So I gave in and said, 'Alright guys, tell me when and where.' They told me to come to the theater around six p.m. because they'd reserved it. So I take my happy-go-lucky ass down there, right? When I arrive, it's just the three of us in there. Bobby says, 'Come sit in the front row, we'll be with you in a second.' I didn't think anything of it. I just walked down the aisle and sat down. A few minutes later they both come out onto the stage. Tommy is holding a handheld device, which allowed him to control lighting, curtains and the cue, the music. So he lowers the lighting, stands center stage and says, 'Bobby and I want to sing two songs for you. We hope you like our interpretation of them.' Then Bobby steps forward and says, 'We did a lot of research and watched a lot of male vocalists sing songs. Thanks to you we were introduced to music that we've never heard before by these two brothers who sang love ballads together.' I'm sitting there searching my memory trying to recall what brother duo sang together. Then, Bobby cues the music and in perfect pitch begins to sing 'Unchained Melody.'"

"That's the song from your favorite movie, *Ghost*, with Patrick Swayze and Demi Moore."

"Girl, you know how much I loved that movie."

"I know. You cry every time you see it." Jasmine laughed.

"Okay, so you know that I was sitting in my seat looking at this young man and saying to myself, please don't ruin my song."

"Did he take you there?" Jasmine asked.

"Girl, I had to toss my hands in the air. He sang the shit out that song. He had me crossing my damn legs and bouncing up and down in my seat. So when he finishes I start clapping like a madwoman because I was so impressed. Then Tommy steps forward and says, 'Hang on, we want to sing a duet for you.' They played around with the lighting a little bit, cued up the music and starting singing again in perfect pitch, 'You've Lost That Loving Feeling.'"

"They were blowing like that?" Jasmine asked.

"Listen to me, Jasmine. I started screaming like some crazed teenager. Never in my life have I ever had a man, let alone two, sing to me."

"Okay!" Jasmine said, fully understanding how Tiffany felt.

"So, they're going on about how I've lost that loving feeling, right. They jumped down off the stage, walk toward me and Tommy gets down on his knees for me. He puts his hand on my knees and spreads my legs open, looks me directly in the eyes and with the most soul-stirring voice shouts out the word, 'Baby.' Bobby responds to the call and yells back, 'Baby.' They sang back and forth and my skin got goose bumps everywhere."

"Aww shit." Jasmine started laughing.

"Aww shit is right! It was at that point that I realized these young men had set my ass up to seduce me. I wiped the perspiration from Bobby's forehead with my fingertips, just as Tommy kissed me on the cheek. Girl, they pulled me up to my feet. One stood in back of me and the other was in front of me. There was no mistaking their intentions. I knew what it was about and went with the motherfucking flow."

"Ahhhh, girl you crazy!" Jasmine screamed.

"Shit, I'm a grown-ass woman. I started swaying my hips and both of them moved with me. They'd gotten my ass hot. The next thing I knew, my blouse was being unbuttoned, and I had each hand on two hard-ass dicks. In no time flat, our clothes were off. I pulled some condoms out of my purse and told Bobby to lie on his back. I rode him while giving Tommy a blow-job. I didn't care whether or not I got caught because I'd always wanted to do two men, but never could find the right two guys. It was like some freaky-deaky and buck-wild porno film, except I was in it. I was the treat. All of that naked, sweaty brown skin turned me on in a way I've never thought possible."

"Girl, were they virgins? I mean, did they have any clue as to what they were doing?"

"They weren't virgins when I was done with them, and they knew enough to give me an orgasm and that's all I'm going to say about that."

"And they didn't care about sharing you?" Jasmine asked again.

"They were twins, Jasmine. I assume they're used to sharing everything. They wore me out though. When I got one to blow his load, I had another hard dick to work with. When I left, girl, I could barely walk. My shit was sore for days, but in a good way."

"I think your name is getting around and young men are approaching you just to see if they can get fucked," Jasmine said with all honesty.

"That may be true, but it's my choice as to whether or not I give in. I'm just having fun right now. I'm not taking any of this seriously. It's just a beneficial arrangement between consenting adults. I like to get down and so do they. However, I did make it very clear that what happened there needed to stay there. They understood the importance of making sure it remained our little secret."

"So what happened after that?" Jasmine asked.

"Nothing. It was truly just one of those moments. The boys think I'm the coolest librarian that has ever walked the face of the earth now, but I already knew that I was fly." Both Tiffany and Jasmine laughed at the authenticity of the comment.

"Girl, I don't even know what to say about you and your sexual explorations," Jasmine said.

"There is nothing you can say. Shit. It is what it is."

Jasmine could hear the smile in Tiffany's voice.

"So what's new with you in the romance department?"

"Well, I wouldn't call it romance as much as I would pure lust. I've got a new fish on the line," Jasmine said.

"Oh really now, what's his name?" Tiffany asked.

"He's a guy I work with."

"Ooo, a freaky sneaky office affair. Is he any good in bed?" Tiffany asked.

"I don't know. We haven't done anything yet, except kiss. But get this... Remember when we were in New York and I was telling you ladies about the guy I met at the bar?"

"Yeah, yeah, yeah. I remember. His drunk friend came over and interrupted your conversation."

"Never in a million years did I ever think I'd see this guy again, but as it turns out, he's a chemist just like me."

"Get the hell out!" Tiffany shouted.

"I'm serious. I almost had a heart attack when I saw him walk in for an interview. He's a brilliant guy. A little bit of a workaholic and slightly obsessed with his work, but other than that, he's a good guy."

"Well, honey, a working man never goes out of style, if you know what I mean."

"Yeah, I understand where you're coming from." Jasmine let her words linger longer than usual. "When he first arrived, he was ignoring me and acting as if he wasn't attracted to me. He kept everything on a professional level and I was truly torn by that. I admired him for being mature about it, but I also wanted him to flirt with me just a little. Anyway, I had to take matters into my own hands and nudge him along. We've agreed to have a very discreet relationship."

"Well, have fun with it," Tiffany encouraged her. "But let me say this. I'm not the one to stop anyone from getting his or her freak on. All I'm saying is be careful with this arrangement because if the relationship sours—"

"I'm going to fire him," Jasmine cut Tiffany off and told her exactly what she'd do if the relationship got out of control.

"Okay, Miss Boss Lady."

"Anyway, I'll keep you up to date about what's going on with that. Have you heard from Millie?"

"I talked to her briefly yesterday, but she said she'd call me back because she was on her way to interview a pool of jurors. I never did hear back from her."

"I know she's going through a lot right now. I'll give her a call later on," Jasmine said as she walked in to her bedroom. She noticed a small light on her cell phone blinking. She picked it up and glanced at the display. Travis had called twice.

"Yeah, we're going to have to keep an eye out for our girl. She's got a ton of drama going on," Tiffany said.

"I'm sure she'll manage it." Jasmine flipped open her phone and saw that Travis had also forwarded her a text message. "Cute."

"What's cute?" Tiffany asked.

"Travis sent me a text message that said, 'Here is a kiss, you can put it anywhere you want to.'"

"Hmph. You should respond back and ask if that kiss comes with tongue."

"You are just a mess, Tiffany." Jasmine grinned wide.

"Hell, that's what I'd do. I'd also tell him the place I want to put the kiss requires more than just one peck. I need that full lip, tongue, and mouth action."

"I am not going to tell him all of that in a text message. I'll just call him," Jasmine said.

"Well, let me get off the phone so you can go handle that. Call me back when he decides to let you up for some air," Tiffany joked.

"Oh, he's not going to have me locked down like that, honey. I'm a Cougar. I'm the one who'll have his ass pinned down."

Jasmine heard Tiffany pop her fingers. "Well all right. I'll talk to you later." The ladies said their good-byes and ended their call.

JASMINE PICKED UP HER PHONE and called Travis back. His phone rang for an unusually long time before he finally picked up.

"Hello?" Travis sounded as if he were out of breath.

"Why are you panting so hard?" Jasmine asked, curious as to what he'd been up to.

"I was in the other room moving furniture around.

I've been cleaning up my apartment up all day. I've finally unpacked the remainder of my boxes," Travis said.

"Were you able to bail your friend out of jail?" Jasmine inquired.

"Yeah, I got his crazy ass out. I spent most of the night talking to him."

"What did he get arrested for?"

"DUI," Travis lied. He didn't want to get into all of the complicated details associated with Alex's arrest.

"Well, that was dumb," Jasmine said.

"I know. I told him that he needed to get his head right and stop doing immature shit and grow up."

"Well, I think you told him right. A good friend does things like that."

"I would not have skipped out on you like that for anyone else. Alex and I are very close."

"I can tell. My sister and I are very close like that. I'd do anything for her and she'd do the same for me." Jasmine positioned her body on her bed.

"So what are you doing now?" Travis asked.

"Laying in my bed."

"Do you want some company?" Travis didn't waste any time trying to hook back up with Jasmine.

"Company would be nice, but right now my house is a mess," Jasmine lied. She had a three-month rule. If a guy made it past three months, then she'd allow him to get a little closer to her.

"Well, I'd like to see you today," Travis said.

"I'd like that."

"Do you want to grab a bite to eat or perhaps catch a movie or something?"

"Dinner actually sounds good," Jasmine said.

"Well, I'm new to this town, so I don't know of many places outside of Wrigleyville."

"I'll tell you what. Since you're relatively still new to Chicago, why don't you give me your address and I'll come pick you up. I know of a great place where we can go."

"Sounds like a plan, but I'm picking up the tab for dinner. I don't want any back-and-forth chatter when the bill comes."

"You're the man," Jasmine said.

"Great. How long will it take you to reach my neck of the woods?"

"Give me about an hour," Jasmine said. Travis gave her his address and they exchanged a few more pleasantries before ending the call.

JUST AS SHE'D PROMISED, an hour later Jasmine arrived at Travis's apartment. She phoned him when she pulled up in front of his building. "I'm here. Come on down because there is no place to park."

"I'll be right down," Travis told her as he grabbed his keys and headed out to greet her. He got into Jasmine's white Jaguar and got situated.

"Nice car," he said.

"Thanks."

"So where are we headed?"

"We're actually doing two things this evening. We're going to go out for dinner and then we're going to see Argentina Tango on Stage at the Harris Theater. Do you like dancing?"

"I have two left feet. I know for a brother to say that is sad, but very true. What about you?"

"I took tango lessons when I was a little girl. Along with ice skating and ballet. Have you ever seen a live tango performance?"

"No. I can't say that I have," Travis said.

"Then you're in for a real treat. The tango is all about sensuality, sex, and seduction. It's about the way a man handles a woman and how they move together as one."

"I can't wait," Travis said as they drove off.

Travis and Jasmine enjoyed their evening out together. Everything went perfectly. Their dinner at Carmen's Italian Restaurant and sensual tango performance offered the perfect combination for a memorable evening. Travis and Jasmine were now sitting in front of his apartment building.

"How long will it take you to get back home?" Travis asked.

"Not too long. Probably about forty or so minutes," Jasmine said as she put the car in PARK and shifted her position so that she was facing him. She focused on his beautiful brown eyes, chiseled jaw line and his full delicious lips.

"Would you like to come up? I could show you what I've done to the place," Travis said, placing his hand on top of hers.

"There is no place to park, Travis," Jasmine said, glancing up the block in which cars lined both sides of the street.

"That's my car right there." Travis pointed. "I'll move it so you can have the parking space and I'll park on the next block."

"You don't have to do that." Jasmine didn't want him to feel obligated.

"You don't understand, Jasmine. I want to do it." Travis leaned in for a kiss and paused just before their lips met, making certain she wouldn't turn away. He kissed her. More tenderly this time. Jasmine's right hand rose up and caressed his cheek. Travis slowly pulled away and looked directly into her amazing green eyes.

"Let me go move my car," he whispered, then turned and exited the car.

As soon as they stepped inside of Travis's apartment, Jasmine had tossed her purse on the sofa, kicked off her high-heeled shoes and pushed Travis back against a wall. She stepped into his embrace, pressed her body against his and began kissing him on his lips and long brown neck. She started unbuckling his belt and pulling his shirt out of his trousers. She couldn't wait to devour every inch of him. Once his jacket and shirt were off, she squatted and placed succulent kisses on his cheek and gently clenched her teeth on his left nipple. Travis moaned as he flexed his pectoral muscles, enjoying the sensation of both pleasure and pain. Jasmine curled her fingers into claws and raked them over his chest and abdomen. Travis shivered as he enjoyed the sensation.

"Oh that feels so damn good," he uttered as Jasmine pulled his slacks and underwear down around his ankles. Travis's manhood was erect and sprang out ready for whatever Jasmine had for him.

"Ooo, you have a pretty dick. It's so long, thick, and chocolate," she said as she stroked it with both hands and kissed the head of it. Travis removed the rest of his clothes leaving them in a pile on the floor. He helped Jasmine get out of the skirt and blouse she was wearing and draped them over the arm of his tan leather sofa. She had on a leopard print thong and matching bra.

"Damn, you have a sexy body," Travis said while admiring her. He was eager to get inside of her warm folds. "Turn around and let me see that ass I've been fantasizing about at work." Jasmine placed her hands on her hips and turned for him.

"Bend over and place your hands on her knees," Travis instructed and Jasmine complied. Her ass was even more beautiful in person. It was full, round and built to take a pounding. Travis had seen more ass than a proctologist and rated Jasmine's as the finest one he'd ever had the pleasure of meeting. Travis lowered himself to his knees. He kissed and nibbled on her caramel derriere.

Jasmine adjusted her stance and stood with her legs shoulder width apart. She leaned forward, resting her hands on the arm of the sofa.

Travis inhaled her sweet scent until his brain memorized it. He moved the fabric of the thong out of the way and nibbled on her butt cheek. He then removed the thong completely, spread her ass cheeks with his hands, and tasted her sweet pussy.

"Reach back and hold your ass cheeks open for me," Travis instructed Jasmine and she complied. Travis made small circles with the tip of his tongue around her anus as he slipped his long middle finger inside of her wetness. Several moans escaped the back of Jasmine's throat as he moved in and out of her with his finger.

"Shit," Jasmine said as she straightened her posture. "Let's take this into the bedroom, baby." Travis led Jasmine to his bedroom. He opened up his dresser drawer and removed a box of condoms. He put one on then turned on his iPod, which was seated in a docking station. Maxwell began singing.

"On your back," Jasmine ordered him. Travis did as she asked and positioned himself in the center of the bed. Jasmine unhooked her bra and ran her hands down her body.

"You are so damn sensual!" Travis spoke as he stroked his Pride with his right hand.

"Standing here watching you stroke yourself is such a turn-on. Your dick looks so damn delicious. The way it's shaped, the way the veins are pulsating and I adore the fact that you've completely shaven all of your pubic hair. It makes me want to put your cock in my mouth, balls and all."

"And I like the hourglass haircut you've given your pussy. You taste better than sweet. The flavor and scent of your essence is like heated brown sugar and it makes my mouth salivate."

"I can't take it anymore. Here is what I want you to do for me," Jasmine said.

"What do you have in mind?"

"Get your spread eagle on, Travis. Open up your legs and spread your thighs." A devilish grin formed on Jasmine's face.

"Oh, you want to get straight up freaky," Travis said as he complied with her request.

"Oh baby, there isn't even a word for what's going on in my head right now." Jasmine positioned herself between his thighs. She put one hand at the base of his cock and stacked the other hand on top of it. She opened her mouth as wide as the sky and took him in.

"Hmmm," she cooed as she swirled her tongue around in a clockwise motion. A healthy amount of saliva was building up in the cave of her mouth so she pulled his dick out and allowed the moisture to trickle down his long shaft.

"Fuck. Do that shit again," Travis begged. Jasmine repeated the move, taking in as much of him as she could until she gagged. She came up, held up his shaft, pushing it against his belly, and licked his smooth testicles. She felt his manhood pulsate in her hand. She knew it was a sign that he wanted to be jerked off so she obliged him.

"Oh damn, I ain't never had my shit sucked like this." Travis didn't want to admit that, but he couldn't help it because she, without a doubt, had perfected the art of giving a blowjob.

Jasmine, with his cock still in her mouth, glided her hands up his muscular abdomen, to his tiny brown and erect nipples. She pinched them between her thumb and forefinger and felt the head of his penis swell in her mouth.

"Not yet," Jasmine said, sensing his attempt to blast his essence into her mouth before she was ready for him to empty his load.

"Oh, I got this under control, baby," Travis said as he tucked his chin into his chest and threaded his fingers through her hair. "It's time for you to serve up some of that brown sugar pussy of yours." Travis pulled her head up. He repositioned himself and rested his back against the headboard.

"Stand up and walk that wet pussy up to my face,"

Travis instructed. Jasmine complied, inching up to him and placing her feet beside his hips. Travis caressed, and spanked her caramel ass as he licked the inside of her left thigh. He brushed the tip of his tongue slowly back and forth in the valley between her thighs and her Goddess.

Jasmine placed the palms of her hands against the wall for balance. "Damn," she cried out as her sweetness began to flow.

Travis masterfully split her labia with the tip of his tongue. He then gently sucked on her moist flesh. He listened to the sound of her body language and matched the rhythm of her movements. He floated his tongue upward and stopped just below her love bead. He inhaled the delicious scent of her sex, then began softly flicking his tongue up and down, over and under her clit.

"Oh damn!" Jasmine cried out and then began whimpering and breathing heavy. Her movements on his face became more pronounced. Travis spanked her ass and Jasmine's body began to quake.

"Uhm-humm, uhm-humm, uhm-humm," Jasmine repeated over and over again. He knew he'd landed on her most sensitive spot. Finally, Jasmine's orgasm sang its beautiful melody for Travis.

"Damn, where did you learn how to eat pussy like that?" Jasmine asked as she collapsed to her knees.

"From the University of Good-Ass Pussy." Travis

felt cocky and confident now that he'd gotten her off and was familiar with the sound of her orgasm. "Get on your hands and knees. I'm going to hit it doggie style."

Jasmine didn't waste any time getting into position. She waited for the breathtaking moment of penetration. The moment his long, thick cock breached the gates of her heaven, she was forced to push her knees out a little wider.

"Oh fuck, Travis. Damn, you're so hard," Jasmine said.

"Come on. You can take this. Give me this pussy. Put your head down and hike your ass up higher."

"Okay baby," Jasmine whimpered as Travis's thoroughbred seemed to touch every inch of her love tunnel. She loved the feel of his strong hands on her ass and how they spread her butt cheeks apart. She pushed her ass back against his stomach and gave him the green light to pound her. She was ready to take all of him and wanted to feel the swell of his cock as it rubbed against the walls of her paradise. She wanted the head of his cock to kiss the back wall of her pussy.

"Come on, baby. Write your name on this pussy," Jasmine told him. She felt Travis pumping her faster, harder, and more aggressively. She released a long continuous moan as her next orgasm was building up to its climax. A few hard thrusts later, Jasmine blasted the head of his cock with her hot and sticky essence.

"Oh yes, baby. I'm just getting warmed up now! Slap my ass," Jasmine demanded and Travis complied.

"Pop, pop, pop." He spanked her. "You like this rough shit, huh?"

"Yes, baby. I love this rough shit," Jasmine answered, panting.

"You have a sexy ass. You have the type of rump that needs a strong dick like mine. I'm going to abuse this big motherfucker."

"Abuse it, baby," Jasmine told him as she got caught up in two successive orgasms. Jasmine pushed her ass back some more. She wanted to swallow as much of him as humanly possible.

"That's right. Fight back!" Travis said as he grabbed a fist full of her hair.

"Yes, yes, yes!" Jasmine couldn't believe how fantastic she felt. Her Goddess kept clutching and squeezing Travis with all of its might. She could feel droplets of Travis's perspiration exploding on her back and ass.

"Damn, girl, you've got me in a damn death grip."

Jasmine didn't respond, she was riding the wave of another big climax. She detonated again. With that release she felt herself nearing exhaustion.

"Where do you want me to cum?" Travis asked. Jasmine could sense that he was about to empty his load.

"Shoot it on my ass," Jasmine cried out. "Shoot it all over my big juicy ass." Jasmine felt Travis squeeze her ass cheeks together with his strong hands. She could feel him clawing it as he pumped her with all of his might. She listened to the quick moans escaping his lips as the pace of his breath quickened.

"You're about to spew it all over me. I can feel it," Jasmine said as she hiked her ass in the air a little more.

"Oh fuck. That's it. Time for the money shot." Travis howled like a wolf barking at the moon as he quickly removed the condom, jerked on himself and spewed a fair amount of cum all over Jasmine's ass and back. Then she saw him collapse and rest on his back. Jasmine flipped over, crawled down to his dick and sucked the rest of his load out.

"Oh damn, damn, damn," Travis wailed as his body trembled. Once Jasmine was sure that he was drained, she mounted him and began kissing him passionately. She pulled away from him and looked down at him, pleased with her conquest. His skin glistened with sweat and she could tell he was completely focused on her.

"Are you ready for round two?" he asked.

"Oh, you've got it like that?"

"Damn right I do," Travis said as he craned his neck upward and began sucking on her erect chocolate nipples.

"What are you trying to do to me?" Jasmine asked, cradling the back of his head.

"Drive you crazy," Travis answered as he felt his manhood come alive again. He rested flat on his back once again. "Reach down and put it back in, I'm ready for you to ride me now."

Jasmine smiled as she placed the palm of her right hand on his chest. She gazed deeply into his eyes and attempted to read his thoughts.

"You want to know what I feel like without a condom on, don't you?"

"You know I do," Travis answered as he flexed his buttocks muscles together, signaling his readiness for her. Jasmine glanced down at his sexy, silky, brown cock and tossed caution to the wind. She had to admit to herself that she wanted to feel him as well. She took hold of his dick and stroked it again until it was unquestionably firm. She took him inside of her mouth and savored the taste of him. She cooed as she sucked and wet his Stallion with her saliva.

"Oh, damn," Travis said as he got lost in the rapture of sexual bliss.

"Your chocolate dick looks extra delicious now that it's all wet," Jasmine said as she lightly raked her fingernails over his balls. Travis shivered as the orgasmic sensation washed over him like a glorious wave of untamed energy.

"I need to feel you now!" Travis demanded that she stop teasing him and give him what he wanted.

"Okay, but I'm going to turn my back to you and ride you reverse cowgirl style."

"That's what I fucking talking about," Travis said excitedly. Jasmine got into position and gave him the ride of his life.

Chapter 16
Travis

After leaving the office late Monday evening, Travis called Alex to see how he was doing, but all he got was his voicemail. He left a message for him to give him a jingle the first chance he got.

❂❂❂

When Travis bailed him out of jail a few days earlier, it was for prostitution. Somehow an undercover law enforcement unit got on the list. An undercover female agent called Alex to request a meeting. When Alex showed up at the W Hotel, he went to the room the woman had given him. The undercover agent asked what was on his menu of services. Alex ran down a list of pleasures and his prices ranging from a body massage to bondage. The agent simply said she wanted her pussy eaten and Alex told her it could cost her three-hundred dollars for one hour. When he accepted the cash, that's when the other cops rushed into the room and arrested him.

"This little incident has fucked me up, man," Alex said to him once the police released him. "I was supposed to fly to Miami today at seven a.m., but obviously that's not going to happen."

"Why were you going around calling yourself a gigolo in the first place?" Travis asked as they exited the police station.

"I'm hurting for money and needed some extra cash," he explained.

"How are you hurting for money? You don't have an ex-wife and kids who are draining you dry. I thought you were doing well."

Alex didn't answer Travis right away. Once they got to Travis's car and got situated, Alex decided to talk. "I'm in deep gambling debt."

"How deep?" Travis asked.

"Half a million dollars," Alex said.

"How in the fuck did you get into that much debt, man?" Travis didn't understand how it was possible to accumulate so much liability.

"I didn't do it all at once. I'd win big, but then lose even bigger. Then I started borrowing money from people to support my addiction."

"How did you even get started?" Travis asked, looking for a reasonable explanation.

"I've been gambling a long time, Travis. Ever since…" Alex paused, then laughed because he'd just had an epiphany. "My uncle, King Solomon, got me into it. I got into the game because of him. He used to take me around to the casinos and poker games in the back room of neighborhood bars. I wasn't even supposed to be in those places but there I was—standing in a corner of the room watching and learning. King Solomon showed me a lifestyle that was so much more fun and exciting than my own. It was fast paced and edgy and thrilling. Looking back on it, I idolized him more than I did my father." Travis released a low laugh as he thought about those days. "I only let you know certain things, Travis. The parts of my life you didn't need to know about, I kept from you. There are still a lot of things you don't know or fully understand."

"Let me get something out of the way real quick. Am I going to get my money back?" Travis asked.

"Yeah, I've got you covered," Alex answered.

"I don't believe you, man. It sounds like you need to get some help for your addiction."

"I'm not addicted and don't ever say that to me again!" Alex was extremely touchy about being accused of having a problem. "Travis, you're going to get your money back. I promise you. I've just got to get my shit in order first."

"It sounds like your shit is fucked up beyond repair. You're not doing a good job of handling your business."

"I'm handling my motherfucking business just fine!" Alex snapped.

"Look, I'm your boy. We've been friends for a long

time and I thought I really knew you. I didn't realize you had a secret side."

"Don't give me that *I didn't know* bull. You know who Hatcher is and what he does. And you know that I do him favors."

"What is the deal with you and that guy? How did you even get involved with him?" Travis asked.

"You don't want to know," Alex said.

"Yes I do. You at least owe me that much now that I've bailed you out of jail."

Alex turned his attention away from Travis who could sense that he really didn't want to discuss this with him.

"Look, man. You're like a brother to me. We're family. I'd do anything for you and I know you'd do the same for me. I've always had your back."

"I know that, man. The shit I'm involved with is just complicated. Have you ever held onto something that was eating away at you inside? You want to tell somebody, but it's too hard because you have to face the truth. It's difficult to take a critical look at yourself and see all of the mistakes you've made and all of the fucked-up situations you've allowed yourself to get into."

"Yeah, I know how that is. Tell you what. I have something that I need to tell you that's probably going to piss you off. I've wanted to tell you for a little while now, but I just couldn't."

"Aww man, please don't tell me you're on the down

low or some wild shit like that, because I don't want to know." Travis waved his hand as if he were swatting a fly.

"You know motherfucking well that I'm not on the down low. Why would you say some shit like that to me, man?"

"I'm sorry. I guess being locked up has my head all fucked up," Alex admitted.

"Then I won't tell you. I'll bring it up at a later time," Travis said.

"No man, tell me. We're at a critical bridge in our relationship. We might as well cross the motherfucker. Let's just lay our cards on the table."

"All right. There is no easy way to tell you this so I'm just going to say it. Remember that Jasmine chick you met a while back in New York?"

"Yeah. What about her?" Alex craned his neck to the left and glared intensely at Travis.

Travis hesitated about being forthcoming, but then decided it had to be done. "She's my new boss and I'm planning to hit that."

"You motherfucker!" Alex punched Travis on the shoulder several times.

"Yo man, chill the hell out!" Travis said, fighting him off while trying to concentrate.

"How the hell did that happen?" Alex said in a disgusted tone.

"It just did, man. I had no clue that she was a chemist. When I went in for my interview, there she was. When

I got the job, I tried to play it cool, but she came at me. And you know that I'm not going to sit back and act like some funky motherfucker who didn't know how to handle himself."

Alex remained quiet as he digested what Travis had just told him.

"I really don't see how you can be that upset because it's not like she's your ex-girlfriend, your sister or your mother. She was fair game, man."

"Whatever, dawg." Alex pouted like a spoiled child.

"Get over it, man. Let's not have a pissing contest about it or fall out like Nino Brown and G-Money did in the movie *New Jack City*."

"You're right and I know you are. I'm still pissed about it, though."

"Well, that's my secret. Now you know. I figured it's better than you coming to visit me and running into her wearing my college T-shirt as pajamas."

"Okay. Let's just drop that conversation. I don't want to talk about it anymore," Alex said.

"Dude, what do you want me to do? She and I are just kicking it." Travis wanted Alex to say what was truly on his mind.

"There is nothing you can do," Alex answered.

"Then can we squash it?" Travis held up his fist for a quick bump of acceptance.

"Yeah man," Alex agreed and they bumped fists.

"So what are you going to do about your current

situation? Did they give you a court date? How are you going to explain this to your employer? Did they call you and hear all of that gigolo stuff on your voicemail?"

"My employer doesn't have my cell number, just my home phone which is programmed to forward a message to my cell phone whenever I get a call. And yes, I have a court date, but I'm not going to show up," Alex answered with a bravado of defiance.

"That's dumb. You'll end up in jail if you do that. I can call around and help you find a good attorney. The judge may go easy on you since it's the first time you've been caught."

"You're not listening to what I'm saying, Travis. I'm not going to court because I'm going to call in a favor. I'll have Hatcher McKean get me out of this."

"Are you sure you want to do that? That may open up a can of worms that you don't want to deal with."

"Travis, that can of worms has been open for a long time. Who do you think I owe the half a million dollars to?" Travis dropped his jaw. He was at a funny crossroads. He knew that Alex was involved with Hatcher, but he didn't know to what extent.

"You said we're like brothers and you wanted to know, right?" Alex was ready to bare his soul to his friend.

"Yes, I want to know," Travis said.

"If I tell you this, the knowledge that you'll have can probably get you killed or indirectly involved in something you may not want to be a part of," Alex warned.

"I just want to understand and perhaps help you if I can. I don't want to see you go to jail or get hurt. I have mad love for you, man. If you're caught up in something, I at least want to know what it is you're dealing with. Maybe I'll be able to think of something you haven't."

"Okay." Alex exhaled. "I got involved with Hatcher when we were in college ten years ago. He liked to gamble on college football games. We'd just won the Aloha Bowl and I scored the winning touchdown. I can still remember that day. There was only twenty seconds left on the clock and the game was tied. It was fourth and long and the coach gave us the 'all or nothing' speech. I broke from the huddle and trotted out to my wide receiver position on the left side of the field. I was nervous as a virgin girl about to have sex for the first time. When the ball was snapped, I got around the defender and shot up the field. I cut towards the middle of the playing field and held my hand up. I knew that if the ball didn't get to me quickly, I'd get sandwiched and that would be it for me. The quarterback cocked his arm and fired the ball at me like a missile chasing a target. I had to leap into the air to pull the ball down. As soon as I secured it, I got whacked but didn't fall. I turned my hips, raised my knees and turned on the jets. I ran down the field like my life depended on it. I dodged several more tackles but got tripped up just before I crossed the goal line. Instead of falling to my knees, I stretched my body out and crossed the goal line."

"I remember that game," Travis said. "It was your junior year and my first year of graduate school."

"That's right. You weren't my roommate anymore at that time. Anyway, I felt invincible that day. I felt as if I could take on the world and knock it flat on its ass. Hatcher, who's also a big gambler, was there for the game. Somehow he got into the team's victory party at one of the frat houses. He blended in among all of the shouting, loud music and cheering. He pulled me to the side and told me that he wanted to become friends with me. That night I wanted to be friends with everyone. He talked about my potential and how he could help me. I was naive and listened to everything he was telling me. He gave me money, around eight thousand, and said it was a present. It was a part of his gambling winnings. He said he'd won two hundred and fifty thousand on that game and wanted to show his appreciation to my teammates and me. Eight thousand might as well have been a million. I should not have accepted it but I did. I watched him as he walked around to a few other teammates and gave them money as well. That was the beginning of my downfall.

"The following season, during my senior year, our team made it to the Citrus Bowl and lost. We lost that game because I purposely fumbled the ball at the goal line. Hatcher didn't want our team to win because he'd bet a substantial amount of money against us with every booking agent in Las Vegas and Atlantic City. He won a ridiculous sum of money from the point-shaving scheme. For my compliance he gave me and several other teammates twenty-five thousand dollars. Everything was going fine. I thought we'd gotten away with it, but the next thing I knew, there was a huge investigation. The team was hauled in for questioning. I kept my damn mouth shut and denied that I ever knew Hatcher and swore I'd never betted on games or accepted money from gamblers. But I was given a chance to come clean because if the federal investigators discovered I'd lied, I would've been convicted. In order to make things easier on myself I pled guilty to gambling, received a suspension and the league overturned all of our victories that got us to the bowl game. With that kind of scandal, it made it much more difficult for me to make it to the pros."

"How come you never told me all of this? I knew some serious shit had gone down but I didn't realize the extent of it," Travis said.

"I didn't want to talk about it, Travis, that's why. I saw my life being flushed down the damn toilet. It wasn't easy dealing with that shit. Hatcher was never caught, and frankly with time, the entire incident sort of just faded away. I'd learn later that Hatcher, through his connections, was able to sweep the incident under a rug. After I graduated, I thought I was done with Hatcher, but I found myself gambling on college and pro games. I got in over my head with a bookie and needed some fast cash. I reluctantly called Hatcher for help. At the time he was in need of a pilot whom he could trust. We made a deal. He took care of my debt and I became his personal pilot. I couldn't bring myself to stop gambling. Like an idiot I kept borrowing money from Hatcher and dug myself into a deep hole that I can't get out of."

"Jesus Christ, man!" Travis said now that he fully understood what Alex was into. "So you've really been flying in drugs for him?"

"I don't ask questions about that. I just know that the plane is loaded and I fly it."

"If law enforcement officials ever got wind of what you were doing, dude, you'd be fucked."

Alex slapped the dashboard of the car. "I'm already fucked, Travis. The question is how in the hell do I get out of it?"

"If you were able to get Hatcher the money, would he let you go?" Travis naively asked.

"Whenever I ask him that, he just smiles sinisterly, slaps my cheeks and says, 'But of course.'"

"Wow." Travis didn't know what else to say.

"Thanks for coming to get me. In all honesty you're the only person whom I can trust and depend on right now. Hatcher believes that my parents are dead and my extended family members were unable to care for me and put me in a foster home."

"So do you think Hatcher is going to get you out of this?" Travis asked.

"I know he is. I'm the best pilot he has and he has too many shipments that need to be delivered. He's going to tack this on to my bill. After this I'll probably owe him close to three quarters of a million dollars."

"Shit!" Travis said.

"I just want my life back, man. Somehow I got lost and now I just don't know which way to turn."

"Go to the police," Travis suggested.

Alex laughed sarcastically. "You don't understand how well Hatcher is connected. He has people in law enforcement and politicians looking out for him. If he even thought I was a snitch, he'd cut my balls off and hand them to me. I want to get out of this man, I really do. I don't know how I'm going to turn this shit around, but I need to find a way to get him his money back with interest, so I can move on."

Travis truly wanted to help Alex, but he had no clue as to how. He'd never had to deal with a complex situation like the one his best friend, whom he loved like a brother, had gotten himself into. He knew overall Alex was a good guy, a little high strung and blinded by his own personality and a series of bad judgment calls, but in general, Travis still loved him enough to do whatever he could for him.

BEFORE LONG, THE END OF THE YEAR had arrived and the holiday season was approaching. Travis and Jasmine were able to maintain a professional relationship and a laid-back intimate relationship. For the moment Travis was content and hadn't gotten bored with Jasmine. Their relationship was based on a mutual agreement to provide each other with intimacy and friendship. Travis liked this arrangement because it wasn't complicated. Jasmine understood the passion he had for his job and she understood how driven he was. She didn't fuss at him for working late or not calling her when he got home. She didn't get fussy at work or accuse him of wanting to be with another woman. Jasmine, from his perspective, was perfect for a guy like him who oftentimes got obsessively lost in the world of experimentation.

TRAVIS WAS IN THE LAB OBSERVING and taking notes on the test subjects he'd injected with a prototype of the aphrodisiac he'd been working on. Jasmine entered the lab and asked him to drop by her office when he had a moment.

"Okay," Travis answered without looking up from his notepad. Time got away from Travis and before he realized, it was close to 8 p.m. He was still working and hadn't stopped in to see Jasmine.

"Shit," he hissed as he exited the lab and walked toward Jasmine's office to see if she was there. When he arrived at her office, she was gone. He walked past his own office and noticed an envelope on his desk. He went in and picked it up. It was from Jasmine. He ripped open the envelope and read the handwritten note inside:

Hey babe. I'm planning a New Year's Eve party. If you're free I'd love for you to come by. You should also bring your friend, Alex. My girlfriends, Tiffany and Millie, are flying in from out of town. I'd love to formally introduce you to them. Let me know if you can make it.

Travis crumpled up the note and tossed it into the trashcan. He pulled out his cell phone and sent Jasmine a text which read: *I'll be there for the party.* Once he forwarded the message, he went back to work.

THE AROMA OF SOUL FOOD WAS WAFTING throughout Jasmine's house. Jasmine had spent most of the day preparing gumbo, collard greens, cornbread, yams, black-eyed peas, macaroni and cheese and an assortment of desserts. Her house was festooned beautifully with holiday decorations that she and Travis had spent putting up the night before. As Jasmine and Travis were both in the kitchen making final preparations for the arrival of guests, Travis was placing dishes in the dishwasher and Jasmine was finishing up placing food on the table. Once Travis was done with the dishes, he went over to the stereo and turned on some music. Donny Hathaway was singing his hit song "This Christmas."

"Babe, turn that up. I love that song," Jasmine requested. Travis turned up the song and then joined her in the dining room.

"Wow, Jasmine, everything looks great," Travis said.

"Do you really think so?" Jasmine asked as she placed her best silverware on the table.

"Yeah, I really do." At that moment the song on the radio switched and now Nat King Cole was singing "The Christmas Song." Jasmine began to sway to the melody as the sound of the doorbell chimed. She immediately turned her attention to the other side of the room and headed toward the door. She opened it to find Millie, Tiffany, and Lauren, who'd picked them up from the airport, standing there with giddy smiles.

"Ahhh!" Tiffany screamed with joy as she stepped inside and tossed her arms around Jasmine and kissed her on the cheek. Jasmine then moved to Millie who was directly behind her and wrapped her arms around her.

"Oh, it's so good to see you," Millie said as they embraced and rocked back and forth.

"I've missed you guys," Jasmine said as everyone walked in. "Come on, I have the guest bedrooms all prepared for you guys." Jasmine escorted them to their rooms upstairs. Once their luggage was set aside, they all came back downstairs.

"Ladies, this is my friend, Travis," Jasmine said as they returned to the dining room.

"Hello, ladies," Travis greeted him with a friendly smile.

"So, you're the lover man Jasmine has been talking about," Tiffany teased. Travis laughed.

"I'm Tiffany, the crazy, sexy and most fabulous one out of the group," she said, extending her hand.

"Hello, it's nice to meet you. Jasmine has most certainly told me a lot about you," Travis admitted.

"Whatever she told you are lies." Tiffany's fun-spirited personality immediately put Travis at ease.

"I'm Millie," she said, sizing Travis up on the sly.

"You're the judge, correct?" Travis already knew the answer to the question, but asked anyway.

"Yes I am, and if you mess up with my girl, I'll sentence your ass to a life of hard labor in prison," Millie said.

"I'd better make sure that I don't mess up then," Travis said.

"And I'm her sister, Lauren. I'm the one with the gun."

"Wow. You're not going to shoot me, are you?" Travis asked.

"No, not unless you get on my bad side. If you do that then, bang—right between the eyes," Lauren said.

"You guys are a rough bunch," Travis said.

"Don't pay them any attention, Travis. They're just giving you a difficult time," Jasmine said, coming to his rescue.

"Don't worry, I can handle myself," Travis said.

"I like a confident man," Tiffany said flirtatiously.

"Tiffany! Don't you dare get started," Millie scolded her.

"What?" Tiffany acted innocently by twirling her hair.

At that moment, the doorbell chimed again. Jasmine went to the window and peeped out.

"Travis, it's your friend, Alex."

"Okay, I'll be right there," Travis said as he walked to the door and opened it. Alex held two bottles of wine.

"What's up, man?" Travis said. He stepped aside to let him in. "I'm so glad you could make it."

"Happy Holidays," Alex said. He stepped inside and waited for Travis to close the door.

"Hello, Alex," Jasmine greeted him for the first time since they'd met on her flight to New York earlier that year.

"You know you should be with me, right?" Alex started in right away.

"Fate had different plans, Alex," Jasmine said as she extended her hands to take the wine bottles. "This is so nice of you to bring a gift, but you didn't have to."

"That's the way I roll. I had to bring something," Alex said.

"Well, hello," Tiffany said while sizing Alex up. "I'm Tiffany. The sexy, crazy, and fabulous one."

"I'm Alex and your pleasure is my business," he said, matching wits with her.

"What kind of pleasure do you give?" Tiffany asked, licking her lips.

"The kind that can turn a woman like you completely out," Alex fired back shifting his weight from one foot to the other while sizing her up.

"You don't look like you have the right equipment to turn a person out." Tiffany placed her hands on her hips.

"Trust me. I'm fully equipped to handle your most daring desires," Alex said slowly and smoothly.

"Oh Lord. You two are cut from the same stone. I see right now you guys are going to go at it all night long." Jasmine chuckled as she took the bottles of wine in the kitchen.

The evening continued on and everyone enjoyed the new friendships being formed. At the stroke of midnight, glasses of wine were poured and everyone toasted in the New Year with cheers and laughter.

"So how do you like working with Jasmine at the pharmaceutical company, Travis?" Millie asked, tucking her hair behind her ear.

"I love it. She and I are working on a new formula that acts as an aphrodisiac for women. The prototype has some real potential, but it's not ready for the market yet."

"An aphrodisiac for women? As in a sexual stimulant?" Alex asked curiously.

"Yeah," Travis answered. "If we can get it tested and approved, it will really help a lot of people."

"Or just make everyone want to fuck each other's brains out all of the time. Not that there is anything wrong with that. I'm just saying," Tiffany joked.

"Well, if it does get approved, I'm positive it will be a popular drug," said Lauren. "How would women use it, though? Is it a cream, liquid or a pill?"

"Right now, it's a liquid. A person would take it thirty minutes before intercourse. It's designed to increase blood flow, heighten a woman's sensitivity to touch, and give a woman a feeling of euphoria so that she relaxes completely. Then there is an ingredient that increases vaginal wetness, eliminating the problem of dryness that many women suffer from."

"That sounds like a damn good drug. When is it going to hit the market?" Alex asked.

"Probably years from now. It takes a very long time for a product to get approved. I have a love-hate relationship with the process. I know that it's necessary, but on the other hand, I want the world to experience what the product can do."

"I'm just totally curious now, but when will you be ready to do a clinical study involving testing of human subjects?" Millie asked.

"Oh, it will be a long time before we reach that point," Jasmine chimed in.

"When you're ready to try it out, call me. I'll be your test subject." Tiffany raised her hand high. Everyone had a hearty laugh at her willingness to be a test subject.

Jasmine and the ladies remained in the dining room while Alex and Travis went into the family room to talk and catch up.

"Travis," Alex called, then leaned in close to his friend so that his voice wouldn't carry. "Do you think you could get me a sample of that stuff?"

"No. The side effects can kill you. The side effects are disorientation, nausea, dehydration, cardiac arrest, and kidney failure, just to name a few," Travis answered.

"But it works, right?" Alex asked.

"Preliminary studies on the lab animals seem to suggest that."

"So let me have some. I don't care about the consequences. Frankly, you can get all types of approved prescription medicines with deadly side effects. I just want to try a little of it. I'm thinking your little experiment may be able to help me straighten out my business with Hatcher McKean."

"You're my friend and I love you, but I can't give you something so impure," Travis said.

"Whatever, man!" Alex said with disgust.

"Don't be like that. Right now, let's just be buddies enjoying a drink together and celebrating the New Year."

"If I don't clear my debt with Hatcher, I may not be here with you next year," Alex whispered.

"What did you say?" Travis asked.

"Nothing, man. I'm just feeling a little tipsy, that's all," Alex lied as he took another sip of wine.

Chapter 17
Jasmine

Spring had arrived and Jasmine had started a new fitness program to lose some of the weight she'd picked up over the long and bitterly cold Chicago winter. She loathed the winter months because weather conditions made it practically impossible to keep a lean and fit body. Her grandmother used to say with absolute conviction that in order to survive winters in Chicago, she needed to eat food that stuck to her stomach. Jasmine was glad to see spring arrive. She'd grown tired of listening to Travis whine about how cold it was. Whenever the temperature dropped below zero, he'd call to complain about having to travel to work under such brutal conditions.

It was now Monday evening and Jasmine had just arrived at the health club. She decided to start leaving work earlier so that she could get back into shape. She hadn't been to the club in a long time and was looking forward to a really great workout. When she walked in, she presented her gym I.D. to the attendant and then walked back to the locker room to change clothes.

After exiting the locker room, she walked back to the main area of the gym and began power walking around the indoor track. As she moved along the back stretch, she peeped through the glass window of the dance studio and saw Harrison teaching his yoga class. He still looked good, but their season was short-lived, and she had no intentions of ever being intimate with him again.

As her body began to heat up, Jasmine quickened her pace and focused on getting her heart rate up. She knew that a solid workout would help manage the stress she was under as well as blow off some steam. Over the past few weeks, she'd been very frustrated with Travis and his fixation on developing a better formula for the aphrodisiac. She had to remind him on a number of occasions that they had other research that required his attention and that he shouldn't focus solely on one project. It had become increasingly clear through the failures of their experiments that the female sexual enhancement project was going to be shelved until further notice. The project was turning out to be a waste of time and resources, and Jasmine strongly felt that it was time to move on.

I'll recommend to Helen that we divert our resources to other drugs which have more promise, potential and a better clinical track record, Jasmine thought as she walked along at a brisk pace. *I'll share with her the results so far, but leave the final decision up to her.*

When Jasmine finished her power walk, she headed over to the free weights area, picked up a set of twelve-pound dumb-bells and sat on one of the benches. Just as she was about to do some lateral shoulder raises, Harrison came over and interrupted.

"Hello, Jasmine," he greeted her politely.

"Hello, Harrison." She tried to sound pleasant when in fact, she'd hoped he wouldn't approach her at all. Jasmine began her reps.

"I haven't seen you here in a long time," he said, watching her every move.

"Yeah, I've been very busy lately and haven't had much time to get in here."

"I can tell," Harrison foolishly said.

"What's that supposed to mean?" Jasmine was all set to fire off several rounds of insults if she discovered that he was poking fun at her because of the extra pounds she'd gained.

"It just means that I see that you haven't been in here in a long time," Harrison quickly clarified what he meant.

"Well, you'll probably see me in here more often. I'm determined to get back into better shape."

"You should come back to my yoga class and work on your flexibility. I wouldn't mind having you back."

"I'll think about it, Harrison," Jasmine said as she sat her weights down.

"I'll be looking for you," Harrison said just as a

woman came up to him and looped her arm around his waist.

"Are you ready to go, baby?" she asked as she smiled at Harrison and then Jasmine. The woman was a Cougar, just like Jasmine. Her complexion was much lighter and her eyes looked like they belonged on a goldfish. It was clear that the woman was being pretentious, as if Jasmine was after Harrison. Jasmine wanted to say something really catty, but decided that it wasn't even worth wasting her breath. Harrison's season with her had come and gone, and she was happy that he'd gotten over her and moved on.

"I'll catch you later, Jasmine," he said as he curled his fingers into a fist and aimed it at her for a fist bump. Jasmine obliged him so that he and his new Cougar could go someplace and play. When Jasmine finished her workout, she was exhausted. She grabbed her belongings from the locker room and headed home.

When she arrived back at her house, she immediately went upstairs into her bathroom and ran a hot bath. When the water was just perfect, she slipped into the water, positioned a comfortable bath towel at the base of her neck, closed her eyes and relaxed. An hour later, she got out of the tub, toweled off, moistened her skin with her favorite scented lotion and resided to her bed. She picked up the new book she'd purchased at a book fair from her nightstand. The novel was *Dangerous Consequences*. The title caught her eye because it spoke to the truth about some of the things going on in her professional life. Just as she was about to start reading, her phone rang. She thought it was Travis calling her, but it was Millie.

"Hey girl," Jasmine answered with a big smile on her face.

"Hey Jasmine, I didn't call you too late, did I?" Millie asked.

"No, I'm just sitting here about to read a book called *Dangerous Consequences*."

"Ooo, that title sounds interesting. Hell, in fact it sounds like that crazy shit I went through with my husband and lover fistfighting a while back." Millie laughed nervously about the ugliness of that particular incident.

"Girl, the title really speaks to a lot of shit going on in my life right now," Jasmine admitted as she placed the book back on the nightstand.

"Sounds like you and I are in the same boat, although my ride on the Titanic is just about over. I signed my divorce papers today. I'm just waiting for Bruce to sign and then it'll all be official. I'll be a single woman once again," Millie said happily.

"Wow, congratulations. What are you going to do with your newfound freedom?"

"Well, the first thing that's going to happen is my young lover and I are taking a much needed vacation to the Virgin Islands. Then after that, who knows."

"Are you going to marry your lover?" Jasmine asked.

"No. I'm not in any particular hurry to get married again. I just want to take it easy, have a little fun, and just take each day as it comes. My boyfriend, Roy, wants me to make a commitment to him, but I'm just not ready for all of that yet."

"Well, good for you. You sound like you're much happier now," Jasmine said.

"Girl, 'happy' isn't a strong enough word. I'm fucking *ecstatic*!" Millie laughed.

"So, how is everything going with the investigation and the allegations of corruption?" Jasmine asked.

"Let's not even talk about that one right now. There is so much shit going on with that investigation that just talking about it makes me dizzy. But I will tell you this. Two other judges that I know are also being scrutinized."

"Oh wow," Jasmine said.

"What about you? How's everything going with you and Travis?"

Jasmine exhaled a long sigh.

"Oh boy," Millie said, sensing that there was something afoot.

"Let me get your opinion on this." Jasmine paused, gathered her thoughts and then began. "There are going to be dangerous consequences if I allow myself to fall in love with Travis."

"Wow! What's that about, Jasmine?" Millie asked

very surprised that Jasmine was thinking along those lines.

"Because…if he ever wants children, I'm so past childbearing years."

"Why are you thinking about children now? I thought you were cool with the fact you didn't have any," Millie asked.

"Trust me, I don't want to have kids at my age. Hell, I really don't think my body would like me very much if I got pregnant, but I'm pretty confident that he wants to have his own biological children."

"Have you had that conversation with him?" Millie asked.

"No. This is just stuff going on in my mind that I've been thinking about. Travis hasn't said anything one way or the other."

"Okay, so what are you worried about?"

"A bunch of things are on my mind. As much as I hate to admit this, I'm in a very funny place. I am competing for Travis's time and attention with our job. Now, doesn't that sound crazy as hell?" Jasmine admitted.

"Yeah, it does. But how exactly is his job your rival. I mean both of you guys work for the same company."

"Travis has a Jekyll and Hyde split personality and one of them needs to be calibrated so that the best parts of him can rule a majority of the time. Millie, I sit at home at night waiting for him to call me just so that I can hear his voice. In fact, when you called I thought you were him. Most nights he doesn't call me at all. At first that didn't bother me because I knew he was at work. But now, I feel like he's working way too much. He's so determined to find the right combination of properties for the aphrodisiac. He works on that more than any of his other research projects. I need Travis to have an internal cutoff switch."

"Okay, but why?" Millie asked still confused as to what Jasmine was driving at.

"Here's what I think: I know that Travis has stronger feelings for me, but he won't express it because he's so absorbed in the work. I think if he had someone like me that he could come home to at a certain time, he'd shut down and come home to me. We've been seeing each other for almost a year so our relationship has grown."

"Does he spend any time with you outside of the bedroom?" Millie asked.

"Of course he does. We go out to dinner, concerts, and plays. But I want more. I don't want to play second fiddle to his work."

"Well, Jasmine, you can't change who he is." Millie pointed out the obvious.

"I don't want to change who he is; I just want to regulate it a little. My biggest competition for his time right now is the sex pill project which is going absolutely nowhere. The project needs to be scrapped and our time and resources need to be redirected to other projects. I think that shelving the project will help."

"Don't you think that's going to upset him?" Millie asked.

"Projects get jettisoned all of the time. There is nothing strange about that."

"So why do you sound worried about bringing the project to a conclusion?"

"Because I don't want him to know that I spearheaded the effort. I really want to have a meaningful relationship with Travis. That's the bottom line and if the only thing keeping us apart is some experiment, then I want it removed from our lives."

"Wow, Jasmine. That could lead to—"

"Some dangerous consequences if it backfires," Jasmine interrupted Millie and finished her sentence.

"Do you think it will come back to haunt you? I mean, what if another project comes up and he gets equally obsessed with that?"

"I'll cross that bridge when I get to it," Jasmine said.

"Okay, so answer this question for me. I'm just putting something on the table for discussion."

"Bring it on," Jasmine said ready to tackle the dilemma Millie was about to present.

"Why doesn't he date women his own age?"

"He says that he finds them to be immature. He likes being with older women," Jasmine answered.

"Okay. Another question for you."

"Shoot."

"What went wrong in his last serious relationship?" Millie asked the killer question.

"You know, Millie. It's very interesting that you brought that up. I've asked Travis about his past relationships, but he hasn't really had any."

"What are you talking about? The guy is going to be twenty-nine years old. There had to be at least one serious relationship in his life."

"I'm telling you, he says that he hasn't. I find that to be rather odd myself. So I asked him who he'd been dating and he says, 'Babe, I did some things in my past that I'm not exactly proud of. I did what needed to be done to move forward with my life and that's all you really need to know.'"

"I don't think I like that answer," Millie said suspiciously. "Are you sure he isn't some ex-con who's murdered people?"

"Girl, you and I think just alike. That's what I thought, too, so one night when he was sleeping over, I got his driver's license number and had Lauren run a check on him to see if anything came up. She told me that he was clean and he had no criminal record. So I figured that he probably never had a real romantic relationship because he was so driven by his work. I want to be his first true love affair. I want him to really love me. What's so wrong with that?"

"There is nothing wrong with being in love. I mean, I believe that a person should take love wherever and whenever it comes into their lives, regardless of age."

"I do, too, but still, I'm at a very tricky crossroads," Jasmine admitted.

"I think everything will work out. Just take your time and communicate how you feel to Travis."

"Do you think I'm being foolish here? Honestly? Am I some old desperate woman trying to snag—"

"Jasmine, stop it!" Millie cut her off. "Don't do that to yourself. Do what you feel needs to be done and go from there. Don't apologize for a damn thing. You're not doing anything wrong."

"Thanks, Millie, I really needed to hear that." Millie and Jasmine talked a little more and then ended their call.

Chapter 18
Travis

"What the fuck do you mean the plug has been pulled on the aphrodisiac project?" Travis was sitting in Jasmine's office. She'd just told him the news about Helen's decision to stop wasting time and resources on the project.

"Will you lower your voice!" Jasmine spoke to Travis in a loud whisper as she rose up from behind her desk and moved swiftly across the floor to close her door.

"We were making real progress, Jasmine. Why would she pull the plug on this? I thought this was the project that she was really behind." Travis picked up an ink pen from Jasmine's desk and began tapping the ballpoint on her desk rapidly and noisily.

"First of all, you need to calm down." Jasmine's demeanor suddenly turned authoritative, but Travis no longer viewed her as his boss as much as he did the woman he was fucking.

"Why should I calm down, Jasmine! I've been blindsided and the rug has been pulled from under my feet! What's really going on? Is there some kind of problem?

Are they giving the project to someone else? I don't understand what the problem is."

Travis made numerous gestures with his hands. Jasmine leaned back in her seat and brushed the tip of her nose a few times with her index finger.

"Travis, projects get pulled all of the time. I can understand how important this particular one was to you, but there are other things that require your attention and mine as well. There is a chance that we'll revisit this later, but for right now, we have to put a hold on this. The side effects of the drug can lead to death. We both know this to be a fact."

"I can fix it, though, Jasmine. I just need more time in the lab. I need this. I've invested too much time and energy into this project. It's all that I think about."

Jasmine tried to look sympathetic. "Travis, listen to me," Jasmine spoke in a calmer tone. "It's not—"

"I'm going to schedule an appointment with Helen to get to the bottom of this." Travis cut Jasmine off.

"You will do no such thing, Travis Adams!" Jasmine snapped. She had no idea just how deeply rooted the obsessive side of his personality was. He spoke like a madman whose lab had just been destroyed by an explosion.

"Why not!" Travis barked at Jasmine as he rose to his feet. She didn't like it one bit.

"Don't you use that tone of voice with me!"

Jasmine stood, too. On the outside she was stern

and direct, but on the inside she worried about him transforming into the Hulk and going on a destruction rampage.

"Look, Jasmine. Listen to me." Travis approached her and placed his hands on her shoulders. "Go talk to Helen for me. Tell her that I need more time on this."

"Travis," Jasmine said, as a look of perplexity formed in the wrinkles in her forehead and the slight turn of her mouth.

"Please," Travis begged.

"Why does this one project mean so much to you?" Jasmine had asked the question she really wanted the answer to.

"If I can create the formula—scratch that; if we, as in you and I, baby, can come up with the right recipe, we'll get prestige, fame, and perhaps win the Nobel Prize for our discovery. Don't you want that? Don't you have the same dream? Isn't that what our profession is all about, making a difference?"

"Travis." Jasmine paused and looked into his blazing brown eyes. "Baby, I want you. I don't want some medal or prestige. Those things are nice, but they don't define who I am. And you shouldn't let it define who you are. You're brilliant without those accolades, don't you know that?"

"You don't understand, Jasmine. I thought you truly understood me." Travis looked as her as if she were a traitor. He had a bewildered gaze in his eyes and felt as if he'd just been shot with a double-barreled shotgun.

"I do understand you. I know you better than you think I do. Travis, you're walking with blinders on. You're so caught up that you barely have time to stop and enjoy life, togetherness, and how to appreciate someone who cares deeply for you. Don't you see me, Travis? Don't you see the beauty of us? Don't you see how this project was getting in the way of giving you one of the best gifts in life? The chemical interaction between a man and a woman, called love?"

"Wait a minute here, Jasmine. What are you saying? I thought we weren't going to go here." Travis didn't like what he was hearing.

"You mean to tell me that you don't feel what we have?" Jasmine whispered out of concern that others would hear them. "I'm trying to reach your tortured soul, baby, and love it like no one ever has." Jasmine placed her hand over her heart and reached for him.

"Look." Travis paused, meeting Jasmine's gaze with his own. "I'm taking the rest of the day off. I need to get out of here."

"Let me go with you then?" Jasmine said.

"No. You don't want to be with me right now. Trust me on that one," Travis growled and walked out the door.

TRAVIS WAS FURIOUS ABOUT THE NEWS Jasmine had shared with him as he drove away from the lab. All of his hard work and efforts were all pointless and even worse, he didn't like that other people could interrupt his work.

"Damn it!" Travis shouted as he punched the dashboard of his car several times with hammer fists. "I hate this shit!"

Travis didn't feel like going home, so he decided to give Alex a ring to see if he was home.

"Hey Travis, what's going on?" Alex answered the phone.

"Where are you, man?" he asked.

"I'm at home right now."

"I'm heading in your direction. Mind if I stop over?" Travis asked.

"No man. Come on through," Alex said with a welcoming voice.

"All right. I'll see you in about twenty minutes."

WHEN TRAVIS ARRIVED, Alex could tell immediately that something was bothering him.

"Wow. Why do you look so crazy? What's the matter with you?" Alex asked as he let him in.

"Fucking bullshit-ass people at work are jerking me around," Travis griped as he plopped down on the sofa.

"Do you want a beer?" Alex asked.

"Yeah, I could use one."

When Alex came back with the beer, Travis took several long gulps and then set the bottle on a glass table in front of him. Travis glanced around the room and noticed that most of the furniture was gone with the exception of the sofa and a chair. All of the art work that adorned the walls was gone.

"What happened to all of your stuff?" Travis asked.

"Sold it," Alex said.

"What for?" Travis asked confused.

"I got fired. When they gave me my severance package, I went to the riverboat casino hoping to change my luck, but instead I lost all of my money. So in order to cover my mortgage I had to have a fire sale."

"Damn, Alex. So I guess getting my money back anytime soon is out of the question," Travis said.

"Why do you want to bring up old shit? I'm going to get you the money, Travis. Besides, you know my situation, man. I've got to get out of this bullshit I'm involved with somehow." Alex shook his head. "Didn't I tell you that I got fired from my job?" Alex sat down in a chair which faced the sofa.

"Aww man. I'm sorry to hear that. What happened?" Although Alex had just told him that he'd been fired, Travis didn't want to be perceived as being apathetic.

"Hatcher is what fucking happened. Flying him all over the place has cost me my job. I don't know what my next move is going to be. It's going to be hard for me to fly for another airline when I got fired for not showing up to transport passengers. When my unemployment runs out, I might have to shack up with one of my Cougars until I can get my shit in order, but even that won't be easy, especially since Hatcher has me flying shipments around for free."

"Why don't you just stop, just go into hiding or something?"

"And do what, man? Live with the fucking wolves?"

"Hey, if things get that bad, you can stay with me," Travis offered.

"Thanks for the offer, but I'm going to try to stay with a lonely woman before I come live with you," Alex said as he leaned back in his seat. "So what's your drama?"

"My issues pale in comparison to what you're going through," Travis said.

"How is your drug coming along? Have you worked out the kinks yet?" Alex asked.

"No, man. They pulled the plug on it. All of my hard work and effort has just gone down the drain."

"Whoa! They can't do that to you, man. You've got to go back there and work that shit out!" Travis noticed that Alex seemed just as upset as he was.

"As far as they're concerned it's pretty much a done deal."

"Then you need to work on that drug on your own. Then once you get the formula tight, they'll be begging you for it and would probably pay through the nose to get it."

"I wish it were that simple. I'd need a lab, equipment, and start-up money, not to mention everything involved with starting a pharmaceutical operation," Travis said.

"What kind of equipment?" Alex asked.

"Why?"

"There are all kinds of labs around this city. Residential houses that have been chopped up for let's say, chemistry purposes. I know of some old warehouses as well."

"Thanks, but no thanks. That's not the way I want to go. However, you did have a good point about continuing my experiments..." Travis's words trailed off and sank to a whisper. Something in his subconscious mind had inexplicably begun speaking to him. It was an ominous and evil voice he heard telling him to keep the project going in secrecy. The more he tuned into the frequency of his darker side, the easier it was to be seduced by the unthinkable. Travis allowed this other side of him to take over. He gave himself permission to soar on the wings of madness.

This is your project, the dark voice said to Travis. *You're the one who truly created the formula. All you need to do is perfect it and then try it out on a human subject. Jasmine would make a perfect test subject. You know it'll work. Just slip the liquid formula in her drink. Once she experiences the mind-blowing pleasure, you'll have the satisfaction of telling her you've solved the mystery of female sexual arousal. She, along with everyone else, will worship the ground you walk on. You are the most brilliant chemist in the world. The world needs to see you as the next Albert Einstein. You are a supreme intellect and you are a genius. Go make the formula and unleash it on the world. No one can stop you. Don't let those bastards control you!*

"Yo man, are you all right?" Alex snapped his fingers in front of Travis' eyes, but got no response. "Travis. What the fuck?" Alex placed his hands on his shoulders and shook him out of his trance. Travis focused on Alex as if he didn't recognize who he was.

"Travis?" Alex's voice was filled with uncertainty. He understood that something strange and off the mark was going on with his best friend.

"What?" Travis's voice was low and heavy like that of a demon. Alex had never heard him sound so wicked.

"What the hell is wrong with you, man?" Alex was clearly freaked out by what he'd just witnessed.

"Nothing. What's the problem?" Travis asked in a monotone voice.

"Shit, you're the problem, motherfucker. You blanked out on me. You just started staring at the fucking wall, man, like you were in some type of otherworldly trance. You had a different look in your eyes. You weren't here just a moment ago. I'm no psychiatrist but I know bizarre when I see it. Are you on something?"

"I'm not on anything, Alex," Travis answered as if he were about to commit homicide.

"Okay, you've officially freaked me the hell out. Stop acting like some weird psychopath," Alex said, not wanting to turn his back on Travis.

"I've always hated that word, Alex. You shouldn't use it in my presence." Travis still spoke in a monotone as if he were reprogramming himself.

"I'm not a very religious guy, never have been. But

if I were, I'd swear that you're acting as if an unclean spirit has taken over your mind."

"No Alex. It's nothing like that. You are right about one thing, though. I suddenly feel different."

"Do you want me to take you to the hospital?" Alex began to cautiously back away from Travis. "I just need to grab my jacket."

"You think I've flipped out, don't you?" Travis asked.

"I don't know what's going on, but I do know this. Over the last few minutes, you've done the Nutty Professor transformation."

"I'm fine, Alex." Travis tried to smile, but it would not fully form. Only his left cheek rose up toward his eye.

"You don't look like it. Seems to me like you might be having a stroke or something."

"I've never felt better, my friend. I should go now. I have a lot of things that need to get done," Travis said as he walked toward the door. Alex grabbed his arm just above the elbow to stop him. He glanced into Travis's eyes again, but still saw something different.

"If you need anything, let me know, all right?" Alex said.

"Of course," Travis answered and gave him a shoulder bump and a pat on the back.

"I love you, man," he said.

"I know," Travis answered and then left.

Chapter 19
Jasmine

It was almost 4:55 p.m. and Jasmine was sitting at her desk still fuming over the way Travis had reacted to her. She couldn't comprehend why he had come out of an ugly bag on her. His behavior was completely irrational and uncharacteristic. She was flirting with the idea of disciplinary action, but she decided to give him a cooling-off period so that he could return to his senses.

As her day drew to its conclusion, she looked forward to heading home so she could relax and forget about how ugly her day had been. Jasmine shut down her computer, gathered her belongings and headed out. When she made it to the lobby, she saw Sam smiling at her. She acknowledged the guard's silent greeting.

"You're not staying with your buddy tonight?" Sam asked.

"Buddy? What are you talking about?" Jasmine eyed Sam suspiciously.

"Dr. Travis Adams," Sam said, grinning at her innocently.

"What are you saying?" Jasmine asked as she approached his counter.

"I'm just wondering if you guys were going to be working late tonight, that's all," Sam explained.

"No. Travis left earlier today," Jasmine said. Before he could respond to her, Sam focused his attention on a woman who was entering the building.

"Can I help you, Miss?" Sam called out to her.

The woman approached. "No thanks, I've found the person I'm looking for."

Jasmine turned her head in the direction of the familiar voice and saw her sister, Lauren. Lauren was still in her DEA gear, but was sporting a pair of dark sunglasses.

"I came to see you," she said, sniffling.

"What's wrong?" Jasmine asked.

"I need to talk to you. Do you have some time for me?" Lauren asked.

"Of course I do. Come on, we can go back to my place," Jasmine said as she began to escort her sister out.

"I'll tell Travis that you've left for the night," Sam blurted before she walked off.

"Travis left earlier today, Sam," Jasmine said.

"Well, he's back. He came in just before you came down. He told me that you guys would probably be working late tonight."

Jasmine paused as creases formed in her forehead. *Why would Travis tell Sam that?*

"Just tell Travis that I'll catch up with him later," Jasmine said before leaving with her sister, who was visibly upset.

A SHORT TIME LATER, Jasmine arrived at her house with Lauren. Lauren went to rest on the sofa in the family room while Jasmine went into the kitchen.

"Would you like something to drink?" Jasmine asked her sister.

"A bottle of Jack Daniel's, if you've got it," Lauren said in the most depressing tone.

"No, I'm not going to let you drink a bottle of Jack Daniel's. Jack is only going to make you feel worse about whatever it is that's bothering you." Jasmine opened her refrigerator. "I've got diet Coke, lemonade, and some sweet tea."

"I'll take the sweet tea," Lauren answered.

Jasmine poured their drinks and then headed to the family room. Lauren had removed her gun belt and shoes and was lying on her back.

"Here you go," Jasmine said as she handed her the drink.

Lauren sat upright and took the glass from Jasmine.

"Take off those dark sunglasses so I can see your face," Jasmine said as she took a seat in a nearby chair.

"You really don't want to see what I look like because I feel like I've been kicked by a mule," Lauren confessed as she combed her fingers through her hair.

"Don't make me come over there and take them off," Jasmine said with a no-nonsense tone of voice. Lauren reluctantly removed her dark sunglasses. Jasmine took one look at her. "Okay, what happened?" Jasmine set her glass of sweet tea down and draped her arm around her sister's shoulder. Lauren turned, embraced Jasmine and began crying.

"Oh come on now. It can't be that bad," Jasmine said as she rocked her sister to help soothe her troubled emotions. Once Lauren let out her pain, she smeared away her tears with the back of her hand. Lauren walked into the kitchen to retrieve a box of Kleenex.

"Here you go," she said, handing her sister the box. Lauren yanked out a few sheets and blew her nose.

"I'm mad, Jasmine. LeMar pissed me the hell off," Lauren said angrily.

"Is there something in the air because Travis snapped out on me earlier today, too," Jasmine said, empathizing with her sister.

"I let LeMar get too close to me. I should've just kept my distance from him. Never in a million years could I have imagined that he'd hurt me like this," Lauren said.

"What did he do?"

"What all men do? He's fucked up big time and he knows it."

"What did he do? Don't tell me he's been shaking down drug dealers for money on the side."

"No, he's not that damn savvy. This idiot has gone out and gotten two girls pregnant: a nineteen-year-old waitress and a twenty-year-old college student." Lauren exposed the dagger that had pierced her heart.

"Oh no he didn't!" Jasmine couldn't believe what she was hearing.

"Yes he did," Lauren said, trying to keep her anger under control.

"Who are they?" Jasmine asked.

"Young girls he was trying to impress and now he's messed around and got caught up."

"How did you find out?"

"One of the girls answered his cell phone while he was in the shower. When I asked who she was, she said, 'I'm Felicia, his baby's mama. Are you Danita, the other girl who's supposed to be pregnant by him, too?'"

"You've got to be kidding me," Jasmine said, not wanting to believe her ears.

"I wish I was, Jasmine. The hurting thing is that when I saw him at work, he acted as if he was so in love with me. He had no clue that I'd talked to Felicia. He was acting as if everything was normal and fine. I tried so hard not to bring the shit up at work, but I couldn't hold it in. I caught him just as he was exiting the washroom and told him that I needed to speak with him. He tried to blow me off, but I insisted we talk. We ducked into a stairwell for a little privacy and he figured that I was just horny and needed to be kissed. When he craned his neck towards me, I slapped the fuck out of him. 'What the hell did you do that for,' he said, sounding all stupid. Then I said, 'Do you have something you need to tell me?' And he says, 'No.' So I asked again and got the same answer. So I just put the shit out there and asked him why didn't he tell me about Felicia and Danita?"

"What did he say?" Jasmine asked.

"He just looked at me all stupid like. Then he rested his back against the door, folded his arms and stared at the floor. He couldn't even look me in the eyes, Jasmine." Lauren snatched more Kleenex from the box. Jasmine remained quiet and waited for Lauren to get herself together so she could finish telling her story.

"I'm a forty-six-year-old woman and I just can't believe I've been duped like this. And then he insulted me by saying, 'Well, I decided that I wanted to have children. I knew you couldn't, so I did what I needed to do.' When he said that shit to me, I snapped out and drop kicked him in the nuts. Ooo, girl, I'm so mad at him and myself. I can't believe I fell in love with his lies."

"He is so wrong for doing you like that," Jasmine said, trying to console her sister. She stroked her hand up and down her back as Lauren began sobbing again.

"When things started getting serious between us, we talked about children and he swore up and down that he didn't want any. He told me that he wanted to build a life with me. I should've known something was up when he didn't come to your holiday party with me."

"I was wondering about that, but I didn't want to pry. I thought perhaps he was spending time with his parents or something."

"No, he was busy fucking Danita—and to think that I was ready to sell my house so that we could buy a new one together. My love life is just fucked up right now."

"Well, you're doing the right thing by breaking it off with him," Jasmine said.

"That's the thing, Jasmine. As pissed off as I am, I still love him. Now what kind of sense does that make? I know it sounds stupid to say that, but it's the ugly truth of the matter."

"Well, what are you going to do?" Jasmine asked.

"I don't know. What do you think I should do?" Lauren asked.

"I think you need some time to get your head right. Once you've had time to think about this, you'll do what's best for you."

"Right now I just want to shoot him and call it a crime of passion," Lauren said.

"You don't want to kill the man because you'll end up in jail and his children will end up fatherless."

"Oh God, why did this happen to me?" Lauren looked to the heavens for an answer.

"It happens to all of us." Jasmine paused. "Travis went crazy on me today at work."

"What?" Lauren asked, sitting upright and dabbing the pool of moisture that had formed under her nose.

"He got upset because one of the projects he was heavily involved with was shelved. When I told him of the decision, he lost it. I never knew that he had a temper until today. He was so upset that he walked out of my office and just left the building."

"That's why you were surprised when the security guard told you he'd returned." Lauren picked up her sweet tea and took a sip. "What do you think he's doing?"

"I don't know and right now, I really don't care. I'm just going to give him some space."

"Why can't men just be honest? Why do they have to lie about everything?" Lauren asked.

"Maybe it's too hard for them to deal with the pain of the truth. I think women look at the truth and confront it head on, but men aren't like that." Jasmine paused in thought for a moment. "I've tried so hard to not let my feelings interfere with my relationship with Travis. It was my intent to just keep him as a cute little boy toy to play around with. But I allowed him to get under my skin to the point that I wanted him. I wanted more out of our relationship. Like you, whether I want to admit it or not, I'm still looking for love. I've lied to myself, made myself believe that I could remove my emotions and just have casual relationships. The lie worked for a while, but my heart knows what's best for me and right now, I have a man who has placed his ambitions before me and I have a problem with that. I want to be the center of his world, not some damned experiment. Am I wrong for feeling that way?"

"No, of course not." Lauren now draped her arm around Jasmine and began rubbing her shoulders.

"Damn, girl, now you've got me crying," Jasmine said as she yanked a few tissues out of the box. "Why do men have such a difficult time expressing their true feelings? I know that Travis is passionate about me. But he doesn't know how to communicate or convey it in a way that lets me know where I stand."

"We're two emotional train wrecks right about now," Lauren said. "We haven't been this confused since we were teenagers back in the eighties."

Jasmine laughed painfully. "How is it that we're both beautiful, educated, and employed women who don't have a bunch of babies on our hip, but still can't find a decent relationship?"

"I don't know, but someone needs to write a book explaining where we went wrong," Lauren said.

"Or better yet, Tyler Perry needs to make a movie about it," Jasmine said, then laughed out loud with her sister.

Chapter 20
Travis

When Travis returned to the office, he was determined to get to the bottom of why his experiments were being shelved. His plan was to confront Jasmine about it once again, but when he arrived, she had already left for the day. Instead of giving her a call, his dark intuition suggested that he enter her office and look through the files on the project. Travis went to Jasmine's office, but the door was locked. He tried to force his way inside, but it was no use.

"Shit," he hissed. He stood outside of her office for a moment and then began to pace back and forth. "How do I get in?" he repeated to himself over and over again until the answer came to him. "Sam," he whispered.

Travis went back down to the security desk to ask Sam if he had a master key to all of the locks.

"Oh hey, Doctor Adams. Jasmine told me to tell you that she was leaving for the evening."

"You saw her?" Travis asked.

"Yeah, she left not too long ago. She was with another woman. I think it was her sister because she was just as shapely as Jasmine, if you know what I mean." Sam chuckled and ribbed Travis playfully.

"Oh yeah. I know what you mean. You'd like to hit that, wouldn't you?" Travis toyed with Sam's lustful nature.

"Ooo, man! If I were to get some of that, I'd probably lose my mind. Jasmine has a sexy stride that very few women have. The way she walks just says, 'let's fuck.' And when she wears a skirt! I'm like, *damn*! She has the butt that goes *pow*! And those big, thick legs. Shit. She can have all of my paycheck." Sam laughed over his words.

"Yeah, she is fine." Travis agreed only to gain his trust. "Listen, Sam, I'm in kind of a jam here. I need to get some information out of Jasmine's office, but she's locked the door. I would call her back, but I don't want her to have come all the way back here."

"Yeah, she probably wouldn't like that, but I would." He laughed like a complete goofball and was getting on Travis's bad side rather quickly.

"Look, do you have a master key?" Travis asked.

"Oh, yeah. I can open the door for you. It's not a problem. Let me get the key out of the back and I'll meet you up there," Sam said.

JUST AS HE'D PROMISED, Sam came up with the master key and opened the door to Jasmine's office. Travis thanked Sam and then shooed him away. He went into

Jasmine's file cabinet and found the folder on female sexual dysfunction. When he opened it, the first thing he saw was a memo to Helen from Jasmine listing all of the reasons why his project should be scrapped.

"Why you sneaky little tramp!" Travis growled as he plopped down in a nearby seat and read the memo in its entirety. "So you really believed that my experiments were total failures! I can't believe you stabbed me in the back like this, Jasmine! This project was my master-piece." Travis was now furious.

"I'm going to get back at you for this. I'll show you. My work is not crackpot science!" Travis rested his elbows on her desk and locked his fingers into a pray-ing position. "I can't take not being in control of my own destiny. From now on, I'm going to do things the way I want them done." With that logic, Travis had made a critical and decisive move. He'd just given himself permission to break all the rules and completely ignore protocol.

TRAVIS DECIDED TO PLAY ALONG with Jasmine's little game of deception. Now that he knew what she'd secretly done, he wanted to see if she'd own up to it or just let him believe that the project was scrapped because of a corporate decision. When he came to work the next day, he immediately went into her office.

"Knock, knock," Travis said as he peeped inside. Jasmine was sitting at her desk writing something.

"Hello, Travis." Her voice was cold and uncaring.

"Do you have a moment?" Travis asked.

"Not right now, Travis. Why don't you schedule an appointment to see me?" Jasmine was giving him the cold shoulder. She didn't appreciate him screaming at her and was even more pissed off that he didn't call her the night before to clear the air.

"This will only take a moment, my love." Travis ignored her insistence on him making a formal appointment.

Jasmine looked up at him and noticed something was a little off. She couldn't exactly put her finger on what was different about him.

"I came to apologize to you. I shouldn't have yelled at you. I'm sorry." Travis worked hard to sell his sincerity to her. There was a long moment of silence before Jasmine finally gave in and accepted his regret.

"You were angry and said some things you probably didn't mean. Let's put the entire incident behind us and let's make sure it doesn't happen again," Jasmine said.

"Deal. Is there anything additional you'd like to say?" Travis was giving her a chance to come clean.

"No," she answered.

"Are you sure?" Travis asked.

Jasmine thought for a moment and then said, "Let's schedule some *us time* this week."

Travis was very disappointed with her but he agreed. "Yes. I'd like that," he said.

"How about Friday evening? I'll cook dinner and we can stay in and watch a movie or something."

"That's sounds wonderful."

"What would you like?" Jasmine asked, feeling as if she was making progress with him.

"How about salmon and pasta," Travis suggested.

"Do you really want fish?" Jasmine asked.

"I think it's appropriate. Especially when there is something fishy going on." Travis laughed, but Jasmine didn't find any humor in what he'd said.

"Are you going to let me in on the joke?" Jasmine asked.

"It's just something I used to always say to my mom when I was a child." Travis winked at her. "I'm going to go into my office and do some work. Ta-ta, my dear," Travis said and walked out.

TRAVIS SPENT A CONSIDERABLE AMOUNT OF TIME working on the formula. He was determined more than ever to get it right and try it out on Jasmine. He was closer to perfecting the serum than she thought.

Friday evening Jasmine and Travis were sitting at her kitchen table enjoying a wonderful dinner. Jasmine was happy because she was getting to spend time with Travis that she felt was important to the continued development of their relationship. Travis, on the other hand, was searching for the perfect moment to try out his aphrodisiac on Jasmine. As soon as they finished with dinner, Travis picked up the plates and placed them in the kitchen sink. He then went to a nearby coat closet and removed a small leather pouch from the pocket of his trench coat. Travis then walked into the bathroom, unzipped the pouch and removed one small jar of a clear liquid. He shook it a few times and then looked at his reflection in the mirror.

Do it, he told himself. *Don't back out now.* Travis took a few deep breaths, then zipped up the pouch that contained several more doses of the liquid.

Meanwhile, Jasmine decided that she wanted to hear some music. She plugged in her iPod into the docking station and selected her love songs play list. The first song that came on was "Chocolate High" by India.Arie & Musiq Soulchild. Jasmine popped her fingers as she listened to lyrics.

"EVERY TIME I HEAR THIS SONG, I THINK ABOUT US," Jasmine admitted as she grooved to the music. "Come dance with me, Travis," she added, feeling good.

"I'll be right there in a moment, babe. Would you like a glass of wine?"

"Yes. There is a bottle on the countertop," Jasmine informed him.

"I see it," Travis said. He removed two wine glasses from the cupboard and filled Jasmine's with both the wine and the liquid. Travis popped a Viagra he'd taken from the supply room at the lab. He walked back into the room and gave her the glass. Without thinking twice,

she drank a healthy amount of it and then looked at the glass strangely.

"Boy, that has a kick to it," Jasmine said, setting the glass down.

"What do you mean?" Travis asked, wanting to know every detail of what she was feeling.

"I don't know, it just has an unusual kick to it," Jasmine repeated.

"Does it taste good?" Travis asked as he took a sip.

"It tastes fine. Actually, I want some more," she said and picked the glass back up to finish off her drink. Jasmine focused her attention back on Travis. She rested her arms on his shoulders and gazed into his eyes.

"Do I make you happy?" Jasmine asked, wanting to hear his words of endearment.

"Yes," Travis said, swaying back and forth with her to the groove.

"Look in my eyes and tell me. Don't look away. Do I make you happy?" Jasmine asked once again. Travis stared into her beautiful green eyes and told her a bold-faced lie.

"Yes, you make me happy."

Jasmine smiled and rested her cheek against his che Travis knew all she wanted was to hear the words, e if his lips were lying to her.

"You make me happy as well and if we make other happy, then we just can't lose. Love will Jasmine said as the song ended.

"Let's go into your bedroom," Travis sugges

"Yeah, let's do that because I'm starting to feel all very hot and naughty."

They walked upstairs and into Jasmine's bedroom. Jasmine sat down on the edge of her bed and patted a spot next to her.

"Come sit next to me."

Travis sat next to Jasmine and looked into her eyes. He noticed that they appeared to be turning a shade greener than normal.

"I want to work on us. I think we have a wonderful relationship. I mean, we're both intelligent people, we get along with each other, we share common ground and we like each other. I want to be with you, so bad." Jasmine stopped talking for a moment. She felt herself getting very hot. "It's hard for me to admit this, but I'm so hooked on you, Travis. I tried not to let my feelings grow, but they have and I think—" Jasmine stood up and started fanning herself with her hand.

"Damn, are you hot?" Jasmine looked back at Travis.

"No," he said, feeling the virile part of him come alive.

"Suddenly I'm having a very bad hot flash," Jasmine said as she reached up and turned the ceiling fan on high. "God, I've got to get out of these clothes." Jasmine started frantically removing her skirt, blouse, pantyhose and undergarments. Once she was completely naked, Travis marveled at her beauty. Her smooth caramel skin, full succulent breasts, and erect chocolate

nipples. Her flat stomach, sexy belly button and the hourglass shape of her pubic hair. Her muscular thighs, drumstick calves and painted toes.

"Ooo, I just suddenly feel like touching myself," Jasmine said as she pinched her nipples with her hand and rubbed her fingers between her thighs. "Damn, baby, I'm just feeling like I need it. Take off your damn clothes!"

Travis was very excited. The formula was working and he couldn't wait to indulge himself and discover a side of Jasmine that was untapped.

"Hurry up!" Jasmine said, stepping toward him and ripping his shirt off. She unbuckled his belt, unsnapped his pants and then pulled them down to his ankles. Travis quickly stepped out of them. Jasmine yanked his underwear down and took his Pride in her hands. The Viagra had kicked in and Travis was erect and ready.

"This dick is so good to me," Jasmine cooed as she put him in the cave of her mouth. She worked her mouth and tongue while stimulating herself and simultaneously rubbing her fingers across her swollen clit. As Jasmine's orgasm began to swell like an ocean tide, she took her mouth off of his cock and screamed while she squeezed his dick. "Ahhhhhh! Shit! Come on, put it in. Hurry up." Jasmine had transformed into a totally different type of lover. She was much more aggressive and passionate in a way that Travis had never seen in any of the women with whom he'd been intimate.

Jasmine bent over at the waist and rested her hands on the bed. "Stop screwing around, Travis, and fuck me." Travis came up behind her and inserted himself into her pussy which was as wet as the ocean.

"Goddamn, Jasmine!" Travis said, amazed at how well the formula was working.

Travis began pounding Jasmine as hard as he could. Her goddess intermittently clutched his manhood with remarkable strength. Jasmine elevated to her tiptoes and raised her ass for him.

"Get in there!" she pleaded with him. Travis squeezed her ass muscles as tightly as he could and extended himself inside her as far as humanly possible.

"Oh, God!" Jasmine screamed at the top of her voice. Travis was amazed by the constant stream of her silky and slick love juices which raged forth like a waterfall. He looked down at his glistening cock, then pulled out of her just in time to witness Jasmine squirting on him and the floor.

"Oh my God!" Jasmine collapsed on the bed. She was out of breath and panting hard. "That's never happened before."

"That's because this dick is so good to you," Travis's over-inflated ego was speaking for him now.

"I've never felt this way in my life," Jasmine admitted as she tried to catch her breath. "What are you doing to me? Why does it feel so good? I want you so bad, baby." Jasmine's emotions began to take over. "I want to do things to you that no other woman ever has. I want to make you feel as good as I do."

"Will you take it in the ass for me?" Travis asked.

"Yes, baby. You can fuck my ass," Jasmine agreed. "I have some lubricant in the top dresser drawer."

"Go get it," Travis said.

Jasmine moved over to her dresser and retrieved the lubricant along with her vibrator.

"Lay down on your back, and bend your knees up to your ears so I can get in your tight ass." Without even challenging the position, Jasmine willingly rolled her knees up to her ears.

"Yeah, that's it. Right there," Travis said as he spread the lubricant between her ass cheeks and around her anus. He then carefully inserted the head of his Pride into her butt. Jasmine cried out.

"Oh my God! I can't believe I'm doing this and it doesn't hurt!" Jasmine cried out.

"You like what I'm doing to you?" he asked her.

"Yes," Jasmine said as she clawed at his legs. "Get all in there. Pound my ass. Please. It hurts so good."

Travis pounded her the way she'd asked. As he pumped in and out of her ass, Jasmine reached for her vibrator and turned it on. The device came alive. The cock-shaped toy had a rotating head and three speeds—low, medium and high. Jasmine set the dial to high. She then inserted it into her soaking wet pussy.

"That's what I'm talking about. Get nasty with it."

At that moment Jasmine had a very strange experience. She felt as if she was outside of her body looking down at herself. She was in a euphoric state of mind. Everything felt marvelous to her. The pain, the pleasure, the feel of Travis's sweat bursting on her skin, the scent of their sex and the vibrations of their lovemaking noises all seemed to clash together and detonate inside of her with the force of a nuclear bomb. Jasmine squirted again, spewing her wetness all over Travis's abdomen. She felt her body go limp, as if her body were a ship adrift in space. It was so quiet, and peaceful. Jasmine never wanted the feeling to end. She believed that Travis's lovemaking ability was so potent that it was addictive. And all she wanted to do was get high off of his love. Travis pulled out and shot his load on her breasts, chin, and stomach. She rubbed it around on her skin and then gobbled up his sweetness off of her fingertips. He tasted so good.

"Put your dick in my mouth," Jasmine whispered. "I want all of it."

Travis complied and for a brief moment, Jasmine wondered why he was still so hard. But then again, she really didn't give a damn. This was her dick, and it was satisfying her in a way she could've never imagined. Jasmine played with his balls as she pulled and sucked him. She was making sure that she got every drop of his love.

Travis began caressing her body. She felt her flame of desire growing again. This second wave felt more intense than the first. It felt as if Travis had a thousand hands touching and fondling her everywhere. Jasmine didn't understand how he could be touching her every place at once. She began to purr like a cat, something she'd never done before, but she couldn't help it. Her purring matched her breathing. Jasmine felt as if she were trapped between the conscious and subconscious world. She wasn't exactly asleep, but she wasn't fully coherent either. The only thing she knew for sure was that she wanted him to be back inside of her forever.

WHEN TRAVIS WENT HOME THE FOLLOWING DAY, he was exhausted. He felt sore and raw. He swore that he and Jasmine had broken some kind of world fucking record. They had gone at it for six hours straight. After getting some much needed rest, Travis went back to the lab. He was excited about his discovery and he wanted to capitalize on it, but he needed more test subjects. He needed to know if the drug worked just as well on other women. He knew that there was no way he could push his formula through for approval through conventional means, especially with his questionable research methods. Still, in spite of the obvious dangers, Travis, for no other reason than his own self-interest, decided to make some more of it. He even created a pill version using a pill press that had the capacity to quickly produce. Travis let the machine run for an hour and made five-thousand pills.

As he drove off in his car he called his friend, Alex.

"Where are you?" Travis asked.

"At home. I'm about to run out to Palwaukee Airport," Alex said.

"You plan on doing any fucking around while you're out of town?" Travis asked.

"I don't know. I'll be with Hatcher and anything is possible," Alex said.

"Well, hold on before you leave. I've got something that I want to give to you."

"What?"

"Something special. You still carrying Viagra around with you?" Travis asked.

"Yeah."

"Good, because you're going to need those," Travis informed him.

"Oh shit, you made the stuff?" Excitement suddenly filled Alex's voice.

Travis just laughed. "I'll be there in five minutes."

When Travis arrived, Alex was waiting for him on the sidewalk in front of his condo. Travis pulled over and got out to greet his friend.

"What's going on, man?" Alex asked as they shook hands.

"I've got something for you. I want you to try this out," Travis said. He gave him a prescription bottle filled with the pills.

"Is this the aphrodisiac?"

"Yeah, and I want you to try it and then let me know

what happens. Oh, and don't let the girls take more than four within a twenty-four-hour period." Travis let out a sinister laugh.

"What is this shit called?" Alex asked.

Travis paused in thought for a moment as he thought of a name for his creation.

"Cougars," Travis finally declared.

"Cougars?" Alex repeated.

"Yeah," Travis said as he started walking back to his car. "Oh, and Alex, be careful with that because it's going to turn the woman into one frisky-ass cat."

"Well, all right then. Good looking out, man. I'll let you know exactly what happens."

"How long are you going to be gone?" Travis asked.

"I'm taking him to South America. I'll be gone for at least a week."

"Cool. I'll see you when you get back," Travis said before he pulled off.

Chapter 21
Jasmine

When Jasmine awoke late in the day on Saturday she had never felt so sick and yet so satisfied her entire life. She felt completely dehydrated; her vagina felt raw from the friction of fucking. Her stomach was in knots, she kept having hot flashes, her eyes were sensitive to light and she had a headache. But in spite of how she felt, her body had the nerve to be aching for more sex. She wanted to get another release, but she felt as if there was no more liquid in her body. She searched her bed for Travis but he wasn't there.

"Travis?" she tried to call him, but her throat was so dry that it hurt to speak. Jasmine massaged her temples and blinked her eyes rapidly to try and focus. She sat up in bed and the room began to spin. Jasmine immediately lay back down and closed her eyes. She curled up into a fetal position and went back to sleep.

By the time nightfall had arrived, she awoke again. The room had finally stopped spinning and her headache was gone, but her stomach was still in knots. She sat upright and tried to swallow her saliva, but it was too difficult. Placing her feet on the floor, she stood up and walked directly to the bathroom and flipped on the light switch. But she immediately turned it off because it hurt her eyes. She turned on the faucet, removed a face towel from the cupboard and washed her face. She took a Dixie mouthwash cup and filled it with water. She sipped some water to moisten her mouth.

"My God. My mouth feels like dry mud," Jasmine said, finally able to speak. "Travis," she called for him, but didn't get a response. She walked out of the bathroom and called for him again.

"Travis," she called as loudly as she could. She made her way down the corridor to the kitchen. She saw Travis writing on a notepad. When he saw her, he quickly gathered up his work and zipped up the leather pouch that was near him.

"What are you doing? Did you hear me calling you?" Jasmine complained.

"No, I'm sorry I didn't. How do you feel?" Travis asked as he helped her to sit down at the kitchen table.

"Exhausted. I feel as if I can barely keep my head up."

"That's because you were such a freak last night," Travis joked.

"My ass hurts, Travis. I'm never letting you do that to me again. I think you did it too hard and now my stomach is messed up. It feels like you've pushed something out of place."

"You'll be fine," Travis assured her.

"No, I don't think so. I think I'm going to make a doctor's appointment. I woke up feeling really bad."

"No!" Travis yelled. The last thing he needed was for her to go to a doctor and get blood work done. "I mean. Give your body a chance to recover. I'm sure you'll be fine. Besides, I'm going to take really good care of you." Travis came up to her and kissed her on the forehead.

"Travis. What happened last night? Why was it so different? Why was I suddenly squirting?"

"You know that's a phenomenon of nature. Some women can do it and others can't. I'm glad that you can. It's such a turn-on," Travis said, stroking her long hair.

"But it's never happened before. Why now?" Jasmine searched her mind for the answers to her questions.

"Who knows, maybe it's just something that occurs." Travis said whatever it took to throw her off and keep her confused.

"How long was I asleep?" Jasmine asked.

"All day," Travis said.

"Then why do I still feel so exhausted?"

"Could it be because you fucked me all night?" Travis joked.

"Whatever, Travis." Jasmine didn't find his humor to be all that funny. "Could you pour me a glass of water?" Travis filled a glass with some ice water and handed it to her.

Jasmine gulped the water down. "Give me another one." She drank nine glasses of water before her thirst was finally satisfied.

"Listen, babe. I'm going to go into the bedroom and change the bedding. Then I want you to lie down and get some rest. I'll come in and snuggle up with you later," he said.

"Yes, that sounds nice." Jasmine stood up and shuffled back to her bedroom.

Chapter 22
Travis

Travis didn't have an ounce of remorse in his body for his involvement with putting toxins in Jasmine's system. He truly believed that what he'd done was a necessary evil, which needed to be performed for the good of science. He knew the drug's side effects, but he was confident that once the drug was out of her system, she'd be back to her old self.

Just as Travis had planned, Jasmine recovered and was back at work by Tuesday of the following week. On her first day, he went to her office and stood in the doorway so he could undress her with his eyes as well as spy on her for any signs of complications.

"Good morning," Travis said while leaning against the door frame.

"Hey, Travis." Jasmine glanced up from her desk.

"Are you feeling better?" he asked.

"Better than I was after Friday night. My stomach is still a little off, but other than that, I'm fine. Thanks for asking."

"Good, I'm glad to hear it. You had me worried there for a minute," Travis lied.

"Well, thank you for your concern, but I'll have to talk to you later. I have a meeting with Helen this morning."

"Is she going to reinstate the project by any chance?" Travis asked.

"No, Travis. That project is dead in the water. I thought this issue was behind us." Jasmine had grown annoyed with Travis's fixation on that particular experiment.

"So you have no idea why she shelved this project, right?" Travis couldn't help it. He wanted her to come clean.

"I don't have time for this right now, Travis," Jasmine said, picking up several folders from her desk. She headed toward him. "Don't ask me about that project again. It's not up for discussion."

Jasmine was stern and direct with him. She was starting to believe that Travis had a real mental issue that needed to be addressed.

"Excuse me," Jasmine said as she moved past Travis and walked down the hallway.

"Fine, Jasmine. Have it your way. If you want to continue to play dumb about the shit, then you must be punished accordingly. I have something very special for you, my dear. You just wait and see," Travis uttered as he lowered his eyes to slits. Misguided revenge and ambition filled his heart. He now believed that Jasmine was trying to play him for a fool.

"I can see right through you, Jasmine. You're trying to make me look incompetent so that I get fired. But that's not going to happen and I'm going to make sure of it!"

Travis was now walking up the block toward his building. Off in the distance he could see flashes of lightning dancing across the sky. The winds suddenly picked up and carried with it the scent of an approaching thunderstorm. Travis quickened his pace as droplets of water began to fall. Just before he reached his building, a man wearing a black suit and dark sunglasses stepped out of a gold Rolls-Royce. Travis had never seen the man and his body language seemed aggressive. Travis's instincts were telling him he needed to be on guard because something about his demeanor screamed *assassin*.

Just as Travis reached his building, the assassin said, "Travis Adams, I need you to come with me." The man's voice was heavy, authoritative, and antagonistic.

"Who the fuck are you?" Travis sized-up the dude, determining if he could defend himself.

"Step this way." He directed Travis's attention to the gold Rolls-Royce. Travis cautiously glanced in that direction, not wanting to fully take his eyes off of the guy.

"Come on, Travis, what are you waiting for?" shouted Alex who'd just rolled down the rear window of the expensive luxury car.

"Alex?"

"Come take a ride with me, dawg," Alex said, inviting Travis to join him.

"Take a ride with you where?" Travis asked as he strolled over to the car.

"Get in before it starts to rain."

Alex opened the car door. Travis ducked inside and got situated on the comfortable leather seats.

"What's going on, pimp?" Alex asked. His attitude was upbeat and energized.

"What a nice car. I've never been in a Rolls-Royce before." Travis was feeling as if he should own a fleet of automobiles of this caliber.

"Dude, this is a 2009 Rolls-Royce Phantom Coupe. This bitch here will hit you for half a million dollars. The ride is so smooth you feel like you're floating on clouds."

"I see," Travis said, running his hands on the soft leather. "So what's this about, Alex?"

"You, man. Whatever that shit was that you gave me is off the hook! I let Hatcher try some of it out on his girls and he can't stop talking about Cougars. He wants to buy a shit load of those pills. I told him that I could hook you two up to talk some business. He's excited about meeting you. I know he's serious because he sent me over here to get you in this." Alex spread his hands out to accentuate the luxury vehicle.

"So he really liked the effects of Cougars, you say?"

Travis asked, smirking with a twisted sense of pride and egotism.

"I'm telling you, that shit had his girls doing all kinds of freakish shit. Hatcher has already been taking orders for it. Man, once that shit hits the streets—*boom*! People are going to lose their minds. At least that's what Hatcher says."

"So where is he? I most certainly want to talk over some things with him."

"We're on our way to see him now. Man, if this works out, it will go a long way in helping me clear my debt with him. So please, whatever you do, don't fuck this up, man," Alex said.

"This isn't about you, Alex. This is about my experiment and my need for more test subjects."

"Fuck the test subjects, man! I'm talking about the money we're going to make from this. Cougars can become more popular than cocaine. Everyone likes to fuck, but not everyone does cocaine."

"Yes, I suppose you're right. It's about the money as well. Especially if I can make a profit from my super pill and live in the lap of luxury."

"See, now you're talking. Now you're starting to think right," Alex said.

They drove to a private airplane hangar and then boarded a small jet.

"Alex, where are we going?" Travis asked as Alex sat in the pilot's seat.

"Relax. This aircraft is fully stocked. Check out the refrigerator back there. We're going to take a quick ride down to Miami. I'll have you back home around midnight," Alex said as he taxied the aircraft out of the hangar and onto the runway.

HATCHER'S HOME WAS GRAND. He lived in a gated community near the boat docks where several major cruise lines departed. Travis and Alex were escorted by a number of men who looked liked they wouldn't hesitate to kill them and feed their remains to sharks. Admittedly, Travis was intimidated and nervous but somehow willed himself to continue on. He was without a doubt covering ground that was foreign to him, but at the same time it seemed surreal, fascinating, and exciting. Travis moved through a grand foyer and out of a set of glass doors. They walked through the yard and toward a dock where there was a white yacht with a helicopter resting on it. Once they boarded, they went into a well-appointed office where Hatcher was waiting on them.

Hatcher was without a doubt a very clever and dangerous man, Travis sensed from the moment their eyes met. He was in his mid-fifties, well-built with black-and-gray curly hair. His moustache was pencil-thin and well-groomed. He was dressed in an expensive-looking white suit and had several expensive rings on his fingers. Hatcher looked of Spanish descent and not

Irish like his last name McKean suggested. It was then that Travis realized that Hatcher was probably one of many aliases.

"Fellas, I'm so happy you could make it," Hatcher said with a slight Spanish accent. "Please have a seat. We're all friends here." Hatcher's eyelids sloped downward as if he'd spent unimaginable time under the blazing hot sun. Both Travis and Alex sat down.

"I'm so glad you're here, Travis."

Travis cleared his throat, then swallowed hard. Then in his most confident voice, he said, "I'm happy to be here, too."

"Alex has told me many things about you. He says you're like a brother to him. That's a good thing because I like Alex and I trust him. If he says you're like a brother to him, then I know that I don't need to bullshit around. Am I right?"

"Of course you don't have to bullshit. This is Travis. He's cool," Alex answered with a nervous and shaky voice. Travis had never seen or heard this particular side of his friend's personality.

"Excellent. Then let me get right to the point. I like to have my way and I always get what I want. Mr. Adams, the moment you stepped into my Rolls-Royce we became business partners. So if you have any business dealings with anyone else in the underworld, speak up so that I can blow your head off right now."

"No. Travis is clean. He doesn't—"

"Alex!" Hatcher shot daggers with his eyes. "I was not talking to you."

Alex tucked his tail between his legs and remained silent.

Travis repositioned himself in his seat. He sat up straight and answered, "No, I don't know anyone in your line of work."

"I like you already. You answered the question directly and didn't give me a bunch of bullshit."

"I don't believe in bullshit," Travis responded, allowing the vile and monstrous side of his nature to come into full bloom.

"You have a product that is very unique and special. There is nothing like it anywhere in the world. It is something that we can make a lot of money with. You do want to make a lot of money, don't you, Mr. Adams?"

At that moment Travis sold what remained of his integrity and his soul to an agent of the devil.

"I want money and respect for my work," Travis said boldly.

"This is good. I like a man who takes pride in his work. Look at me. Look around inside a small corner of my empire. In this world I am a king with wealth and riches at my feet. I have people who respect me, fear me, and admire me. In many ways, to many people, I am a prophet."

"So do you want to talk business or do you want to talk religion. You don't have to explain your power or importance. I already know that."

Hatcher leaned back in his seat, and placed his index finger to his temple. He glared at Travis for a long moment and Travis unyieldingly glared back.

"Check him," he said to one of his aides who stepped over and frisked Travis.

"He's clean," answered his henchman.

"You know from your profession that the drug trade is a billion-dollar business that has two sides: the legitimate side and the dark side; one cannot exist without the other. Pharmaceutical companies spend millions of dollars each year on research in hopes of finding new medicines that will make them a large profit. Those big companies don't want to find a cure for diseases; they only want to relieve the symptoms. This keeps their customers coming back time and time again. In my business I don't give a damn about giving people false hope for miracle cures. I give them what they want. I give them the ability to escape from their reality and misery. And you, my friend, have created something that everyone will want."

"If someone overdoses on it, they will die," Travis said.

"So fucking what! You can die taking prescription medicine just as easily as you can illegal drugs. In the end, we all die." Hatcher let his words linger in the air.

"You will make Cougars for me and only me. I will distribute it around the world and together we'll introduce something more powerful than cocaine or heroin."

Hatcher snapped his fingers. One of the henchmen

placed a large briefcase on Alex's lap. "I'm going to assign some people to you and Alex. I want you to make me one-hundred-thousand pills. There is a lot of money in that briefcase. It should be enough to get the job done. And Travis, don't stop working your day job just yet. I have something I want you to do for me." Hatcher popped his fingers again and another person brought in a bottle of wine and glasses. "Let us drink to our arrangement," Hatcher said. All three men held up their glasses and toasted to the moment.

Chapter 23
Jasmine

Jasmine stood in the bathroom mirror putting the finishing touches on her makeup. She was waiting on her sister, Lauren, to come pick her up because they decided it was time for a girls' night out. They were heading to a nightclub for an evening of fun, laughter, and anything else that came their way. Jasmine had decided to wear her sexy blue jeans, which accentuated her behind and long legs. She also had a pair of favorite gladiator high-heeled shoes and a low-cut top. Once she was finished with her makeup, she squirted on some of her most seductive perfume. She then walked into her bedroom and selected a small purse to carry. As she exited her bedroom and descended the staircase, her doorbell chimed.

"Hey babe," Jasmine said as she greeted her sister wearing a blue jean miniskirt with a green top and strapless heels. Jasmine looked her sister over and gave her approval.

"You're showing off all of your big, sexy legs," Jasmine said.

"You're damn right, I am. I am too damn sexy to just sit around the house being grumpy. Are you ready?" Lauren asked.

"Just about," Jasmine said, walking over to a nearby closet and grabbed a light jacket. "Let's go."

"I'm so tired of being upset over LeMar. Tonight I just want to go out, have myself a few drinks, dance with some young men and just do whatever," Lauren explained as she opened her car door.

Once they got situated inside, Jasmine said, "Girl, I don't know what is going on with Travis and me. He acts so hot and cold. One minute he behaves as if he wants to be with me, then the next he's as cold as the Antarctic. I'm the type of woman who has a high sex drive and I need the dick on a regular basis. I can't deal with him just wanting to keep shit casual. I got things a little twisted by suggesting that we get a little more serious. But I couldn't help it. I swear his dick is so damn good that I had a damn out-of-body experience fucking him. That's the type of lovemaking that can screw a woman's head up."

"What do you mean you had an 'out-of-body experience'?"

"Girl, I've done some shit with Travis that I've never done with any man. It's just something about him that I just can't shake. We had anal sex and I have never in my life wanted to do that. But he was putting it down so excellently and I was so damn hot that I took it. I was sick and my stomach was uneasy for a few days, but after that I was cool," Jasmine said.

"Girl, I just can't do that anal thing. More power to you on that tip. Would you do that again, or was that one of those one-time-only deals?" Lauren asked.

"I'd let him do it again, but he'd have to be more gentle."

"Well, let me just say this and then I'm going to leave the shit alone. I get a funny vibe when I'm around Travis. I don't know what it is, but something about him just doesn't sit right with me." Lauren stated what was on her mind.

"I'll admit he can be a little arrogant, but overall he's an okay guy. Of course from my perspective, his best asset is his dick. For some reason, his shit is like gold to me." Jasmine laughed.

"What has he been up to?"

"Actually, it's funny you should mention that. He's been assigned to work with another team. Some other special project the president of the company put him on because he complained about having his research interrupted. He works on a different floor, so I don't see him as much at work. I've been poking his ass every day on Facebook though." Jasmine laughed and then continued talking. "As pathetic as this may sound, I still want to fuck him. We haven't spent any intimate time together in weeks. And like you, I have my needs. Ever since we did the anal thing, I have been craving dick. I mean I've really been hot. It's like my sexual desire has kicked into overdrive. My vibrator has been getting a serious workout." Jasmine chuckled.

"Oh Lord, Jasmine, that was really too much information."

"Whatever, but I do know this, I'm not going to keep calling him to ask for some of his precious time because Jasmine Sallie does not sit around waiting on some man to bring the beef. If I'm forced to go out and hunt down some new dick, I will."

"Amen to that," Lauren said as she turned up the radio. The old school jam "It Takes Two" by Rob Base was playing.

"Old school for life, baby. When I was in college, this song here was the shit," Jasmine shouted as she grooved to the music.

"My favorite college song was 'Wild Thang' by Tone Loc. Do you remember how I'd go around just saying that phrase?" Lauren asked.

"Oh yeah, between that and your obsession with the movie *I'm Gonna Git You Sucka*, you drove me crazy." Jasmine laughed.

"Come on, you've got to admit that movie was funny as hell. I still laugh every time I think about the part where the dude went into prison in the seventies and then when he got out it was like a decade later," Lauren said.

"Oh yeah and he had the fish swimming in his shoes." Jasmine started laughing aloud with her sister.

"Yeah, yeah, yeah. Now that was some stupid shit, but it was just too damn funny."

"Damn, Lauren, we were in our twenties back then and didn't have a care in the world. And the sorority parties we went to. God, those were good times. Where does the time go?"

"Time is never on our side. The more we want it to slow down, the quicker it moves," Lauren said as they drove down the highway toward their destination.

WHEN JASMINE AND LAUREN ARRIVED AT THE CLUB, there was excitement and energy on the streets. The weather had finally warmed up and waves of partygoers were walking in the streets traveling from one club to another. Lauren used the nightclub's valet service to park her car. When they entered the club there was loud music, flashing lights, and a massive gathering of people dancing to Rick James' "Super Freak." Jasmine and Lauren maneuvered their way through the crowd and found a spot at the bar. They ordered themselves something to drink. No sooner than Lauren's drink arrived did some young man come up to her and ask for a dance.

"Go on. Have fun," Jasmine said as she encouraged her sister to enjoy herself.

"I'm a super freak, I'm super freaky yow!" Lauren said as she made her way to the dance floor.

As the night continued on, Jasmine and Lauren had danced to many songs and had a particularly grand time dancing to the Casper Slide.

"Okay, everyone, this is DJ Boogie Child. How y'all feeling tonight?" The DJ interrupted the music to try to get the crowd pumped up.

"Is anyone celebrating a birthday tonight?" A loud roar arose from the crowd again. DJ Boogie Child decided to have a contest to see which male had the sexiest chest. He stopped the music for a moment and selected volunteers from the crowd.

"Come on, let's move closer. I want to see this," Jasmine said to her sister. They moved closer to the stage so they could see. Four young men stood before them; all of them looked scrumptious to both Jasmine and Lauren.

"Who do you think is going to win?" Lauren spoke purposely in Jasmine's ear.

"I don't know, we'll have to wait and see what they're working with."

"Now, I'm going to play some music for each of these guys. As I play the music they're going to do a strip-tease, taking off only their shirts."

"Let them take it all off," Lauren yelled out and the crowd agreed with her. All of the young men on the stage laughed with embarrassment. The first guy stepped forward and danced to Justine Timberlake's "Sexy Back." He had a strip of hair down the center of his chest, but his pectoral muscles were very well-developed. The next guy danced to a song by Kanye West called "Love Lockdown." His chest was nicer looking, but he needed to work on his abs. The third guy danced to a song called "Body on Me" by Nelly.

"Oh, now he has a nice body," Jasmine said to Lauren as she admired the sensual way he moved.

The fourth guy danced to "Whatever You Like" by T.I.

"Yeah, baby, work it!" Lauren screamed out for the fourth guy who actually had mannerisms like the iconic rapper. His chest and shoulders were filled with tattoos and he was very skinny.

It was clear that the third guy had the sexiest chest. He had smooth chocolate skin, a six-pack, strong shoulders and defined biceps. The third guy won the contest with ease.

"Okay, what's your name, man, and how old are you?" asked DJ Boogie Child before placing the microphone in front of the young man's lips so he could answer.

"My name's Paul and I'm twenty-four," he answered.

"Now, Paul, I've got a can of whipped cream in my hand." The DJ held it up to show everyone. "I'm going to spray some on your chest and I want you to pick a woman out of the audience that you think will lick it off of you." The audience exploded with a loud roar.

"I can choose anybody, right?" asked Paul as he searched the crowd.

"Yeah, but it has to be someone who you think is freaky enough and bold enough to do it."

"Right there. I think she'll do it." Paul pointed into the crowd.

"Who? The one wearing the blue top?" asked DJ Boogie Child.

"Nah, sexy right there with the long hair and green eyes," Paul said, pointing directly at Jasmine.

"Oh, shit girl, he's talking about you?" Lauren laughed and then pushed her forward.

"Yeah, her," Paul said.

"Go on up there, girl, and show him a thing or two." Lauren laughed out loud.

"Do I have a sign on my back that says 'Freak of the Week' or something?" Jasmine asked.

"Will you do it?" DJ Boogie Child asked.

Jasmine looked at Paul who looked like he couldn't wait for her to agree.

"Young guys. Always ready to take on something that's a little too much for them to handle," Jasmine said aloud as she approached the stage.

Lauren and the rowdy crowd cheered loudly.

"What's your name, baby?" DJ Boogie Child asked.

"Jasmine."

"Okay, Jasmine. I'm going to spray your name on his chest, and I want you to lick it all off before he cums in his pants and before the whipped cream slides all the way down his belly."

"I want to lick it off of his stomach," Jasmine said.

The crowd cheered. Paul spread his legs, placed his hands behind him and arched his back so that his chest pushed forward. The whipped cream was sprayed on and Jasmine took her time and traced the letters with her tongue. Paul was clearly enjoying the erotic moment because Jasmine noticed that he was trembling with delight. Jasmine, who had gotten hot, had decided to increase the intensity by rotating the palm of her left hand in a circular motion around his crotch. By the time Jasmine got to the letter "M," Paul's knees buckled under the titillating pleasure of Jasmine's tongue. DJ Boogie Child made fun of the young man for not being able to handle it and then gave them both tickets to an upcoming concert.

Jasmine left the stage laughing and then rejoined her sister at the bar.

"You are so crazy," Lauren said, shaking her head.

"I'm having such a good time. Thanks for getting me out of the house," Jasmine said.

"I need to run to the bathroom," Lauren said.

"Okay, I'll come with you."

As they made their way toward the restroom, Paul grabbed hold of Jasmine's hand.

"Can I talk to you for a minute?" Paul asked, licking his lips.

"Lauren, I'll be there in a second."

Lauren acknowledged her and then continued on her way. Paul pulled Jasmine over toward a corner of the room. He leaned his shoulder against the wall and looked at Jasmine lustfully.

"Can I help you, Paul?" Jasmine knew that he was

undressing her with his eyes, and she got a kick out of knowing he desired her.

Paul licked his lips. "Do you think we can hook up?"

"When?" Jasmine asked.

"Tonight. I don't live too far from here." Paul was moving in for the kill.

"Paul—"

"Wait a minute." Paul shivered a little bit. "I can still feel your tongue on me. I want to experience that again."

"We've just met and—"

"Shhhh," Paul interrupted and then leaned in closer to her ear. "I've got some Viagra and I've got some Cougars for you. Come on now. I know that I want you and I know you're just dying to have a little fun."

"What is Cougars?" Jasmine had never heard of that.

"Oh, you haven't heard?" Paul asked.

"No, I'm afraid that I haven't."

"Cougars is like…" Paul searched the heavens for an answer. "It's like a mind-blowing stimulant that just makes sex seem like an out-of-this-world ride."

"No thank you, Paul. I think I want to stay *in* this world," Jasmine said as she stepped away from him.

"Hey, don't knock it until you try it. It's the best shit out here," he spoke loudly which caused Jasmine to move away at a quicker pace.

She went into the bathroom and freshened up. Once she was done, she and Lauren decided to go to another club. They drank some more, danced to a few more songs, and flirted with men. Even at the new club as Jasmine danced with another guy, he mentioned that he had Cougars if she wanted to have mind-blowing sex with him. Jasmine declined and wondered if she'd gotten too old for the game because she had no idea what Cougars was.

By the time Jasmine got back to her house, she insisted that Lauren stay for the night.

"You know that I am," Lauren said as she walked into the house. "I'll see you in the morning. We'll go out and have breakfast."

"Girl, by the time we wake up, it will be dinner-time," Jasmine joked.

"You're probably right. We'll just have to play it by ear," Lauren said and then walked toward the guest room.

Jasmine got out of her clothes, relaxed on her bed and turned on the television. As she adjusted her head on her pillow, she turned up the volume to catch the rebroadcast of the evening news. A reporter Angela Rivers was standing outside of Stroger Hospital giving her report.

"There is a new drug out on the black market that's causing quite a scare among health officials. It's a sexual enhancement pill called Cougars and ingesting it can lead to serious health problems and even cardiac arrest."

A news clip of a woman being rushed through the emergency room doors appeared on the screen.

didn't want to sound desperate. She exhaled, placed a pillow between her thighs and fantasized about Travis.

THE NEXT MORNING JASMINE AWOKE WITH A HANG-OVER. She lazily walked into her bathroom, opened up the medicine cabinet and removed a bottle of aspirin.

"Jasmine, girl, you've got to slow down a little," she said to her reflection. She filled a Dixie cup with water and took two tablets. She walked out of her bathroom and down the hall to the guest bedroom. She peeped inside the room and noticed that Lauren was flat on her back and snoring.

"She's getting louder in her old age," Jasmine whispered to herself as she stepped away. She went back to the bathroom and freshened up. Afterward, she headed down to the kitchen where she decided to cook breakfast. She turned on a nearby countertop radio and listened to an old school cut by Stevie Wonder, "Living for the City." She sang along with the melody as she prepared their food.

Thirty minutes later, just as she was pulling the butter-flaky biscuits out of the oven, Lauren dragged her tired self into the kitchen.

"What did you cook?" Lauren asked, still sounding sleepy.

"Oh, I didn't cook anything for you," Jasmine said. She waited for the disappointed look to form on her sister's face.

"I know good and damn well you didn't get up this

morning and only cook some food for yourself." Lauren was all set to be totally pissed off. Jasmine laughed.

"You know I wouldn't do you like that," Jasmine joked with her a little more.

"Don't you have a hangover like I do?" Lauren asked as she sat down and rested her forehead in the palm of her hand.

"I did wake up with a headache a while ago, but I took some aspirin. There is some upstairs in my bathroom."

"Good, because I certainly need some. Do you have any coffee here?" Lauren asked. "You know I can't function without my morning cup of coffee."

"By the time you go freshen up and come back down, I will have brewed some for you."

"Are the extra clothes that I brought over still in the back coat closet?" Lauren asked.

"Yeah, they are. I put your door key to my house in your duffle bag. You must've left it from another time that you stayed over."

"Okay, I'll be sure to put it back on my key chain," Lauren said as she walked away.

FIFTEEN MINUTES LATER, Lauren and Jasmine were sitting down enjoying their meal. They talked about the wild events of the previous night before talking about their lovers.

"In all seriousness, is it really over between you and LeMar?" Jasmine asked.

"Hell yeah, it's over. Shit, he's gotten two girls pregnant. I can't date a man who's got baby mama drama, and he's got plenty of it. His stupid ass," Lauren said with a sour taste in her mouth.

"When I came home last night, I checked to see if Travis had called me, but he hadn't. No text message or nothing. I guess I thought we could at least be cordial with one another if things didn't work out. I don't have the foggiest idea why I thought an office romance would stand the test of time. That's one of the oldest traps in the book."

"Do you know what we need?" Lauren asked.

"No, what?"

"A vacation. We should take a trip to Europe."

"Now that's what I'm talking about. I'll probably find myself a hot, young piece of ass over there," Jasmine joked.

"I'm serious about that. I think we'd have a blast and I know Millie and Tiffany would love the—"

At that moment Lauren's cell phone rang, interrupting the conversation. She looked at the caller ID and saw that it was her boss.

"Hey, what's going on?" Lauren asked, wondering why she was being called on her off day. "No, I didn't hear that. When did it happen? You're kidding. Okay, give me twenty minutes and I'll be there," Lauren said and then hung up the phone.

"What was that about?" Jasmine asked.

"Senator Yolanda Cobb has been found dead. It looks like she went into cardiac arrest. The rumor is that she was taking Cougars."

"You've got to be kidding me. I just saw a news report on this and a strange thought—"

Lauren cut Jasmine off before she could finish her sentence. "No. If it turns out to be true, the media is going to have a field day with it. I've been assigned to the case. There goes our vacation plans," Lauren said as she gulped down her coffee. Lauren went back to the room where she'd slept and changed clothes. She grabbed her duffle bag and then headed toward the door.

"I'll be in touch," Lauren said as she rushed out of the house.

Chapter 24
Travis

Travis was stunned with how quickly his concoction had hit the streets, spread and become popular. Within the first two weeks, Hatcher was able to provide him with a substantial amount of cash money that was more than double his annual income as a chemist. Travis knew that at some point he'd need to have a conversation with Hatcher about increasing his percentage of the profits. It was all too easy for Travis to fall in love with dirty money and the lies that come with it.

Travis, Alex, and Hatcher's men set up a lab in one of Hatcher's many ill-gotten properties around the city. Alex ran the pill press while Hatcher's men bagged the pills for distribution. Travis paid off an employee who oversaw ordering materials that the pharmaceutical company purchased; he also paid off Sam the security guard. Travis had the employee order extra material for his needs. The shipments would be left on the dock for a late-night pickup by Hatcher's men. Sam would open up the dock for them so they could load their truck. On the weeknights and weekends, Travis spent the remainder of his time creating large amounts of a powdered substance which would later be pressed into the Cougars pills by Alex. Travis attempted to show Alex how to create the powder one day while they were in the makeshift lab, but Alex wasn't interested. His interests were two-fold: He wanted a cut of the profits and he wanted to get away from Hatcher.

"Hatcher has me doing this shit for free, man. I'm not getting a cut of the profits. He said that since I owe him so much money, I'd better do as he says or face the consequences. I hate that motherfucker, man. If I'm not available for his every little need that fool will kill me. I don't want to die, Travis. I just want to get my life back. I thought when I introduced this Cougars shit to him, we'd call it even. I mean, if it weren't for me he would've never met you. But he doesn't see it like that. I've got fucking bills to pay and flying his cargo all over the place is going to land my black ass in a federal prison."

"Maybe I can talk to him for you. And neither one of us is going to prison so get that shit out your head. I don't want you to think it or speak it into existence," Travis said.

"Fine, I won't say it or think about it, but diplomacy doesn't work when you're dealing with Hatcher—the guy's an agent of the devil!" Alex raised his voice in anger.

"Just calm down, okay? We'll figure something out," Travis assured him.

"That's easy for you to say. I'm the one taking all of the risks! Pressing these damn pills, then flying them around to drop-off points. Shit, I want to get paid for my stress and anxiety, too. You're getting paid. Why can't I?"

Alex sat down in a chair that was positioned against a wall in the basement. He placed his face in his hands for second, clenched his teeth, then slapped his forehead with the palms of his hands. "I feel like I'm going crazy. I can't believe that I've fucked up my life like this. I want to run away from all of this, Travis, but I don't have any money. I'm flat broke."

"Don't fucking flip out on me now, Alex. I need you. If you'll just hang in there a little while longer, I will have made enough cash for the both of us to disappear for a long time. Selling this shit can easily turn into a million-dollar-a-week empire! Now get your shit in check!" Travis snapped. "I'll give you some money. How much do you need?"

"Shit, man, how much do you have?" Alex glanced up at him.

"Enough for now," Travis answered. "Will five thousand hold you for a minute?"

"Make it ten thousand," Alex requested.

"Fine. I'll get the money to you," Travis agreed without blinking an eye.

"Just like that." Alex popped his fingers. "You suddenly have ten grand you can let go and not miss?"

"Yeah, I have it like that now. You're my boy. If you'd just stand by my side a little longer, you'll never have to worry about money again."

"How do you figure?" Alex didn't want promises; he wanted to know the details and the plan.

Travis walked over to Alex and kneeled down beside him. "I'm working on an ever stronger version of Cougars at work. I just about have the right mixture, too."

"I thought you said they shelved the project?" Alex didn't understand how Travis was able to continue his research.

"I'm fucking the president of the company on the side," Travis confessed.

"How in the hell did that happen, and what about Jasmine?" Alex asked.

"I'm still fucking Jasmine. I'm not done with her yet."

"You shouldn't do Jasmine like that, man, but I'm not going to get in your business about that. What I want to know is how did you get the president of the company in the sack?" Alex just had to know.

"I joined the Sex Club List again, but this time I used an alias. I got a call one night from a very lonely woman. We agreed to meet. I popped some Viagra and went to the hotel. When I knocked on the door of Room 1865, Helen, the president of the company, opened it. She was a bit embarrassed and there was an awkward moment. I suggested that we order a bottle of wine from room service and just talk for a little while. She was reluctant, but agreed to it. While we waited for room service she didn't say much. She was rather distant with me and gazed out the window at traffic moving along Lake Shore Drive. I turned on the little clock radio and that classic Phil Collins song, 'In the Air Tonight,' filled the room. I guess the melody was soothing to her because she started singing along.

"When the wine was delivered I stepped out into the hallway and told the employee I'd take it from there. Once he was gone, I crushed up a pill and sprinkled it into her wineglass and filled it up. She drank the entire glass and asked for another. By the third glass, she'd loosened up and told me that she thought something was wrong with her because she'd been suffering with female sexual dysfunction. She said that she hadn't had an orgasm in a long time. Her girlfriend introduced her to the Sex List and that night was her very first time using it, which was why she was so nervous and utterly shocked when she saw me.

"I approached her from behind, began kissing her shoulders and neck," Travis continued. "I caressed her breasts and took off her blouse and bra, then unzipped her skirt. Next I squatted down and told her to step out of it. I liked her red pumps so I told her to leave them on. I quickly got undressed, then got down on my knees.

I ran the tip of my tongue around the curvature of her calf muscle, and up the back of her legs, and over the hump of her ass, to the bow in her back. I could hear how her breathing pattern changed and how warm her skin had gotten. I knew the drug was taking effect. I rose to my feet, pressed my dick between the cheeks of her ass and combed my fingers through her pubic hair. I toyed with her clit and slipped a finger inside of her. She asked me what I was doing to her and I said, 'I'm about to give you everything you've been missing.' I turned her around, lifted her up and pressed her back against a window. She wrapped her legs around my waist and said, 'I can't believe how wet I am. I'm usually very dry.' It took me a minute to get my dick into her tight pussy but when I did, I could tell she hadn't had dick in a long time. By the time Phil Collins bellowed out 'Oh Lord' and the drums sequence hit its climax, I was fucking her hard against the glass. Her hips popped and she began moving wildly, as if all of her untamed energy had been unleashed. She was a squirter and before I knew it, my feet were sliding around in a puddle of her juices. She was biting, clawing at my back, and screaming out my name. We went at it for hours before we both were just too damn exhausted to do anything else.

"When I saw her at work, I asked if I could be moved to a different team, citing personality differences between Jasmine and me. Helen was more than happy to move me. She gave me a bigger office and told me I could continue my research, but to keep it under my hat."

"Damn," Alex said totally blown away by Travis's account of events. "Did she get sick like some of the other people who've taken the drug?"

"I believe so because she didn't show up at work for a couple of days," Travis said.

"Do you feel guilty about people getting sick and even dying from taking this?" Alex cautiously asked, then saw Travis's eyes turn cold.

"Even prescription drugs have side effects, Alex. Drug seekers know the risks before they even start using narcotics. Cocaine and PCP can kill you just as easily as Cougars can, but people still want to get high. People will even mix prescription medicine to get high." Travis walked back toward the pill press machine. "They'll even take something as simple as cough syrup and mix it up until it becomes something stronger. So no, I don't feel guilty at all."

There was a moment of silence in the room, but it was interrupted when one of Hatcher's men came down to tell Alex he was needed at the airport.

"See what I mean, man?" Alex griped. "I'm tired of this shit." Alex rose to his feet and walked away.

TRAVIS WAS DRIVING OVER TO JASMINE'S HOUSE to pay her a visit. It had been weeks since they'd spent any serious time with each other and he, being driven by his lust for her, wanted to be inside of her warm folds. In spite of the wild sex he'd had with Helen, she had nothing on Jasmine. It was something about the way Jasmine could look into his eyes and see his soul. In his mind he believed that she'd always want him. As narcissistic as it sounded, Travis knew that Jasmine loved the way he made love to her. Even before he'd drugged her up and given her a dose of Cougars, she was completely into him and was trying to take the time to get to know his heart. He was no longer angry with her, especially now that he was able to continue his work. That is what really mattered to him most and it was the drive behind everything he did. Jasmine had to learn that she should never compete with his career, because she'd lose out every time. She'd have to live with being second to that.

TRAVIS UNDERSTOOD THAT AFTER WEEKS of only speaking to Jasmine casually on Facebook whenever the mood hit him, that he couldn't just waltz back into her life empty handed. So to help get back into her good graces, he stopped at Tiffany's Jeweler and had the saleswoman assist him with picking out something nice that read, "I apologize." After looking at a selection of bracelets and rings, Travis found the perfect gift. It was a pair of Elsa Peretti open heart earrings with pavé diamonds. The gift cost him five-thousand dollars, but he didn't mind because he knew Jasmine was worth it. In his grand scheme, he was seriously considering a place for Jasmine in the twisted castle he was building for himself.

Travis knew that when he arrived unannounced with a Tiffany's bag in one hand and a selection of roses in the other one, Jasmine wouldn't be so quick to turn him away. There was also one additional factor motivating Travis and that was the improved Cougars formula. Since Jasmine was his very first human test subject, he thought it appropriate for her to be his guinea pig for a second time. He didn't want to give Jasmine a choice in the matter. His mind had become twisted like that. He felt as if, to a certain degree, he owned her.

Travis pulled his car into Jasmine's driveway and parked it directly next to hers. He glanced at himself in the rearview mirror just to make sure he looked good one last time and then stepped out of his car. He rang her doorbell and waited. When the door swung open, Jasmine, who was wearing soft sweatpants and a clingy Mary J. Blige concert T-shirt, looked as sexy as ever to him.

"How are you doing, sexy?" Travis grinned at her. Jasmine folded her arms across her chest and shifted her weight from one foot to the other.

"What do you want, Travis? And why are you coming over unannounced?" Jasmine's voice was edgy and fully of confrontation.

"I came to see you, babe. I've missed you. I've been lonely without you," Travis explained.

"Yeah right. Go tell that line to some chickenhead. You didn't miss me." Jasmine didn't believe him.

"Yes I did, Jasmine. I swear to God I did. I've just been so busy at work and I brought you this. I'm making time to see you. Doesn't that mean something?" Travis gave her the sad puppy dog look.

"You do not look cute doing that, so just stop." Jasmine wasn't behaving the way he'd hoped.

"Can I come in?" he asked.

"For what?" Jasmine glanced down at the blue Tiffany's bag.

"So that I can give you these flowers and a gift I've picked up for you." Travis held them both up. Jasmine gazed past the gifts and directly into his eyes. Travis shook the gifts a little so she'd focus on them and not him. "Aren't you at least curious as to what I got for you?"

"You can't buy your way back into my life, Travis. Maybe I've moved on. It certainly appears that you have someone new. Don't think that I haven't heard about the rumors floating about Helen's sudden interest in you."

"Now why would you think that Helen and I have something going on?" Travis flat out denied the accusation.

"I have people who let me know things," Jasmine answered sarcastically.

"Who?"

"You don't need to know who, you just need to know that there are rumors floating around."

"Well then, that's just what they are: *rumors*." Travis lowered the gifts.

"Well, Sam says—shit," Jasmine said as she had slipped up and ratted out Sam.

"Sam the security guard?" Travis started laughing. "You're going to believe that punk over me. Come on now, Jasmine, don't get played like that." Travis challenged her common sense. "You know that boy has the hots for you and is probably just trying to throw salt on me because he's undoubtedly heard rumors about us."

Jasmine thought about what he said and then gave him the benefit of the doubt. "Well, I am curious as to what you've picked out. Come on in." Jasmine stepped aside and shut the door behind him.

She followed him into the kitchen and then pulled down a vase for the flowers.

"What are you in here doing?" Travis asked.

"I'm cleaning out the closet in my bedroom," Jasmine answered as she placed the flowers in the vase. Travis approached her from behind and set the Tiffany's box on the countertop in front of her.

Jasmine stared at it for a moment and tried to determine if she should accept his gift.

"Go on, open it. I got it for you," Travis encouraged her as he placed his hands on her shoulders and placed sweet kisses on the back of her ear. Jasmine's body immediately reacted to his touch. She pulled her shoulders up to her ears and paused as goose bumps of sensitivity formed everywhere. When the feeling subsided, she opened the box.

"Oh wow, Travis. These are beautiful," Jasmine said, taking them out of the box. "These must've cost you a small fortune."

"They weren't cheap," Travis joked.

"I can't accept this. It's too much." Jasmine tried to return the gift.

"Don't do that to me, Jasmine. This is how I say how sorry I am. Can you forgive me?" Travis asked.

Jasmine closed her eyes and felt Travis's fingers slip under the fabric of her sweatpants. She wasn't wearing any underwear and his long fingers quickly found what they were searching for.

"Yes." Jasmine gave in to the moment. "I forgive you."

TRAVIS AWOKE AT 6 A.M. THE NEXT DAY to the sound of his cell phone ringing. He attempted to ignore the call, but whoever was trying to reach him was insistent on talking to him. He was exhausted from making love to Jasmine. The improved formula was certainly more powerful than its predecessor. Travis got out of bed and walked over to retrieve his pants which had his cell phone hooked to the belt. He removed his phone. Hatcher was calling. Travis exited Jasmine's bedroom and went downstairs so that he could talk in private.

"Hello," Travis answered.

"We have a fucking problem, Travis." Hatcher didn't calibrate his words.

"Problem? What are you talking about?"

"Your boy, Alex, has fucked up and pissed me off. He was supposed to make a delivery and he didn't. I found him at a casino spending my money."

"Shit," Travis hissed. "How much did he spend?" Travis asked, thinking that perhaps he could settle the debt.

"That doesn't matter. No one steals from me. Alex right now is paying for his mistake. Hear, listen."

Travis heard horrific screams. It sounded as if Alex was being tortured in the most gruesome way possible.

"You hear that, my friend?" Hatcher got back on the phone.

"Oh my God, what are you doing to him?" Travis got very nervous and upset as Alex's dreadful shrieks got louder.

"It's amazing what people tell you when you've broken their knees, and cut off their fingers."

"Oh God!" Travis covered his mouth with one hand. He didn't like the way Alex sounded.

"Alex tells me you've made an advanced formula. It sounds like you're trying to do business on the side without me."

"Hatcher, no, that's not true," Travis quickly explained.

"Look at it from my perspective. If the drug companies

approve it, I'm out of business. I told you to keep your job so that you could order supplies until I got an inside connection for us. Who told you to improve it without my fucking permission!"

"I wanted to do it on my own!" Travis snapped back.

"You don't do shit unless I tell you to!" Hatcher shouted. "Pull out his teeth with the wrench!" Hatcher barked orders to his men.

"For yelling at me, your friend is going to lose his teeth."

A moment later, Travis heard the shrill of Alex's agony. "Your friend is in misery."

"Hatcher!" Travis tried to reason with him.

Hatcher started laughing. "You should hear the way he's cried for you. Listen."

"Travis, please, man. I don't want to die like this. Please, help me, man. Please, please, please," Alex howled again as another tooth was pulled.

"Okay, I get your point, Hatcher," Travis said now fully understanding what Alex was trying to tell him. Hatcher was evil to his very core.

"No, you don't get my point. That's the problem."

"What can we do to fix this?" Travis asked. There was a long pause, then Hatcher laughed sinisterly.

"I'll tell you what. A life for a life. Your life for his. You come work for me in South America or your best friend dies."

"What if I just give you the formula in exchange for his life?" Travis asked.

"My terms are non-negotiable. That's going to cost your friend his big toe," Hatcher said. Travis pulled the phone away from his ear because he couldn't stand to hear what was happening to his only friend.

"I'm on my way. Okay! Just stop torturing him. Please!" Travis said. Hatcher laughed.

"Alex is pretty fucked up, right? If you're not at the Palwaukee Airport in twelve hours, Alex will be dead and you'll be hunted down like a dog and killed. And bring me all of my cash back!"

Hatcher then hung up the phone. Travis's knees buckled beneath him and he fell to the floor. He began to have a panic attack. His breathing became labored and he clutched his chest. It never occurred to him that things would get this far out of control. Travis's first inclination was to take the money and run, but he couldn't turn his back on Alex. Not after he'd begged him for help like that.

"Jasmine. I need you, baby," Travis called out. He ran back upstairs and tried to wake her, but the drug had placed her in a very deep sleep. "Come on, baby, wake up. I need you. I need your help." Travis slapped her face several times, but Jasmine didn't wake up. He put his ear to her chest to make sure she was still breathing. Thankfully she was.

"Jasmine!" Travis screamed out her name, but Jasmine was out of it. "Fuck, fuck, fuck, fuck!" Travis screamed out. He paced the floor and tried to think of what his next move should be.

"Fuck it!" he said and walked over to Jasmine. He removed the earrings that he'd gotten her, gathered his belongings, and rushed out of her house. The small container he'd kept the Cougars pills inside had fallen out of his pocket.

Chapter 25
Jasmine

Forty-five minutes after Travis left, Jasmine awoke feeling very sick. The mucus in her mouth was very thick and blocking her airway. She rolled onto her side, gagged and then vomited on the floor. She felt dizzy and confused. Her body was twitching uncontrollably and she felt as if her nerves were ablaze. She tried to sit up but couldn't. She vomited voluntarily again on the floor. Her vision became blurred and the room started spinning out of control. Then unexpectedly her ears began ringing. Jasmine began to panic because she didn't know what was going on. With all of the strength she could muster she willed herself to stand to her feet, but slipped on her own vomit and fell to the floor. The ringing in her ears was constant now. She didn't know if the noise was in her head or if it was her doorbell. She couldn't tell. Jasmine began heaving again. Once she stopped, she reached up and tried to pull herself back up by using a nearby nightstand as support. She fell back to the floor hard. Jasmine cried for a moment and then as best as she could, crawled out of her bedroom. She now realized that someone was ringing her doorbell. Crawling over to the staircase, she saw someone step inside of her home. She thought it was Travis and tried to call to him.

"Jasmine!" She recognized Lauren's voice, but then blacked out.

WHEN JASMINE AWOKE AGAIN, SHE WAS FEELING BETTER. Her mouth and throat were very dry and she wanted a drink. She slowly rolled her head to the right just as her sister, Lauren, was walking into the room. Jasmine slowly raised her right hand which had some type of tubing attached to it.

"I'm here." Lauren quickly grabbed her hand. Jasmine had a difficult time keeping her eyes open, but was glad that she could see her sister clearly.

"Water," Jasmine whispered and then winced because her throat was so dry. Lauren grabbed a cup already filled with water from the bed stand and helped Jasmine to drink it. Jasmine savored the taste of liquid and then closed her eyes briefly.

"Jasmine," Lauren called to her.

Jasmine opened her eyes again and focused on her sister. "Yeah."

"What happened?" Lauren asked.

"I don't know," Jasmine answered wearily.

"The doctor says you're very lucky that I found you when I did. You could've died," Lauren whispered as

Jasmine coughed. "I let myself into the house with the spare key because you didn't answer. I just sensed something was wrong."

"I'm glad you had that key," Jasmine whispered.

"So am I."

"I'm so blessed to have a sister like you who comes to check up on me. I didn't know what to do." Jasmine started crying.

"Don't cry. It's okay," Lauren said as she grabbed a Kleenex and wiped the tears that were rolling toward Jasmine's ear.

"Funny thing is, I'd come over there to show you the toxicology report from Senator Yolanda Cobb. I wanted to ask you how a person would go about making such a strong poison like Cougars. Never in a million years would I have ever thought you were taking the drug. But I'm here for you and I'm going help you get through this addiction of yours."

"I just woke up feeling horrible. I'm not taking Cougars," Jasmine said.

"Jasmine, the poison was in your bloodstream. The doctor told me himself. I even saw the toxicology report. Plus there was a pill bottle filled with the drug on your floor by the door."

Jasmine started crying again. She now realized what Travis had done. Now she understood that he'd poisoned her with the experimental aphrodisiac he'd been trying to perfect.

"It's going to be alright, Jasmine." Lauren stroked her sister's hair. Once Jasmine got her emotions under control, she looked into her sister's eyes.

"Travis poisoned me. Those are his pills. I didn't know he even had them. He probably made them himself," Jasmine explained. As she spoke, it became clear to Lauren what had happened.

"I'm going to call his ass in for questioning!" Lauren pulled out her cell phone to let her colleagues know that Travis Adams was a person of interest in the narcotics case they were investigating as well as a wanted man for attempted murder.

"What's Travis's address?" Lauren asked. Jasmine gave it to her and Lauren relayed the message. "It's two p.m. I'll meet you at his residence in an hour. I want to be there when he's picked up," Lauren said before she hung up the phone.

"I have to go, but I'm coming back," Lauren said as she kissed Jasmine on the forehead. "I've called Tiffany and Millie. They both dropped everything and are on their way."

"Go get that bastard and drop-kick his ass for me. I'll be okay," Jasmine whispered. Lauren gathered her belongings and headed out the door in a rush.

Chapter 26
Travis

When Travis left Jasmine's house, he stopped by the pharmaceutical lab and grabbed all of the files and notes he could find on the experiments he'd been doing. On his way out, Sam stopped him and asked, "Is everything alright?"

Travis didn't bother to answer him; he just walked out of the building as fast as he could. He then drove back to Jasmine's house to see if she was awake yet. When he turned onto her street, he stopped the car and put it in reverse. Travis positioned his sedan so he could view the activity from a distance. He saw paramedics bringing a body out on a gurney. Travis feared the worst.

"I've killed Jasmine. She probably overdosed on Cougars." Unwilling to face the consequences, Travis drove off in a reckless manner.

It was 2:45 P.M. Travis was at his apartment trying to gather up as much of his belongings as he could. He raced around his apartment shoving clothes and money into a large suitcase. Now he looked forward to going with Hatcher because it was better than facing murder charges. Out of nervousness, he glanced out of his front window and saw two squad cars pull up.

"Fuck! How did they find me so quick?" he howled. He grabbed his suitcase and rushed out the back door. Glad that he'd parked his car in the alley, he tossed his suitcase in the trunk and hurried around to the driver's side of the car.

"Travis, stop!" he heard Lauren scream. Travis had no intention of doing so. He fired up his car and sped down the alleyway.

Before long there was a line of police cars pursuing him. Driving like a madman, Travis did everything he could to outrun them: ran red lights, sideswiped cars and almost ran down several pedestrians. He had no regard for anyone's life but his own. Travis got on the Kennedy Expressway and cut off an eighteen-wheeler. His sedan was no match for the speed and training of the police officers pursuing him. Travis tried to shake the police officers by swerving abruptly to exit the highway. He turned the wheel too hard and crashed into a concrete barrier. Airbags deployed, the front of the car was smashed and a section of the dashboard collapsed onto his legs. Pleased that his legs weren't crushed, Travis quickly maneuvered himself out of the car via the passenger door. He started running down the exit ramp as fast he could. He raced across several lanes of traffic and was narrowly missed by several vehicles that swerved to avoid hitting him. Travis raced through the parking lot of a fast-food restaurant, climbed over a chain link fence and continued on. He had no idea where he was running. Travis ducked into a gangway between two brick apartment buildings. He stopped, pressed his back against one of the structures and leaned over to catch his breath. It was then he noticed that one pants leg was soaked with blood. There was a tear in his pants and a nasty gash on the side of his right leg.

"Fuck!" he growled angrily. He knew his badly injured leg would not take him much farther.

Once his breathing regulated, he began looking around for a place to hide. He knew the police were not far behind because he could still hear sirens wailing. Seeing no safe harbor, he cautiously continued on toward the rear of the buildings. He made it to the alley and looked in both directions making sure no police were present. He limped as best as he could toward a safer location. When he reached the end of the alley, he saw several teen boys standing around a car listening to loud music.

"Damn, man! Your leg is fucked up!" shouted one of the boys who pointed at him.

"Shhhh! Can I get a little help?" Travis asked.

"Hell no! I don't fucking know you!" snarled the young man as he and his buddies got inside the vehicle and drove off.

"Fuck it then!" Travis barked as he continued on, dragging his leg as if it was a heavy sack. He came across a backyard and noticed the back door to the house was open. An elderly woman stood at the sink washing dishes. Her back was turned to him so she didn't notice Travis was there. Desperate and deranged, Travis gave himself permission to do the unthinkable. He was going to force his way into the house and strong arm the elderly woman into helping him. He opened the gate to the yard and hobbled toward the open door. In his hastiness he didn't see the two pitbulls resting in another corner of the yard. By the time Travis spotted the hounds, they were charging toward him and barking viciously.

"Oh fuck!" Travis hollered out. He quickly turned and hauled ass as fast as he could before the dogs reached him. Travis continued on, but only made it to the end of the street before collapsing from a combination of blood loss, pain and exhaustion.

Moments later, Travis was surrounded by police officers. Once he was handcuffed, he was yanked to his feet when he saw Lauren approaching him. Travis smiled smugly as if none of what was happening was of real concern. When Lauren got within striking distance, she punched him in the face.

"That's for trying to kill my sister, you sick bastard! You're lucky she didn't die because if she had, I'd put a bullet between your eyes!"

"She's alive? That means it worked." A deranged expression formed on Travis' face. Lauren felt as if her message had not gotten through his thick skull, so she kicked him in the balls to drive her point home.

"Fuck you, too, bitch. This is police brutality. My rights have been violated." Travis argued as he coughed and gasped for air.

Lauren ignored him and began reading him his Miranda Rights. "Travis Adams, you have the right to remain silent. Anything you say or do can and will be used against you in a court of law. You have the right to an attorney. If you cannot afford an attorney, one will be appointed to you."

"I don't have a damn thing to say!" Travis glared at Lauren with arrogance and superiority as he was marched over to an emergency medical team who had just arrived for treatment.

TRAVIS WAS TAKEN INTO CUSTODY and driven to the police station where he was placed in an interrogation room. A short time later Lauren entered with another agent and sat down on the opposite side of the table.

"I don't have to tell you why you're here. You already know what this is about, am I correct, Travis?"

"I'm not saying a word without a lawyer," Travis answered insolently.

"Travis, the evidence found in the car you were driving will pretty much serve as the nails in your coffin. Why don't you make it easier on yourself and tell us how and who helped you distribute the drugs."

"I'm not saying anything until my attorney is here and a deal can be made." Travis stared directly into Lauren's eyes.

"Fine. We'll wait for your legal counsel to arrive. But answer this one question for me. Why did you do Jasmine that way?" Lauren had to know.

Travis squirmed around in his seat and tilted his head upward trying to decide if he should answer the question.

"Tell you what. Off the record, tell me why?" Lauren gave him another option.

Travis met her gaze once again. As he stared at her, he thought about how brilliant he was. Then his mind split and the psychopathic spirit within took full control.

"What's wrong with you? Why do you suddenly look like an insane lunatic?"

"I'm perfectly fine, Lauren." Travis inhaled deeply, then exhaled loudly as if he were taking in air for the very first time. "In fact, I've never felt better."

"Then answer my question."

Travis laughed and then said, "It was for the good of science. It was a necessary evil. Besides, she tried to control me and keep me from fulfilling my destiny…I couldn't have that."

Chapter 27
Jasmine

Three days after she'd been poisoned, Jasmine was at home and feeling much better. The toxins were now out of her system and thankfully, the test results from the blood, which was drawn before she was released, had come back normal. The attending physician explained to her how fortunate she was to still be alive because she could've easily gone into cardiac arrest.

Tiffany and Millie had both taken time out of their busy schedules to visit with her and nurse her back to good health. They'd cleaned up her house, cooked for her and done anything else which needed to be taken care of.

They were now all sitting on lawn chairs in Jasmine's backyard enjoying the beautiful warm day and drinking sun tea.

"I still can't believe that psychopath almost poisoned you to death," Millie said as she tried to comprehend Travis's madness.

"I just feel so stupid right now," Jasmine admitted. "I was his fool. I tried not to be but I was. I didn't want to think that he could stoop so low. He seemed so sincere and I believed in him. I'm still having a difficult time wrapping my mind around why he allowed himself to go down the road of madness."

"Because he was a crazy motherfucker, that's why." Tiffany chimed in. "He thought he was above the law and couldn't get caught."

"Hello, ladies," Lauren greeted everyone as she stepped through the sliding-glass patio door.

"Come here and let me give you yet another hug," Jasmine requested. Lauren approached her, leaned over and hugged her sister. "I love you so much." Jasmine started crying.

"I know," Lauren answered.

When Jasmine finally let her go, she noticed that both Millie and Tiffany were teary eyed. "I love you guys, too," Jasmine said.

There was a long moment of silence before Millie broke it. "So how's the investigation going?"

"It's not pretty." Lauren exhaled as she sat down.

"Not to change the subject here, but how did the probe into your case-fixing allegations turn out? Well, obviously it turned out fine; you're still a judge but what was that about?" Lauren asked.

"Honey, that's a long story for another day but the short of it is this: Another female judge who I didn't get along with started all of the bull. Apparently she used to date the young intern I was having an affair with.

He broke up with her just before he started dating me. You can pretty much fill in the blanks on why she tried to ruin my name," Millie explained. "Then there was the issue of my husband and his affair and oh, it was just one big mess. However, I'm happy to be divorced, single and available."

"Vindictive women. Ugh, they make my stomach turn." Tiffany scowled.

"So you're not seeing anyone right now?" Jasmine asked.

"No. After my husband and lover had a fistfight on the front lawn, that incident was pretty much the nail in the coffin on both relationships."

"I'm so sorry I wasn't there for you like I should've been," Jasmine said.

"Don't do that. There was nothing you could've done. That's behind me now and I want it to stay there," said Millie.

"Do you want to know what's going on with Travis?" Lauren asked.

"Yes. I want to know," answered Jasmine.

"We all want to know," Tiffany chimed in.

"Travis had all of his research documentation in his possession when he was arrested. He also had nearly a quarter of a million dollars stuffed in a suitcase. It is clear that the drug is something he designed and sold. He says that drug kingpin Hatcher McKean is responsible for distributing Cougars. When we apprehended

Travis, he was on his way to meet up with Hatcher in order to save his friend Alex's life."

"Why would he poison the hell out of Jasmine but try to save his boy? That sounds crazy," Millie said perplexed.

"There is no rhyme or reason to Travis's actions. He was ambitious and arrogant that caused him to blindly jump into the ring and wrestle with the devil. Needless to say, he lost the battle."

"So how's Alex mixed up in all of this?" Jasmine asked.

"That's the really tragic part. Alex had a gambling problem and got into debt with Hatcher. In order to repay him, Alex flew cargo, money, or whatever for Hatcher."

"So has Alex been arrested, too?" Tiffany asked.

"No. Alex is dead."

Jasmine gasped. "What?" She didn't believe what she was hearing.

"Yeah. Another unit found his remains in an airport hangar. He was tortured to death," Lauren explained.

Jasmine felt sorrowful and buried her face in her hands. She took a few deep breaths. "His family must be devastated."

"That's another bizarre thing about Alex. From what I understand, he came from a good family that had money. He didn't have to do what he did, he chose to."

"So what about Hatcher? Has a warrant been issued for his arrest?" Millie inquired.

"We don't truly know the real identity of Hatcher McKean. Travis and his lawyer have been cooperative with sharing information but whoever Hatcher is, he's well connected and was informed about Travis's arrest. He was able to stay a step ahead of us because the make-shift lab where Cougars was being made burned to the ground. Travis gave us the location of the houseboat in Florida where he met Hatcher, but the houseboat is gone and the property itself blew up in a suspicious gas line leak. Authorities in Florida are conducting a full investigation into how that happened."

"So Travis is going to be the fall guy for everything," Jasmine asked, wanting to make sure he paid the price for what he'd done.

"There is a very strong case against him. Sam, the security guard where you work, has also come forward with information after he'd heard about what Travis did to you. I think he was also afraid of being implicated for his role. But we're not interested in him," Lauren answered honestly as she reached over and placed her hand on top of her sister's.

"Don't you want to go and see the son-of-a-bitch and ask him why he tried to kill you?" Millie asked.

"I don't care if that asshole rots in his prison cell, so I definitely don't want to see him. I'm just as pissed off with him, as I am myself. I should've known better. I should've seen the signs but I put blinders on and chose to see what I wanted to."

"Well, I asked him why when I was interrogating him," said Lauren.

"What was his response?" asked Millie.

"He said it was your fault, Jasmine," Lauren answered.

"My fault? How am I responsible for all of this?" Jasmine couldn't believe Travis had said that.

"He says that you deceived him. He is very angry and bitter about your role in shelving his experiments. So he wanted to get even with you and prove a point," Lauren explained.

"The experiments were failures. He created poison and he knows that. For Christ's sake, Cougars has killed people. That's not science, that's madness." Jasmine growled and clenched her teeth. "If I could shoot that bastard and get away with it, I would."

"Okay, let's change the subject," Tiffany blurted. "What we need to do is celebrate the fact that we're all here together. We need to be thankful because this situation could've turned out worse."

"Amen to that, Tiffany," Jasmine supported her position. "We should celebrate the fact that this isn't *my* damn funeral. Travis Adams is a chapter in my past. Like Millie, I'm flipping the page because I know the best is yet to come."

About The Author

National bestselling and award-winning author Earl Sewell has written twelve novels including *Have Mercy, The Good Got to Suffer with the Bad, Through Thick and Thin, The Flip Side of Money, When Push Comes to Shove, Keysha's Drama, If I Were Your Boyfriend, Lesson Learned, Love Lies and Scandal,* and his debut title *Taken For Granted,* which was originally self-published through his own publishing company, Katie Books. His work has also appeared in four separate anthologies including *On the Line, Whispers Between the Sheets, Sistergirls.com* and *Afterhours: A Collection of Erotic Writing by Black Men.* He has written numerous romantic short stories for *Black Romance* magazine and has been featured in *Black Issues Book Review* and *Upscale* magazine. Recently the African American Arts Alliance presented Sewell an Excellence Award for outstanding achievement in literature for his novel *The Flip Side of Money.* He is also the founder of a travel agency, Earl Sewell's Travel Network, (www.earlsewellstravelnetwork.com). In addition Earl is a lifelong athlete who has completed several marathons and triathlons. Earl lives in South Holland, Illinois with his family. To learn more about Earl Sewell, visit his websites at www.earlsewell.com, www.aabook clubs.ning.com and www.myspace.com/earlsewell

If you liked "Cougars," we encourage you
to try another novel by Earl Sewell.
Please enjoy this excerpt from

Have Mercy

By Earl Sewell

Available from Strebor Books

-Chapter 1-
Carmen

Carmen swiveled her wrist to glance at her wristwatch as she shuffled up the steps of Nikki's apartment building. It was 6:00 a.m. on Saturday and the Chicago air was already heavy with sweaty humidity.

"I hate this sticky and clammy weather," Carmen complained as she wiped perspiration from her forehead and the base of her neck. "Nikki had better have her behind out of bed," Carmen muttered as she noticed a peculiar, scruffy-looking man exiting the brick building. The man was wearing a green T-shirt and cutoff blue jean shorts with black grime stains on the thighs. The grungy man had a face that only a mother could love and reminded

Carmen of the scrawny rock and roll icon Mick Jagger. As she approached the entrance, he held the door open for her.

"Thank you," she whispered as she eased by him and walked over and pressed a silver button on the wall to call for the elevator. She stared mindlessly at the orange elevator light, paused on the eighth floor. She sighed impatiently, then turned around to look out a nearby window while she mulled over her thoughts. Carmen was disillusioned with the fact that Nikki wasn't doing anything useful with her life. Her baby sister had a day job at an adult bookstore as a peep show girl and an evening job as a stripper at a seedy gentlemen's club. Carmen was sure their parents had to be turning over in their graves, knowing that Nikki was making a living exposing her body to men old enough to be her grandfather. That wasn't the way either of them were raised. *Yeah*, Carmen whispered to herself as she continued to glance out the window. *Nikki's life is dreadful, in my opinion.*

Carmen shouldered much of the blame for Nikki's appalling lifestyle, and the guilt she toted around was a heavy burden on her heart. Carmen continually attempted to clear the unspoken tension between her and her sister, but reconciling with Nikki was turning out to be a monumental task.

Their mother had passed away years ago from a combination of cancer and being a perpetual worrywart. Two years later, their father, Anthony, died. At the time of his death, Carmen was twenty-one years old and became guardian of her then fifteen-year-old sister, Nikki. The untimely loss of their father was the root of the tension between them. Nikki blamed Carmen for the death of their father and she knew it, although Nikki hadn't verbalized it as much lately. Blame and guilt were parasites eating away at Carmen's soul and she was tired of toting around her baggage of unhappy feelings. Carmen exhaled, hoping the shift in her breathing pattern would rid her mind of the unwanted and haunting thoughts. She turned back around to check the progress of the elevator and noticed that the scrawny man who had held the door for her was still hovering around the doorway, glaring at her. He licked his lips, flicked his tongue at her a few times, sounding like a dog slurping up water, and brushed his fingers across the stubble on his chin. Carmen translated the glint in his lustful eyes and realized he was having a sexual fantasy about her in his mind.

"Go to hell," Carmen snarled at him as she flipped up her middle finger. "Damn weirdo." The man didn't seem to mind Carmen's harsh words because he continued to glare at her. "Nikki has to stop moving into these apartment buildings filled with freaks and crackpots," she muttered as the bell on the elevator chimed.

Carmen stepped inside the elevator and pressed the third-floor button. When she got off the elevator, she noticed that the hallway carpet was wet. She wrinkled her nose because the musty and moldy odor was overpowering. She moved quickly down the enclosed corridor toward Nikki's apartment. Curling her fingers into a fist, Carmen drummed on the door with her knuckles. A short moment later, Frieda, Nikki's roommate, answered the door.

"Hey, Frieda," Carmen greeted politely as Frieda allowed her access to their small, cluttered, two-bedroom apartment. The place was littered with piles of laundry that needed to be either cleaned or folded but Carmen couldn't tell which.

"Is Nikki out of bed yet?" Carmen asked, crinkling her

nose while comparing the untidiness of the apartment to Nikki and Frieda's chaotic and messy lifestyle.

"Why are you asking a question that you already know the answer to?" Frieda scraped her fingernails up and down her belly before releasing a loud yawn that assaulted the already stale air with the rotting smell of her morning breath.

"You know damn well Nikki and I are vampires and function only after the sun goes down." Carmen tried to inconspicuously cover her nose with the palm of her hand. Frieda's breath literally smelled like spoiled food and its foul odor was making her dizzy.

"Well, she's the one who told me to be here this early. I've got to drop my car off at the repair shop, and she promised me that she'd drive over there with me, so that I wouldn't have to sit there and wait while a mechanic worked on my car."

"Yeah, yeah, yeah," Frieda answered as she scratched the side of her neck. "She told me all about it. I think that she would have left work earlier but this older dude walked into the tavern and started paying her some attention. And you know how Nikki has a soft spot for older men."

"I know," Carmen answered. She wasn't giving her full attention to what Frieda said because she didn't want their conversation to last longer than necessary. The only thing she wanted her to do was to stop talking. Carmen sauntered into the kitchen area and inspected a banana sitting on the countertop. After checking it thoroughly for bruising, she decided that it appeared safe enough to eat.

"He was a nice-looking man," Frieda continued, to Carmen's annoyance. "He looked like he used to play football or something. You know the type that probably has a large stash of money hidden somewhere."

"Humm," Carmen coyly answered, hoping that Frieda picked up that she didn't want to continue their conversation. Carmen noticed a chair that wasn't cluttered with clothes positioned in a corner of the room. She decided to sit down and wait for her sister.

"You don't seem like you're in a talkative mood. But then again, you never are. I'm going to go back to my room. Besides, Francisco came over early this morning and gave me some grown-man loving. My body trembles just thinking about having my ass in the air while he sucks on my sweet, juicy Spanish pussy." Carmen could not have cared less about Frieda's sex life; and if her pussy was as funky as her breath, Francisco had to be one nasty motherfucker to put his face anywhere near her smelly ass.

"Yeah, whatever. You're telling me way too much information," Carmen said and began to leave. She was glad Frieda was taking her body funk back into the bedroom.

"There is no need to be jealous, honey."

Oh, Lord, here we go, thought Carmen. *Now she thinks that I'm being insulting.*

"You and your stuck-up attitude will get a man to fuck you right one of these days. Hopefully he'll be able to mellow you out some. How long has it been now since that no-good professor dumped you? What, nine years? Or is it ten?" Freda snickered. "He had your head all messed up when he cancelled the wedding on you after you'd spent all of your money planning this elaborate event, which you specifically told me I wasn't invited to. I still haven't forgotten that evil shit. I'm glad he cracked your prissy little face and left you all broken up. You needed to be taught a lesson." Frieda used threatening hand gestures to emphasize her point.

"Frieda, it's too damn early in the morning to dig up

old shit and start a fight with me. I didn't come over here for that." Carmen was more than willing to bare her claws and stir up an ugly argument if Frieda didn't back down. "Trust me; you do not want to toy with me this morning."

Frieda chuckled. "You don't scare me, honey. Not one bit." Frieda said her peace and then made her way down a narrow corridor to the bedrooms. She banged hard on Nikki's bedroom door.

"Your snooty-ass sister is here," Frieda said, loud enough for Carmen to hear her. The animosity between Frieda and Carmen was like a knife in her back that she couldn't reach. In fact, as Carmen saw it, Frieda was a part of the reason that her relationship with Nikki was so sour at times.

——

After the death of their parents, Nikki and Carmen moved into an apartment in the Ravenswood community on Chicago's North Side. Carmen, who had always been more mature than her years, worked as an audiovisual supervisor at a branch of the Chicago Public Library and attended Truman Community College in the evening. Carmen was responsible, levelheaded, and ambitious. Nikki, on the other hand, was an impressionable and rebellious high school sophomore who didn't respect her older sister as her guardian. Nikki was an untamed free spirit who was fascinated and seduced by Chicago's night-life and the freedom it represented. She would often sneak out of the house on school nights and hang out with her friends at the beach, someone else's apartment, or a neighborhood park where she and her friends would loiter and be loud as well as rude. One night, after waking up and discovering that Nikki had once again snuck out of the house, after she'd specifically told her not to, Carmen decided she'd had enough of Nikki's disobedience. She went searching for Nikki to confront her and perhaps physically fight her, if that's what it took to make Nikki abide by her rules.

"Nikki! I am not going to allow you to hang out on street corners all night with your friends and come home whenever you feel like it!" Carmen shouted at Nikki after she'd located her and forced her to come home against her will. Carmen had spent an hour combing neighborhood streets, and her temper had reached its boiling point.

"Are you listening to me?" Carmen barked at her sister as they reentered their small apartment. Nikki's ears were completely closed to Carmen's ranting. She stood defiantly in the center of the living room with her arms folded across her chest and her eyes fixed on a wooden support beam in the ceiling.

"What are you trying to do? Get pregnant and drop out of high school?" Carmen continued her ranting, not worrying about whether or not her neighbors would make a phone call to the police and report a domestic disturbance.

"For your information, I am not trying to do anything, especially get pregnant. It's boring around here and I'm just having fun." Nikki had no respect for her older and wiser sister.

"No, not yet, but if you stay on the path that you're on, you will end up being another teenage mother, or even worse, some young girl locked up."

"Please! I'm not even going out like that. Your comment proves how little you know me," Nikki answered defiantly.

"Then who are you? Tell me; I want to know. Tell me what you're about, Nikki. What do you want to do with yourself? Help me understand." Carmen genuinely wanted answers but wasn't sure if Nikki even had a clear idea of who she was or what she wanted to do with life, outside of aggravating the hell out of her.

Nikki responded by working her neck and allowing her body language to speak as loudly as her words.

"There isn't anything for you to understand except that I've got my own life. And I control what I do, when I do it, and how I do it. So get off of my damn back and leave me the hell alone!" Nikki said her peace and felt as if she'd finally put Carmen in her proper place. Nikki was about to step away, but Carmen blocked her path.

"You may have your own life, but you don't have a pot to piss in or a window to throw it out of. I pay the bills here, Nikki. I am the one who is making sacrifices so that you can complete school. I'd like to go out and party, too, but I can't because I have to set an example for you. Don't you understand what I'm trying to do? Don't you care about the sacrifices I'm making for you?"

"Carmen, you're trying to be someone that you're not! You're not my mama and you're not my daddy. And if you keep trying to control me, I'm going to make you regret the day you were born." Before Carmen could stop herself, she hauled off and whacked Nikki with the palm of her hand as hard as she could.

"I'm tired of your damn mouth and attitude, Nikki. If you don't get your shit together, you and I are going to do something we'll both end up regretting!" Carmen howled at her baby sister.

Nikki's chest began heaving with anger and resentment. She lowered her eyes to slits as she allowed her rage to consume her.

"Oh, you've done it now!" Nikki hollered out as she

allowed her fists to fly and fight Carmen back. The two of them fought and flung each other around the apartment, knocking over furniture, until they finally wrestled to the floor. They pulled each other's hair and clawed at each other's skin. They shouted angry words as they tried to gain an advantage over each other. After struggling on the floor for a long moment, they both stopped once they'd reached exhaustion. Although Carmen had gotten the best of Nikki, she wasn't willing to concede her loss. When Nikki finally had enough, she asked Carmen to let her go. Carmen stopped pressing her elbow against Nikki's neck and allowed her to stand. Once she was on her feet, Nikki went directly to the bathroom. Carmen lightly touched her stinging face, then looked at her fingertips that were spotted with blood.

"She's scratched me all up," Carmen uttered as she took a glance around their modest apartment, which now looked like a train wreck.

— —

After their confrontation, Carmen went into her bedroom, picked up the phone, and called her girlfriend Millie. Millie was special and unique; she was an Irish girl who was raised by a black family. Millie was twenty-six and five years older than Carmen. Millie was Carmen's confidante as well as a close friend.

"I don't know what I am going to do with Nikki," Carmen explained to Millie. "We actually had an all-out brawl tonight. I'm surprised no one called the damn cops. I pushed her so hard against the wall that there is a big body imprint in it now. After I did that, I thought she'd had enough, so I turned my back to her. She snatched a lamp off of the end table and smashed it against my back and shoulder," Carmen said, still fuming with anger.

"Do you think it's safe for you to stay there?" Millie asked.

"Yes, it's safe. I'm not afraid of Nikki. After she smashed the lamp against my back, I lost it. I was on her like flies on shit and I damn near choked her to death. I am not going to allow Nikki to run me out of this house."

"Have you guys ever considered going to a therapist? You know, to get some professional help?"

"Trust me, there will be no need for professional help if she tries to fight me again. I will put her six feet under and that's no joke." Carmen was filled with anger and vengeance.

"You don't really mean that. She's your sister and siblings fight sometimes. Although you guys really take it to the extreme."

"Millie, I tell you, I'm doing everything that I can to get her through high school. I'm tired of being nice; I'm putting my own happiness on hold to make sure she has a fighting chance and she doesn't appreciate any of it. She's a selfish and trifling little girl who thinks she knows everything. I can't tell her anything. She will not listen and it's frustrating. I think she's bipolar."

"She's not bipolar. A little high-strung, but not bipolar." Millie wasn't about to support Carmen's rationale. "Maybe it's the crowd she's hanging around with. Maybe she's under a lot of peer pressure; that's always difficult to deal with. Who was Nikki with when you found her tonight?"

"Her tack-headed friend named Frieda. The daughter of the devil, in my opinion. Frieda is a rough-looking girl who has been in and out of juvie countless times. She's standoffish, has a nasty attitude, and is quick to jump to her own conclusions."

"She sounds like a real piece of work." Millie cleared her throat. "This Frieda girl might be the cause of the tension between you and Nikki, if you think about it. When you and your sister first stepped out into the world on your own, everything was going smoothly. Then, when she transferred to her new school and hooked up with this Frieda chick, everything seemed to spiral out of control."

"You could have a point there, now that I think about it. I remember Nikki telling me that she had a hard time making new friends and how everyone at the school seemed to have it in for her. It could be that she's behaving like this to prove that she's tough enough to hang out with this Frieda girl and her clique."

"Maybe you should consider moving. Getting Nikki into a different environment might help."

"Millie, I'm not Rockefeller. I don't have the resources right now to make a move. Besides, I don't want to go through the hassle of breaking the lease. Even if I did move, I wouldn't be able to go far. I need to stay close to my job and school. But Nikki and I are going to have to work out our problems before we kill each other." Carmen paused and then rotated her neck to release some of the tension that was trying to provide her with a massive headache. "Look, I don't want to talk about Nikki any more. Let's talk about something else. How are things with you and Chuck, now that you guys are shacking up?"

"Things are going good, although he's still talking about moving back to Kansas City so that he can be closer to his family."

"Well, what are you going to do if he does?" Carmen

asked as she moved over to the mirror and inspected her wounds. Her face was rather red and she could clearly see where Nikki had scratched her. *I should kill that girl*, she thought to herself as she reached for a towel.

"I'm not going anywhere until I finish school. I only have two semesters left at Truman Junior College and then it's on to a four-year university. After that, I plan to go to graduate school," Millie said with absolute certainty.

"So what's up with you and the English professor? Why did he want to see you after class the other night?"

"To ask me out on a date." Carmen laughed nervously.

"You're kidding me. Why didn't you say something to me?" Millie was upset that Carmen had failed to mention this.

"I'm frustrated and at my wit's end with Nikki. It slipped my mind. I meant to tell you about it."

"Look, girl, Nikki is going to be Nikki. When that girl turns eighteen, she is not going to be worried with you, especially if she continues to defy you as she's been doing lately. I know that you want the best for her and all, but you have got to think of yourself as well."

"It's hard for me to let go. I feel such a sense of responsibility for her. Especially now since both Mom and Dad are gone." Carmen paused as she briefly thought about her parents. She missed them deeply and longed for the chance to talk to either of them one more time. She stopped thinking about her parents and answered Millie.

"Anyway, Professor Green is a nice man but—"

"I had a feeling that the professor had a thing for you," Millie interrupted. "He is a handsome-looking man and you're a beautiful woman. If you guys hit it off, you're going to be a hot couple. If I were you, I wouldn't let him get away."

"Can I tell you something, Millie? Something personal?" Carmen asked.

"You know I'm your girl. I know that we haven't known each other all that long but I truly feel as if I've known you for much longer. So ask as many questions as you'd like; I'm all ears."

"I like Professor Green a lot, but I'm afraid of dating him. He is thirty years old and more experienced."

"What does his age have to do with anything? You're twenty- one and he's thirty. So what?"

"I see with you, I have to come right out and explain it."

"Come right out with what?" Millie asked, utterly puzzled.

"He's experienced and I'm not. He's probably been with other women and I've never been with a man. I'm afraid that I will not know what to do or he may not like my body. Do you catch my drift now?" Carmen asked.

"You're still a virgin?" Millie chuckled. "That explains a lot."

"What's that supposed to mean?" Carmen had taken offense to the comment.

"It means that I can tell that you haven't been getting it; that's all. You're all wound up. But there is nothing wrong with being a virgin. If I could turn back the hands of time, I'd be a virgin, too. I wouldn't have given in to peer pressure."

"I've been with boys before, so I'm not at a total loss. I've never gone all the way. I've come close a few times, but I changed my mind." Carmen sighed. "So, what was your first time like?"

"I'm not going to lie to you. My first time was supposed to be perfect, but it wasn't—the first time happened when I was seventeen and going into my senior year at Proviso

West High School. I gave up my virginity to a college boy named LeMar. We were at his house in his bedroom one afternoon while his parents were at work. I got caught up in a Luther Vandross song called 'Superstar.' Luther's voice was sweet and clear and LeMar was positioned on top of me, nibbling on my ear and telling me how much he loved me. I remember feeling his hands gently gliding over my nakedness and getting goose bumps while I spread my legs open a little wider for him. LeMar had a mighty chest, strong shoulders, and an ass that had dimples in it. I caressed his ass and thought that his strokes were going to feel so strong and powerful. LeMar was an excellent kisser and when he held my face in his hands and kissed me tenderly, my body responded immediately. I raised my legs in the air, wrapped them around his body, and locked my legs at the ankles. He positioned himself just right and began to enter me. I thought, '*Oh my God. This is it. I'm actually going to do it.*' The first moments of penetration made me cringe."

"So, what did you do? I mean, when it was hurting," Carmen asked.

"LeMar wasn't a rough guy who jumped up and down on my stomach. When I said that it hurt, he stopped. He was very patient with me. It took a few more tries before he actually penetrated me. I'm not going to lie and tell you that my first time made me see stars. I think I was so wound up and nervous at the time. When we tried again later, I'd learned how to relax and it felt better."

"So what ever happened to LeMar?"

"Unfortunately, our romance was a summer thing. We spent a lot of time together during the summer, but then he went back to school in the fall. He completed his bachelor's degree in Texas. We kept in touch with each other for a little while. We talked on the phone and wrote love letters. Then his parents divorced and he ended up living in Fort Lauderdale with his mother."

"Did you love him?" Carmen asked.

"I have loved every man I've ever laid down with. That's not to say that I have a bunch of skeletons in my closet, but I believe in love and I believe that there is someone for everybody. LeMar was special, though. Although he wasn't my best lover, he was my first, and you never forget the first person you made love to." Millie paused and there was a brief moment of silence. "So, do you think that you're going to give Professor Green that opportunity?"

Carmen laughed nervously. "I believe I will let him take me out on a date. Lord knows that I haven't been on one in ages and I'm way too young to be sitting around the house like some old woman. And as much as I hate to admit it, Nikki is probably getting more action than I've ever gotten." Millie and Carmen chuckled.

"Thank you for listening to my madness, Millie," Carmen said, truly appreciating Millie's attention.

"You don't have to thank me for that. As much as you've listened to me ramble on about all of my issues, it's welcoming to hear someone else's drama for a change."

Carmen could hear the smile in Millie's voice, and the image of Millie's smile blanketed her and made her feel warm and at ease.

⎯ ⎯

Carmen's train of thought was interrupted by Nikki, who came out into the living room wearing blue sweat pants, a "TLC" sweatshirt that said "Ain't too Proud to

Beg," a baseball cap, and dark black sunglasses. Nikki had not matured much since she'd been on her own. She still liked marching in the opposite direction of what was normal.

"Nikki, it's humid, hot, and sticky outside. You're going to sweat like a pig in those clothes."

"It's okay. I got the air conditioner in my hoopty-mobile fixed. One of my neighbors, who looks like Mick Jagger, fixed it. I can turn it on if I get too hot, but you know me. I'm always cold so it's unlikely that I'll get hot."

"That guy doesn't look like the mechanical type." Carmen gave her sister a sarcastic glance.

"And what's that supposed to mean?" Nikki instantly picked up on her sister's sarcasm. "Why are you always judging people?"

"Never mind," Carmen uttered. She was not in the mood for an argument. "Let's go, so we can drop off my car and get it repaired."

"Yeah, let's go before you piss me off." Nikki moved past her sister and walked out of the apartment.

Carmen pulled her blue Dodge Daytona into the parking lot of the Magic Muffler and Brake Shop on Stony Island Boulevard. It was a quarter to seven and there were already five people standing in line at the door because service was given on a first-come, first-served basis. Carmen parked her car and then stood in line and waited with the other patrons. A few moments later, she saw Nikki creeping into the parking lot in her rusted-out Nissan Sentra with one red door and one white door. Carmen noticed that all of Nikki's car windows were rolled down. It was a clear indication to her that her air conditioning wasn't working at all.

The shop owner finally opened the door and began

attending to customers in the proper order. While the owner was out inspecting the car of another customer, Carmen noticed one of the mechanics arriving. Carmen stared at the brawny man wearing a blue mechanic's suit that zipped up the front. His skin was the color of gingerbread, and he had sizable arms, a wide chest, and broad shoulders. He didn't appear to be the type that worked out at the gym; his burly build seemed to be more genetic. The brawny man went to the back of the garage where the supplies were stored and then reappeared a few moments later behind the front counter.

"Who's next?" he asked, with a forceful tone in his voice.

"I am," Carmen answered.

"What kind of car do you have?" he asked without looking up, as he rested his fingers on the computer keyboard, eager to input her information.

"Dodge Daytona," Carmen answered and watched the man's thick brown fingers slowly peck the information into the computer. Carmen didn't understand why she imagined his thick fingers toying with her womanhood. She had to quickly ease the thought from her mind.

"What's your address?" he asked.

"1642 East Fifty-sixth Street."

"Oh, you stay over in Hyde Park. That's Obama's neighborhood," he commented. "How long have you lived over there?" He took his eyes off of the computer screen and met her gaze. She noticed that his skin had become slightly glossy with sweat from the humidity. His face was unyielding and his expression was uncompromising. She suddenly felt as if she were being interrogated rather than flirted with.

"I've lived there a little over a year now. I teach first

grade at Bret Harte Elementary School." She didn't want to tell him that, but for some reason, she couldn't make herself shut up. Maybe it was because of his strict glare. It had somehow overpowered her and caused her to say more than she wanted to. She offered a Pollyannaish smile in an attempt to break the intensity of his glare. That didn't help. He kept his blazing eyes on her. Carmen suddenly wondered what had gone wrong in his life.

"What kind of problems are you having?" He broke eye contact abruptly and continued to peck at the keyboard.

"When I press the brakes, I hear a scrubbing sound," Carmen answered, with a soft voice.

"It is a scrubbing or squeaking sound?"

"No, it's definitely a scrubbing sound. And the brakes almost touch the floor before the car begins to stop." Carmen noticed the monogrammed lettering on his overalls. His name was stitched in yellow letters. Luther was his name. He typed in some more information and then asked for her car keys.

"I need to test drive it before I pull it in and get it in the air."

"Okay," Carmen said as she handed over her car keys. Luther walked out to her car, got in, and drove off. A few minutes later, he returned and pulled her car into the far stall. Carmen observed from a distance through a glass window in the lobby as he pressed the air drill to the wheel lugs and removed the tires one by one. Carmen then felt a light tap on her shoulder.

"Do they have a soda machine in here?" It was Nikki. She picked up a muffler brochure from the countertop and began fanning herself as if she were sitting in church trying to keep cool.

"No, I don't think that they do. There is an Amoco gas

station across the street. I think that they sell cold drinks," Carmen said.

"Do you have any idea of how much longer it's going to take to get an estimate?"

"It shouldn't be too much longer. He has my car in the air right now."

"Well, I'm going to run over to the gas station and get me something to drink. It's hotter than hell out here."

"I told you that your ass was going to burn up."

"Whatever," Nikki answered. "I'll be right back." Nikki turned and left without saying another word. Carmen turned her attention back to her car and saw Luther was waving his hand, signaling for her to come and take a look at what he'd found. Carmen walked through the garage toward Luther.

"You're going to have to get the front brake pads replaced. The rotors need replacing as well." He pointed to the silver disk that the pads rubbed against in order to bring the car to a stop. "The scrubbing sound that you were hearing was the sound of metal rubbing against metal."

"Shit!" Carmen hissed, because it was starting to sound as if the repairs were going to set her back financially.

"How long has the brake light on the dashboard been on?" Luther asked as he continued his inspection.

"I don't know—three, maybe four weeks." Carmen shrugged her shoulders.

"If you had brought the car in sooner, you wouldn't have this problem." Luther didn't mean to be cold with his answer; he was only telling her the truth. Carmen's mood changed in that instant.

"How much is this going to cost me?"

"I don't know. I'll have to look at the cost of the parts." Luther was now inspecting the rear brakes.

"I don't want to spend a small fortune on repairs; I'm letting you know that right now." Carmen became stand-offish. She hoped her attitude would indicate that she'd done some kind of research on brake repair jobs and wasn't going to pay one cent over what she considered to be a fair price.

"Your rear brakes will last a little longer, but not too much longer. You'll probably need to replace them by this winter." Luther continued his inspection. He was now focusing on the muffler system.

"Do you see this?" He pointed to a brown rust spot in the muffler pipeline. That's the beginning of a hole. By the time the winter sets in, you're going to have to replace this pipe or your car will sound like a tank coming down the street." Luther did one more check to make sure that everything was tightly secure. Carmen stood with her arms crisscrossed. Her irritation level was rising with each second that ticked by. She simply wanted to know the cost of fixing the brakes; she could not have cared less about the muffler. Her main concern was that her car came to a stop when she pressed the brake pedal.

"Let's go back up front and I'll give you an estimate."

Luther stepped back behind the counter, began looking up the cost of the parts, and calculated the cost of the labor involved. He leaned toward her, resting his arm on the countertop and began explaining the itemized list he'd placed before her.

"The brake pads are seventy-nine dollars and ninety-nine cents. The new rotors are one hundred dollars each; you need two of those. The labor will cost you seventy-five dollars. There is a two-dollar disposal fee, plus tax, brings your total to this right here." Luther circled the number.

"Three hundred eighty-seven dollars and ninety-nine cents!" Carmen blurted out the words before she had a chance to adjust her tone. "Don't you have some kind of discount or sale going on?"

"No." Luther was sharp and abrupt with his answer.

"Well, I think that you're robbing me and charging me way too much!" Carmen got loud with Luther. There was no way she was about to let him take advantage of her like this. She wanted him to look at the estimate again and give her some type of discount, especially if she was about to spend damn near four hundred dollars.

"Look, lady!" Luther barked. He had an evil glare and viciousness in his voice. "I wasn't the one who was driving around in the damn car for a fucking month with the motherfucking brake light on. I don't set the goddamn prices; the factory does!" Carmen flinched with fear. She thought for sure the mechanic had lost it. She was not expecting to get an explosive reaction from him. At that moment, the shop owner walked back in with a customer. He'd overheard Luther and quickly pulled him into the garage area for a private conversation.

"What the fuck is wrong with you, man!" Carmen overheard the owner rip into Luther as the door to the garage area slowly shut. "You don't talk to my customers like that!"

Luther glanced at Carmen and his eyes were blazing with resentment. Carmen wanted to leave, but she couldn't because her car was still in the air. The owner cupped his hand and placed it at the back of Luther's neck so that he could hold his gaze.

"She can kiss my ass, man!" Luther howled out loud enough for Carmen to hear.

"That's it. Get out of here!" the owner shouted back.

"Fuck you, man. I didn't need this shitty-ass job any-damn-way!"

——

Carmen watched as Luther gathered his belongings and left. A moment later the owner came back and spoke with Carmen.

"Look, ma'am, I'm so sorry that he yelled at you like that. I'm only going to charge you a flat three hundred dollars for the repairs to your car. Is that fair enough?"

"Okay, but where is Luther going?"

"Ma'am, he had two strikes against him already." The owner paused.

"But I was the one who provoked him. I don't want the man to lose his job because of me." Carmen felt horrible.

"Miss, we get upset customers all the time. It's part of the business and he knows that. He should not have used that threatening tone with you. I've spoken with him about his tone of voice on several occasions and warned him about it. He had a final warning yesterday. I'm a small business owner and how my customers are treated is very important for my referral and repeat customers. I don't want my customers to have a bad experience when they come here. Do you understand where I'm coming from?"

"But…" Carmen's voice trailed off.

"Ma'am, do you want your car repaired or not? I can get another mechanic started on it right away."

"Yes," Carmen answered as she watched Luther chase down a Stony Island bus that was heading north.

-CHAPTER 2-
LUTHER

Luther located an empty seat at the rear of the bus. Once he got himself situated, he slid open a window so that a breeze would cool off his hot and sticky skin. He crumpled his front pants pockets, listening carefully for the sound of crinkling plastic. He reached into his right pocket and pulled out a wrinkled pack of cigarettes and a lighter. He removed a cigarette, pinched it between his lips, and spun the wheel of his lighter. Luther slumped down in his seat and allowed the nicotine to relax him. He was about to close his eyes and free his mind of all his problems and issues. When his eyes connected with the disapproving gaze of an elderly woman sitting in front of him, he paused. She'd twisted herself around in her seat to find the source of the repulsive scent of smoke. The upset elderly woman pointed to the posted "no smoking" sign, but Luther didn't give a damn.

"Go on; say something! I dare you to," Luther snarled at the older woman who was clearly frightened by his aggressiveness. To avoid any additional altercation with him, she got up and moved to another seat.

Luther took a long drag and blew the smoke out of the open window. "I can't believe my day has gotten fucked up," he uttered to himself. He noticed that it was almost his stop, so he reached up and pulled the cord, which alerted the driver. When the driver stopped, Luther bolted out of the rear door and flashed across the street to make his connection with the Sixty-third Street bus. He rode the bus down to King Drive, which was filled with the usual crowd of vagrants, drunkards, addicts, and young drug pushers cruising about in luxury cars. Luther lived nearby in a rundown apartment building on Prairie Street where rent was cheap. His shabby dwelling consisted of three musty rooms, all of which had soiled green shag carpet with matching wall paint. The paint on the walls had chipped and left jagged designs. White pipes from other apartments snaked across the ceiling of his unit like a complicated spider web. The pipes hissed constantly and sprung leaks wherever they saw fit.

Luther entered the vestibule of the building and saw his electric bill on the floor with a shoe print on it; it had been opened. *One of the crackhead squatters no doubt had opened it thinking that it was some kind of check*, he thought to himself as he pushed his basement apartment door open. Luther walked down a few creaky steps and flipped on his lights. A polluted odor of cooking gas attacked his nose and he thought the stovepipe had cracked. He went to the kitchen and opened the small window above the stove to allow some fresh air to come in. He noticed a cluster of cigarette butts, matchsticks, and booze bottles on the ground outside of his kitchen window. *Damn vagrants have been loitering outside of my window drinking and smoking again*! Luther hissed to himself. He began pulling the stove away from the wall but stopped when he noticed the sink had backed up and the basin was filled with brown water.

"Damn," he said to himself.

He stooped down, opened the cabinet doors under the

sink, and grabbed the plunger. He plugged the sink fero-
ciously until the brown murky water retreated down the
drain. He went into the living room to sit and think. He'd
attend to the issue of the stovepipe once he got his thoughts
in order. The only furniture he had was his bed, a folding
chair, and a small color television, which sat on the floor.
He flipped on the television and watched a mindless program about cops who patrolled beaches. A short while
later, there was a thundering knock on his door.

"Who is it?" he asked, with a hostile voice.

"Mr. Packard is outside and he wants to see you." It was
a strange woman and her voice was filled with nervousness.

"Shit!" Luther cupped his hands and buried his face in
them. Nervous adrenaline shot through him like a river
and he could feel his anxiety rising. Packard was the last
person he wanted to see.

"Okay. Tell him I'll be out there in a minute," responded
Luther.

"Come on, man! He promised me a little something if
I got you right away." The woman pounded the door
again. At that moment, Luther realized that Packard had
put some junkie up to this for the promise of drugs.
Packard was foul and evil like that.

"Hurry up, man!" The woman was now desperate. Luther
attempted to organize his thoughts. *Why does Packard
want to see me?* he wondered. The woman began kicking
the door with her foot. The thudding sound echoed
throughout the basement apartment.

"Come on, brother! Where are you at, in the bathroom
or something?!" the woman shouted. Finally, Luther
opened the door and saw a boney woman with large
almond eyes. Her hair was uncombed and matted, a clear

indication that her addiction meant more to her than her appearance. The two of them stepped out of the building and the woman rushed over to Packard's black Chevy Blazer.

"See, I got him for you, baby. I got him; he's right there." She impolitely pointed at Luther while laughing nervously. Packard had one of the men in the back seat hand her what she'd worked for. The woman snatched the narcotic out of the man's hand and rushed off down the block.

Packard was a former cop who'd turned into a drug dealer and a gangster who was not to be toyed with on any level. He was an unyielding barracuda of a man who was old enough to be Luther's father. His facial features were strong and imposing, like he'd seen more tragedies than most would see in their lifetime. His eyes appeared to be sun beaten but were as sharp as a hawk's. Packard was a former amateur bodybuilder and his physique was well-maintained. He didn't look his age because he still spent a fair amount of time at the gym. He had been abusing and terrorizing Luther with fear and intimidation since he was a small boy. Today was not the day Packard planned on putting an end to the seeds of fear he'd planted in Luther years ago.

Packard signaled for Luther to move closer. Luther attempted to place a smile on his face to give the illusion of being happy to see him.

"How old are you now, Luther?" Packard's eyes were red with anger.

"Twenty-nine," he answered, feeling his shoulders tense up. He could tell Packard was in an evil mood.

"Who hooked you up with the mechanic's job?" Packard asked.

"You did." Luther was jittery and spoke softly like a child. He hated himself for being so weak. "Packard, let me explain."

"Did I ask you to explain?" Packard cut him off. Luther stood silently like an obedient pet.

"Whose apartment building are you living in for practically nothing?" Packard asked.

"Yours," Luther responded.

"And what were you doing before my divine intervention blessed you with a job and a roof over your head?"

"I was working at a car wash for peanuts."

"And what else?" Packard pressed the issue.

"I also begged people for money," Luther answered, ashamed of his inability to be more of a man.

"And who was the one who got the attempted robbery incident erased from your record?"

"You," Luther answered again.

"That's right, Luther, me. And look at how you repay me for my kindness. I put my solid reputation on the line for you and you make me look like a damn fool. I'm the one who called in a favor so that you could get the job at Magic Muffler. Do I look like a fool to you, Luther?" Packard's voice was much more vicious than ever.

"No." Luther suddenly felt the urge to pee.

"No! Is that what you said?"

"Yes."

"No, Luther. I must look like a fool to you because you're trying to play me for one. And you know I can't let that happen. You know that I can't let these people on the street think that I'm soft."

"I'm sorry." Luther quickly offered his apology as he backed away from the car door. He feared that Packard would shoot him down where he stood.

"Sorry! That's right, Luther. You are about the sorriest son-of-a-bitch I've ever known. How long were you working at that job?"

"Seven months."

"Seven months," Packard repeated in disgust. "Your big, dumb, sorry ass could only keep a job for seven months."

"It wasn't my fault," Luther tried to explain once again.

"It wasn't your fault?" Packard glared at Luther. "It's always your fault, Luther. It's always your fault because I say it is and don't you ever forget that. You hear me, boy?!"

"Yes," Luther answered, staring at the ground. He didn't like being belittled. In the back of his mind, he told himself that one day he'd get his revenge and make Packard respect him; one way or another.

"The only reason I stuck my neck out for your sorry ass is because I feel somewhat responsible for how useless you are. But you know what? I'm done with giving charity to your pitiful soul."

Luther gritted his teeth and clenched his fist. He was contemplating whether or not he should hit Packard with a solid right hook to the jaw and deal with the consequences later. *After all*, he thought, *I don't have shit to lose.*

"What? You want to do something? I see that look in your eyes, boy! Come on, take your best shot." Packard held up his gun to show Luther that he meant business. "I'll put a bullet in your ass and stuff your body down a damn sewer," Packard barked at him. Luther could see that Packard was determining whether or not to end Luther's life.

"I'm sorry." Luther once again offered up an apology.

"Good. For a minute there I thought I was going to have to commit homicide this afternoon," Packard said as he put his firearm away. "But I am going to evict you."

"Don't put me out on the street, man. I don't have any place to go," Luther pleaded. Packard released a wicked laugh.

"You've got exactly two weeks to pack up your shit and get the hell out of my place. Oh, and, Luther, if I were you, I'd make sure that I didn't stay the full two weeks. Strange things happen to old buildings like the one you're living in. Sometimes buildings like that one mysteriously burn to the ground." Without sharing any additional information, Packard sped off down Prairie Street.

Luther loathed himself for not having enough courage to stand up to Packard. Luther ground down hard on his teeth as he held back the sensation of shouting out in anger and frustration at the complications of his miserable life. He walked back inside his shabby apartment and lay down on his bed. He curled up into a fetal position and hugged himself for comfort. He focused his eyes on the feet of the silver radiator in the corner and began to think about his mother, Sugar, and the event that had altered the course of his life.

— —

On his tenth birthday, Sugar had promised to take him shopping for fresh workout clothes and a football so that he'd be ready when football tryouts were held at a local neighborhood community center. Luther, knowing how short-tempered and forgetful Sugar could be, wanted to be on his best behavior so she'd keep the promise she'd made to him. On the morning of his birthday, he got up extra early and assembled the best breakfast their bare cupboards had to offer. He made two scrambled eggs, toasted the last slice of bread and covered it with strawberry jam. He made sure everything looked perfect on the white paper plate before he walked toward her bedroom. The moment he opened her bedroom door, he wrinkled his nose, not wanting to inhale the musty odor wafting in the air. As he approached his mother, who was resting on her back, Luther noticed a syringe dangling from the joint of her left arm. He knew right away that Sugar had been shooting up again. Still not wanting to give up hope of having a good birthday, he swallowed down his edgy emotions and called to her.

"Mama?" he whispered softly. He set the plate of food down on the bed next to her hip, then gently rocked her bony shoulder. Sugar's eyes flipped open suddenly and startled Luther. Her eyes were filled with hell's fire and Luther quickly realized that he'd made an awful mistake.

"What in the hell do you want, boy?" Sugar snapped at him, causing him to bow his head down and project his voice toward the floor in shame.

"I…" Luther had trouble getting his words out. "Nothing. I mean…I didn't want anything. I mean—"

"Speak up. I can't hear your dumb ass!" Sugar berated her son.

"I was wondering if you're ready to go to the store. And I made you some breakfast." Luther pointed to the food near her hip.

"That football and some new clothes are the only things you care about, isn't it?" Sugar continued to scold her son for putting unwanted pressure on her.

"No, Mama. I just…" Luther paused to get his thoughts together. "You promised you would—"

"I don't remember making you any promise." Sugar began coughing violently.

"But you did. You said we could go shopping today."

"You want that stuff really bad, don't you?" Sugar stopped coughing and glared at him with contempt.

"I'll work for it," Luther answered, attempting to strike a new deal. "I'll clean up; I'll do the laundry; and I'll be quiet when you have company over. I can wait outside, or something, when Packard is here. I won't make a sound, I promise."

"Let me think about it," Sugar said and turned her back to him. "Leave the food. I'll eat it in a minute. And shut my door on your way out," she told him as she removed the syringe from her arm and began scratching uncontrollably.

Later, Sugar and Luther walked four miles to a local sporting goods store. Luther followed Sugar toward the back of the store where all of the sports equipment was stocked. He picked out the brown-and-white leather football he wanted and watched Sugar as she stuffed the ball inside of a large bag she'd brought with them. Sugar marched over to the sporting apparel aisle, located Luther's size, and quickly shoved some items into the bag.

"Carry this and come on." She gave Luther the items she'd gotten for him, then snatched his hand and raced toward the front door. Neither Luther nor Sugar noticed that a security guard had been watching their every move. When the guard yelled for them to stop, Sugar dropped Luther's hand and took off running. Before Luther could react and run out of the door, the guard nabbed him. Sugar rushed out the door, disappeared into the crowd of pedestrians, and never looked back. When it became clear that Sugar wasn't going to return, the police were called. Later, a squad car and two officers took Luther back to his home address. When the police gained entrance to the apartment, what few possessions Luther and Sugar had were gone. The only thing left was a plastic bag filled with his clothes in the center of the floor. It was clear to both Luther and the police officers that Sugar had left in a hurry and had no intentions of ever returning to see about Luther's well-being.